# Jeeves and Company

P. G. Wodehouse

# Jeeves and Company

Favorite Stories

*featuring*

Jeeves, Reggie Pepper,

Archie Moffam *and* the Oldest Member

Pandion Press

# Contents

**Reggie Pepper** ....................................... 7

*Helping Freddie* ...................................9

*The Test Case* ....................................28

**Jeeves** ...................................... 51

*Leave It to Jeeves* ...............................53

*The Aunt and the Sluggard* ........................77

*Jeeves and the Chump Cyril* .....................110

*Jeeves in the Springtime* ........................136

*Sir Roderick Comes to Lunch* .....................158

**Archie Moffam** .......................... 179

*The Man Who Married a Hotel* ...................181

*Dear Old Squiffy* ................................197

*Washy Makes His Presence Felt* ..................220

**The Oldest Member** ...................... 249

*The Clicking of Cuthbert* .........................251

*Ordeal by Golf* ..................................271

*The Long Hole* ..................................296

# Reggie Pepper

BETWEEN 1911 AND 1915, P. G. Wodehouse wrote seven short stories featuring Reggie Pepper, a wealthy but not particularly bright young dandy.

Reggie resembles the later character of Bertie Wooster, Jeeves' employer. Indeed, according to Wodehouse, Bertie "started out as Reggie Pepper, and I don't know why I changed the name." He later rewrote some of the Reggie Pepper narratives as Jeeves and Bertie stories.

*My Man Jeeves* (1919) contains four tales featuring Reggie Pepper. All seven tales appear in the posthumous anthology *Enter Jeeves* (1997).

# Helping Freddie

I DON'T WANT TO BORE YOU, don't you know, and all that sort of rot, but I must tell you about dear old Freddie Meadowes. I'm not a flier at literary style, and all that, but I'll get some writer chappie to give the thing a wash and brush up when I've finished, so that'll be all right.

Dear old Freddie, don't you know, has been a dear old pal of mine for years and years; so when I went into the club one morning and found him sitting alone in a dark corner, staring glassily at nothing, and generally looking like the last rose of summer, you can understand I was quite disturbed about it. As a rule, the old rotter is the life and soul of our set. Quite the little lump of fun, and all that sort of thing.

Jimmy Pinkerton was with me at the time. Jimmy's a fellow who writes plays—a deuced brainy sort of fellow—and between us we set to work to question the poor pop-eyed chappie, until finally we got at what the matter was.

As we might have guessed, it was a girl. He had had a quarrel with Angela West, the girl he was engaged to, and she had broken off the engagement. What the row had been about he didn't say, but apparently she was pretty well fed up. She wouldn't let him come near her, refused to talk on the phone, and sent back his letters unopened.

I was sorry for poor old Freddie. I knew what it felt like. I was once in love myself with a girl called Elizabeth Shoolbred, and the fact that she couldn't stand me at any price will be recorded in my autobiography. I knew the thing for Freddie.

"Change of scene is what you want, old scout," I said. "Come with me to Marvis Bay. I've taken a cottage there. Jimmy's coming down on the twenty-fourth. We'll be a cozy party."

"He's absolutely right," said Jimmy. "Change of scene's the thing. I knew a man. Girl refused him. Man went abroad. Two months later girl wired him, 'Come back. Muriel.' Man started to write out a reply; suddenly found that he couldn't remember girl's surname; so never answered at all."

But Freddie wouldn't be comforted. He just went on looking as if he had swallowed his last sixpence. However, I got him to promise to come to Marvis Bay with me. He said he might as well be there as anywhere.

Do you know Marvis Bay? It's in Dorsetshire. It isn't what you'd call a fiercely exciting spot, but it has its good points. You spend the day there bathing and sitting on the sands, and in the evening you stroll out on the shore with the gnats. At nine o'clock you rub ointment on the wounds and go to bed.

It seemed to suit poor old Freddie. Once the moon was up and the breeze sighing in the trees, you couldn't drag him from that beach with a rope. He became quite a popular pet with the gnats. They'd hang round waiting for him to come out, and would give perfectly good strollers the miss-in-baulk just so as to be in good condition for him.

Yes, it was a peaceful sort of life, but by the end of the first week I began to wish that Jimmy Pinkerton had arranged to come down earlier: for as a companion Freddie, poor old chap, wasn't anything to write home to mother about. When he wasn't chewing a pipe and scowling at the carpet, he was sitting at the piano, playing "The Rosary" with one finger. He couldn't play anything except "The Rosary," and he couldn't play much of that. Somewhere round about the third bar a fuse would blow out, and he'd have to start all over again.

He was playing it as usual one morning when I came in from bathing.

"Reggie," he said, in a hollow voice, looking up, "I've seen her."

"Seen her?" I said. "What, Miss West?"

"I was down at the post office, getting the letters, and we met in the doorway. She cut me!"

He started "The Rosary" again, and side-slipped in the second bar.

"Reggie," he said, "you ought never to have brought me here. I must go away."

"Go away?" I said. "Don't talk such rot. This is the best thing that could have happened. This is where you come out strong."

"She cut me."

"Never mind. Be a sportsman. Have another dash at her."

"She looked clean through me!"

"Of course she did. But don't mind that. Put this thing in my hands. I'll see you through. Now, what you want," I said, "is to place her under some obligation to you. What you want is to get her timidly thanking you. What you want—"

"But what's she going to thank me timidly for?"

I thought for a moment.

"Look out for a chance and save her from drowning," I said.

"I can't swim," said Freddie.

That was Freddie all over, don't you know. A dear old chap in a thousand ways, but no help to a fellow, if you know what I mean.

He cranked up the piano once more and I sprinted for the open.

I strolled out on to the sands and began to think this thing over. There was no doubt that the brain-work had got to be done by me. Dear old Freddie had his strong qualities. He was top-hole at polo, and in happier days I've heard him give an imitation of cats fighting in a back-yard that would have surprised you. But apart from that he wasn't a man of enterprise.

Well, don't you know, I was rounding some rocks, with my brain whirring like a dynamo, when I caught sight of a blue dress, and, by Jove, it was the girl. I had never met her, but Freddie had sixteen photographs of her sprinkled round his bedroom, and I knew I couldn't be mistaken. She was sitting on the sand, helping a small, fat child build a castle. On a chair close by was an elderly lady reading a novel. I heard the girl call her "aunt." So, doing the Sherlock Holmes business, I deduced that the fat child was her cousin. It struck me that if Freddie had been there he would probably have tried to work up some sentiment about the kid on the strength of it. Personally I couldn't manage it. I don't think I ever saw a child who made me feel less sentimental. He was one of those round, bulging kids.

After he had finished the castle he seemed to get bored with life, and began to whimper. The girl took him off to where a fellow was selling sweets at a stall. And I walked on.

Now, fellows, if you ask them, will tell you that I'm a chump. Well, I don't mind. I admit it. I am a chump. All the Peppers have been chumps. But what I do say is that every now and then, when you'd least expect it, I get a pretty hot brain-wave; and that's what happened now. I doubt if the idea that came to me then would have occurred to a single one of any dozen of the brainiest chappies you care to name.

It came to me on my return journey. I was walking back along the shore, when I saw the fat kid meditatively smacking a jelly-fish with a spade. The girl wasn't with him. In fact, there didn't seem to be any one in sight. I was just going to pass on when I got the brain-wave. I thought the whole thing out in a flash, don't you know. From what I had seen of the two, the girl was evidently fond of this kid, and, anyhow, he was her cousin, so what I said to myself was this: If I kidnap this young heavy-weight for the moment, and if, when the girl has got frightfully anxious about where he can have got to, dear old Freddie suddenly appears leading the infant by the hand and telling a story to the effect that he has found him wandering at large about the country and practically saved his life, why, the girl's gratitude is bound to make her chuck hostilities and be friends again. So I gathered in the kid and made off with him. All the way home I pictured that scene of reconciliation. I could see it so vividly, don't you know, that, by George, it gave me quite a choky feeling in my throat.

Freddie, dear old chap, was rather slow at getting on to the fine points of the idea. When I appeared, carrying the kid, and dumped him down in our sitting-room, he didn't absolutely effervesce with joy, if you know what I mean. The kid had started to bellow by this time, and poor old Freddie seemed to find it rather trying.

"Stop it!" he said. "Do you think nobody's got any troubles except you? What the deuce is all this, Reggie?"

The kid came back at him with a yell that made the window rattle. I raced to the kitchen and fetched a jar of honey. It was the right stuff. The kid stopped bellowing and began to smear his face with the stuff.

"Well?" said Freddie, when silence had set in. I explained the idea. After a while it began to strike him.

"You're not such a fool as you look, sometimes, Reggie," he said handsomely. "I'm bound to say this seems pretty good."

And he disentangled the kid from the honey-jar and took him out, to scour the beach for Angela.

I don't know when I've felt so happy. I was so fond of dear old Freddie that to know that he was soon going to be his old bright self again made me feel as if somebody had left me about a million pounds. I was leaning back in a chair on the veranda, smoking peacefully, when down the road I saw the old boy returning, and, by George, the kid was still with him. And Freddie looked as if he hadn't a friend in the world.

"Hello!" I said. "Couldn't you find her?"

"Yes, I found her," he replied, with one of those bitter, hollow laughs.

"Well, then—?"

Freddie sank into a chair and groaned.

"This isn't her cousin, you idiot!" he said.

"He's no relation at all. He's just a kid she happened to meet on the beach. She had never seen him before in her life."

"What! Who is he, then?"

"I don't know. Oh, Lord, I've had a time! Thank goodness you'll probably spend the next few years of your life in Dartmoor for kidnapping. That's my only consolation. I'll come and jeer at you through the bars."

"Tell me all, old boy," I said.

It took him a good long time to tell the story, for he broke off in the middle of nearly every sentence to call me names, but I gathered gradually what had happened. She had listened like an iceberg while he told the story he had prepared, and then—well, she didn't actually call him a liar, but she gave him to understand in a general sort of way that if he and Dr. Cook ever happened to meet, and started swapping stories, it would be about the biggest duel on record. And then he had crawled away with the kid, licked to a splinter.

"And mind, this is your affair," he concluded. "I'm not mixed up in it at all. If you want to escape your sentence, you'd better go and find the kid's parents and return him before the police come for you."

BY JOVE, YOU KNOW, TILL I started to tramp the place with this infernal kid, I never had a notion it would have been so deuced difficult to restore a child to its anxious parents. It's a mystery to me how kidnappers ever get caught. I searched Marvis Bay like a bloodhound, but nobody came forward to claim the infant. You'd have thought, from the lack of interest in him, that he was stopping there all by himself in a cottage of his own. It wasn't till, by an inspiration, I thought to ask the sweet-stall man that I found out that his name was Medwin, and that his parents lived at a place called Ocean Rest, in Beach Road.

I shot off there like an arrow and knocked at the door. Nobody answered. I knocked again. I could hear movements inside, but nobody came. I was just going to get to work on that knocker in such a way that the idea would filter through into these people's heads that I wasn't standing there just for the fun of the thing, when a voice from somewhere above shouted, "Hi!"

I looked up and saw a round, pink face, with grey whiskers east and west of it, staring down from an upper window.

"Hi!" it shouted again.

"What the deuce do you mean by 'Hi'?" I said.

"You can't come in," said the face. "Hello, is that Tootles?"

"My name is not Tootles, and I don't want to come in," I said. "Are you Mr. Medwin? I've brought back your son."

"I see him. Peep-bo, Tootles! Dadda can see 'oo!"

The face disappeared with a jerk. I could hear voices. The face reappeared.

"Hi!"

I churned the gravel madly.

"Do you live here?" said the face.

"I'm staying here for a few weeks."

"What's your name?"

"Pepper. But—"

"Pepper? Any relation to Edward Pepper, the colliery owner?"

"My uncle. But—"

"I used to know him well. Dear old Edward Pepper! I wish I was with him now."

"I wish you were," I said.

He beamed down at me.

"This is most fortunate," he said. "We were wondering what we were to do with Tootles. You see, we have the mumps here. My daughter Bootles has just developed mumps. Tootles must not be exposed to the risk of infection. We could not think what we were to do with him. It was most fortunate your finding him. He strayed from his nurse. I would hesitate to trust him to the care of a stranger, but you are different. Any nephew of Edward Pepper's has my implicit confidence. You must take Tootles to your house. It will be an ideal arrangement. I have written to my brother in London to come and fetch him. He may be here in a few days."

"May!"

"He is a busy man, of course; but he should certainly be here within a week. Till then Tootles can stop with you. It is an excellent plan. Very much obliged to you. Your wife will like Tootles."

"I haven't got a wife," I yelled; but the window had closed with a bang, as if the man with the whiskers had found a germ trying to escape, don't you know, and had headed it off just in time.

I breathed a deep breath and wiped my forehead.

The window flew up again.

"Hi!"

A package weighing about a ton hit me on the head and burst like a bomb.

"Did you catch it?" said the face, reappearing. "Dear me, you missed it! Never mind. You can get it at the grocer's. Ask for Bailey's Granulated Breakfast Chips. Tootles takes them for breakfast with a little milk. Be certain to get Bailey's."

My spirit was broken, if you know what I mean. I accepted the situation. Taking Tootles by the hand, I walked slowly away. Napoleon's retreat from Moscow was a picnic by the side of it.

As we turned up the road we met Freddie's Angela.

The sight of her had a marked effect on the kid Tootles. He pointed at her and said, "Wah!"

The girl stopped and smiled. I loosed the kid, and he ran to her.

"Well, baby?" she said, bending down to him. "So father found you again, did he? Your little son and I made friends on the beach this morning," she said to me.

This was the limit. Coming on top of that interview with the whiskered lunatic it so utterly unnerved me, don't you know, that she had nodded good-bye and was half-way down the road before I caught up with my breath enough to deny the charge of being the infant's father.

I hadn't expected dear old Freddie to sing with joy when he found out what had happened, but I did think he might have shown a little more manly fortitude. He leaped up, glared at the kid, and clutched his head. He didn't speak for a long time, but, on the other hand, when he began he did not leave off for a long time. He was quite emotional, dear old boy. It beat me where he could have picked up such expressions.

"Well," he said, when he had finished, "say something! Heavens! man, why don't you say something?"

"You don't give me a chance, old top," I said soothingly.

"What are you going to do about it?"

"What can we do about it?"

"We can't spend our time acting as nurses to this—this exhibit."

He got up.

"I'm going back to London," he said.

"Freddie!" I cried. "Freddie, old man!" My voice shook. "Would you desert a pal at a time like this?"

"I would. This is your business, and you've got to manage it."

"Freddie," I said, "you've got to stand by me. You must. Do you realize that this child has to be undressed, and bathed, and dressed again? You wouldn't leave me to do all that single-handed? Freddie, old scout, we were at school together. Your mother likes me. You owe me a tenner."

He sat down again.

"Oh, well," he said resignedly.

"Besides, old top," I said, "I did it all for your sake, don't you know?"

He looked at me in a curious way.

"Reggie," he said, in a strained voice, "one moment. I'll stand a good deal, but I won't stand for being expected to be grateful."

Looking back at it, I see that what saved me from Colney Hatch in that crisis was my bright idea of buying up most of the contents of the local sweet-shop. By serving out sweets to the kid practically incessantly we managed to get through the rest of that day pretty satisfactorily. At eight o'clock he fell asleep in a chair, and, having undressed him by unbuttoning every button in sight and, where there were no buttons, pulling till something gave, we carried him up to bed.

Freddie stood looking at the pile of clothes on the floor and I knew what he was thinking. To get the kid undressed had been simple—a mere matter of muscle. But how were we to get him into his clothes again? I stirred the pile with my foot. There was a long linen arrangement which might have been anything. Also a strip of pink flannel which was like nothing on earth. We looked at each other and smiled wanly.

But in the morning I remembered that there were children at the next bungalow but one. We went there before breakfast and borrowed their nurse. Women are wonderful, by George they are! She had that kid dressed and looking fit for anything in about eight minutes. I showered wealth on her, and she promised to come in morning and evening. I sat down to breakfast almost cheerful again. It was the first bit of silver lining there had been to the cloud up to date.

"And after all," I said, "there's lots to be said for having a child about the house, if you know what I mean. Kind of cozy and domestic—what!"

Just then the kid upset the milk over Freddie's trousers, and when he had come back after changing his clothes he began to talk about what a much-maligned man King Herod was. The more he saw of Tootles, he said, the less he wondered at those impulsive views of his on infanticide.

Two days later Jimmy Pinkerton came down. Jimmy took one look at the kid, who happened to be howling at the moment, and picked up his portmanteau.

"For me," he said, "the hotel. I can't write dialogue with that sort of thing going on. Whose work is this? Which of you adopted this little treasure?"

I told him about Mr. Medwin and the mumps. Jimmy seemed interested.

"I might work this up for the stage," he said. "It wouldn't make a bad situation for act two of a farce."

"Farce!" snarled poor old Freddie.

"Rather. Curtain of act one on hero, a well-meaning, half-baked sort of idiot just like—that is to say, a well-meaning, half-baked sort of idiot, kidnapping the child. Second act, his adventures with it. I'll rough it out tonight. Come along and show me the hotel, Reggie."

As we went I told him the rest of the story—the Angela part. He laid down his portmanteau and looked at me like an owl through his glasses.

"What!" he said. "Why, hang it, this is a play, ready-made. It's the old 'Tiny Hand' business. Always safe stuff. Parted lovers. Lisping child. Reconciliation over the little cradle. It's big. Child, center. Girl L.C.; Freddie, up stage, by the piano. Can Freddie play the piano?"

"He can play a little of 'The Rosary' with one finger."

Jimmy shook his head.

"No; we shall have to cut out the soft music. But the rest's all right. Look here." He squatted in the sand. "This stone is the girl. This bit of seaweed's the child. This nutshell is Freddie. Dialogue leading up to child's line. Child

speaks like, 'Boofer lady, does 'oo love dadda?' Business
of outstretched hands. Hold picture for a moment. Freddie crosses L., takes girl's hand. Business of swallowing
lump in throat. Then big speech. 'Ah, Marie,' or whatever
her name is—Jane—Agnes—Angela? Very well. 'Ah, Angela, has not this gone on too long? A little child rebukes
us! Angela!' And so on. Freddie must work up his own
part. I'm just giving you the general outline. And we must
get a good line for the child. 'Boofer lady, does 'oo love
dadda?' isn't definite enough. We want something
more—ah! 'Kiss Freddie,' that's it. Short, crisp, and has
the punch."

"But, Jimmy, old top," I said, "the only objection is,
don't you know, that there's no way of getting the girl to
the cottage. She cuts Freddie. She wouldn't come within a
mile of him."

Jimmy frowned.

"That's awkward," he said. "Well, we shall have to
make it an exterior set instead of an interior. We can easily
corner her on the beach somewhere, when we're ready.
Meanwhile, we must get the kid letter-perfect. First rehearsal for lines and business eleven sharp tomorrow."

Poor old Freddie was in such a gloomy state of mind
that we decided not to tell him the idea till we had finished coaching the kid. He wasn't in the mood to have a
thing like that hanging over him. So we concentrated on
Tootles. And pretty early in the proceedings we saw that
the only way to get Tootles worked up to the spirit of the
thing was to introduce sweets of some sort as a sub-mo-
tive, so to speak.

"The chief difficulty," said Jimmy Pinkerton at the end
of the first rehearsal, "is to establish a connection in the

kid's mind between his line and the sweets. Once he has grasped the basic fact that those two words, clearly spoken, result automatically in acid-drops, we have got a success."

I've often thought, don't you know, how interesting it must be to be one of those animal-trainer Johnnies: to stimulate the dawning intelligence, and that sort of thing. Well, this was every bit as exciting. Some days success seemed to be staring us in the eye, and the kid got the line out as if he'd been an old professional. And then he'd go all to pieces again. And time was flying.

"We must hurry up, Jimmy," I said. "The kid's uncle may arrive any day now and take him away."

"And we haven't an understudy," said Jimmy. "There's something in that. We must work! My goodness, that kid's a bad study. I've known deaf-mutes who would have learned the part quicker."

I will say this for the kid, though: he was a trier. Failure didn't discourage him. Whenever there was any kind of sweet near he had a dash at his line, and kept on saying something till he got what he was after. His only fault was his uncertainty. Personally, I would have been prepared to risk it, and start the performance at the first opportunity, but Jimmy said no.

"We're not nearly ready," said Jimmy. "Today, for instance, he said 'Kick Freddie.' That's not going to win any girl's heart. And she might do it, too. No; we must postpone production awhile yet."

But, by George, we didn't. The curtain went up the very next afternoon.

It was nobody's fault—certainly not mine. It was just Fate. Freddie had settled down at the piano, and I was leading the kid out of the house to exercise it, when, just as we'd got out to the veranda, along came the girl Angela on her way to the beach. The kid set up his usual yell at the sight of her, and she stopped at the foot of the steps.

"Hello, baby!" she said. "Good morning," she said to me. "May I come up?"

She didn't wait for an answer. She just came. She seemed to be that sort of girl. She came up on the veranda and started fussing over the kid. And six feet away, mind you, Freddie smiting the piano in the sitting-room. It was a dash disturbing situation, don't you know. At any minute Freddie might take it into his head to come out on to the veranda, and we hadn't even begun to rehearse him in his part.

I tried to break up the scene.

"We were just going down to the beach," I said.

"Yes?" said the girl. She listened for a moment. "So you're having your piano tuned?" she said. "My aunt has been trying to find a tuner for ours. Do you mind if I go in and tell this man to come on to us when he's finished here?"

"Er—not yet!" I said. "Not yet, if you don't mind. He can't bear to be disturbed when he's working. It's the artistic temperament. I'll tell him later."

"Very well," she said, getting up to go. "Ask him to call at Pine Bungalow. West is the name. Oh, he seems to have stopped. I suppose he will be out in a minute now. I'll wait."

"Don't you think—shouldn't we be going on to the beach?" I said.

She had started talking to the kid and didn't hear. She was feeling in her pocket for something.

"The beach," I babbled.

"See what I've brought for you, baby," she said. And, by George, don't you know, she held up in front of the kid's bulging eyes a chunk of toffee about the size of the Automobile Club.

That finished it. We had just been having a long rehearsal, and the kid was all worked up in his part. He got it right first time.

"Kiss Fweddie!" he shouted.

And the front door opened, and Freddie came out on to the veranda, for all the world as if he had been taking a cue.

He looked at the girl, and the girl looked at him. I looked at the ground, and the kid looked at the toffee.

"Kiss Fweddie!" he yelled. "Kiss Fweddie!"

The girl was still holding up the toffee, and the kid did what Jimmy Pinkerton would have called "business of outstretched hands" towards it.

"Kiss Fweddie!" he shrieked.

"What does this mean?" said the girl, turning to me.

"You'd better give it to him, don't you know," I said. "He'll go on till you do."

She gave the kid his toffee, and he subsided. Poor old Freddie still stood there gaping, without a word.

"What does it mean?" said the girl again. Her face was pink, and her eyes were sparkling in the sort of way, don't you know, that makes a fellow feel as if he hadn't any bones in him, if you know what I mean. Did you ever tread on your partner's dress at a dance and tear it, and see her smile at you like an angel and say: "Please don't apologize. It's nothing," and then suddenly meet her clear blue eyes and feel as if you had stepped on the teeth of a

rake and had the handle jump up and hit you in the face?
Well, that's how Freddie's Angela looked.

"Well?" she said, and her teeth gave a little click.

I gulped. Then I said it was nothing. Then I said it was
nothing much. Then I said, "Oh, well, it was this way."
And, after a few brief remarks about Jimmy Pinkerton, I
told her all about it. And all the while Idiot Freddie stood
there gaping, without a word.

And the girl didn't speak, either. She just stood listening.

And then she began to laugh. I never heard a girl laugh
so much. She leaned against the side of the veranda and
shrieked. And all the while Freddie, the World's Champion Chump, stood there, saying nothing.

Well I sidled towards the steps. I had said all I had to
say, and it seemed to me that about here the stage-direc-
tion "exit" was written in my part. I gave poor old Freddie
up in despair. If only he had said a word, it might have
been all right. But there he stood, speechless. What can a
fellow do with a fellow like that?

Just out of sight of the house I met Jimmy Pinkerton.

"Hello, Reggie!" he said. "I was just coming to you.
Where's the kid? We must have a big rehearsal today."

"No good," I said sadly. "It's all over. The thing's finished. Poor dear old Freddie has made an ass of himself
and killed the whole show."

"Tell me," said Jimmy.

I told him.

"Fluffed in his lines, did he?" said Jimmy, nodding
thoughtfully. "It's always the way with these amateurs.
We must go back at once. Things look bad, but it may not

be too late," he said as we started. "Even now a few well-chosen words from a man of the world, and —"

"Great Scot!" I cried. "Look!"

In front of the cottage stood six children, a nurse, and the fellow from the grocer's staring. From the windows of the houses opposite projected about four hundred heads of both sexes, staring. Down the road came galloping five more children, a dog, three men, and a boy, about to stare. And on our porch, as unconscious of the spectators as if they had been alone in the Sahara, stood Freddie and Angela, clasped in each other's arms.

DEAR OLD FREDDIE MAY have been fluffy in his lines, but, by George, his business had certainly gone with a bang!

# The Test Case

WELL-MEANING CHAPPIES at the club sometimes amble up to me and tap me on the wish-bone, and say "Reggie, old top" — my name's Reggie Pepper — "you ought to get married, old man." Well, what I mean to say is, it's all very well, and I see their point and all that sort of thing; but it takes two to make a marriage, and to date I haven't met a girl who didn't seem to think the contract was too big to be taken on. One and all, they have tied a can to me and requested me to stand aside and let the rest of the waiting line get action. Well, if you see what I mean, after a few years of this sort of thing, a fellow gets discouraged; and nowadays I'm rather by way of being the stern, soured man who's jolly well fed up with the sex. If any girl wants to marry me now, she has got to come after me with a rope.

Looking back, it seems to me that I came nearer to getting over the home-plate with Ann Selby than with most of the others. In fact, but for circumstances over which I had no dashed control, I am inclined to think that we should have brought it off; and I'm bound to say that, now that what the poet chappie calls the first fine frenzy has been on the ice for awhile and I am able to consider the thing calmly, I am deuced glad we didn't. She was one of those strong-minded girls, and I hate to think of what she would have done to me. The other day I saw the fellow she did marry. I was at the club-window, meditatively sipping something or other, when a Woman's Suffrage procession came along; and there, in the very first rank, carrying an enormous banner and looking licked to a splinter, he marched; and the sight gave me such a turn — thinking that it might have been me — that I had to press the bell and have two more in rapid succession.

At the time, though, I was frightfully in love, and, for quite a while after she definitely gave me the mitten, I lost my stroke at golf so completely that a child could have given me a stroke a hole and got away with it. I was all broken up, and I contend to this day that I was dashed badly treated.

Let me give you what they call the data.

ONE DAY I WAS lunching with Ann, and was just proposing to her as usual, when, instead of simply refusing me, as she generally did, she fixed me with a thoughtful eye and kind of opened her heart.

"Do you know, Reggie, I am in doubt."

"Give me the benefit of it," I said. Which I maintain was pretty good on the spur of the moment, but didn't get a hand. She simply ignored it, and went on.

"Sometimes," she said, "you seem to me entirely vapid and brainless; at other times you say or do things which suggest that there are possibilities in you; that, properly stimulated and encouraged, you might overcome the handicap of large private means and do something worth while. I wonder if that is simply my imagination?" She watched me very closely as she spoke.

"Rather not. You've absolutely summed me up. With you beside me, stimulating and all that sort of rot, don't you know, I should show a flash of speed which would astonish you."

"I wish I could be certain."

"Take a chance on it."

She shook her head.

"I must be certain. Marriage is such a gamble. I have just been staying with my sister Hilda and her husband—"

"Dear old Harold Bodkin. I know him well. In fact, I've a standing invitation to go down there and stay as long as I like. Harold is one of my best pals. Harold is a corker. Good old Harold is—"

"I would rather you didn't eulogize him, Reggie. I am extremely angry with Harold. He is making Hilda perfectly miserable."

"What on earth do you mean? Harold wouldn't hurt a fly. He's one of those dreamy, sentimental chumps who—"

"It is precisely his sentimentality which is at the bottom of the whole trouble. You know, of course, that Hilda is not his first wife?"

"That's right. His first wife died about five years ago."

"He still cherishes her memory."

"Very sporting of him."

"Is it! If you were a girl, how would you like to be married to a man who was always making you bear in mind that you were only number two in his affections; a man whose idea of a pleasant conversation was a string of anecdotes illustrating what a dear woman his first wife was; a man who expected you to upset all your plans if they clashed with some anniversary connected with his other marriage?"

"That does sound pretty rotten. Does dear old Harold do all that?"

"That's only a small part of what he does. Why, if you will believe me, every evening at seven o'clock he goes and shuts himself up in a little room at the top of the house, and meditates."

"What on earth does he do that for?"

"Apparently his first wife died at seven in the evening. There is a portrait of her in the room; I believe he lays flowers in front of it. And Hilda is expected to greet him on his return with a happy smile."

"Why doesn't she kick?"

"I have been trying to persuade her to, but she won't. Most women are doormats, and Hilda's one of them. She just pretends she doesn't mind. She has a nervous, sensitive temperament, and the thing is slowly crushing her. Don't talk to me of Harold!"

CONSIDERING THAT she had started him as a topic, I thought this pretty unjust. I didn't want to talk of Harold. I wanted to talk about myself.

"Well, what has all this got to do with your not wanting to marry me?" I said.

"Nothing, except that it is an illustration of the risks a woman runs when she marries a man of a certain type."

"Great Scott! You surely don't class me with Harold?"

"Yes, in a way you are very much alike. You have both always had large private means, and have never had the wholesome discipline of work; and consequently you have never had to exercise your brains. A man who has never done that is an unknown quantity; he may do anything absurd and irritating."

"But, dash it, Harold, on your showing, is an absolute nut. Why should you think that I would be anything like that?"

"There's always the risk."

A hot idea came to me.

"Look here, Ann," I said, "suppose I do something which proves that I'm not the total chump you consider me, how about it then? Suppose I pull off some stunt which only a deuced brainy chappie could get away with? Would you marry me then?"

"Certainly. What do you propose to do?"

"Do! What do I propose to do! Why, I propose—well, to be absolutely frank, at the moment I don't quite know."

"You never will know, Reggie. You're one of the idle rich, and your brain, if you ever had one, has atrophied. Better not worry yourself, trying to think. Go on sitting in your club-window, watching the traffic and sucking a cane."

Well, that seemed to me to put the lid on it. I didn't mind a heart-to-heart talk, but this was mere abuse. I changed the subject.

"What would you like after that fish?" I said coldly.

You know how it is when you get an idea. For a while it sort of simmers inside you, and then suddenly it sizzles up like a rocket, and there you are, right up against it. That's what happened now. I went away from that luncheon, vaguely determined to pull off some stunt which would prove that I was right there with the gray matter, but without any clear notion of what I was going to do. Side by side with this in my mind was the case of dear old Harold. When I wasn't brooding on the stunt, I was brooding on Harold. I was fond of the good old lad, and I hated the idea of his slowly wrecking the home purely by being a chump. And all of a sudden the two things clicked together like a couple of chemicals, and there I was with a corking plan for killing two birds with one stone: putting one across that would startle and impress Ann, and at the same time healing the breach between Harold and Hilda.

IT WAS LIKE THIS: I happened to be passing a big candy shop, and in an idle sort of way I recalled that old yarn they pitch to you when you're a kid, about how they make certain that the people who sell the stuff don't go pinching the stock. You know the stunt. When a new hand is taken on in a candy-shop, the boss tells him or her to go right ahead and help himself. "This is the life," says the new hand, and proceeds to cut a wide swath through the stuff. By the end of a week he has had all the candy he wants in a life-time, and wouldn't touch so much as a marsh-mallow if you offered him a handsome reward.

And I had hardly brooded over this yarn for more than a minute or so, when something seemed to say to me, "This is the dope for dear old Harold."

You see what I mean? My idea was that, in a case like this, it's no good trying opposition. What you want is to work it so that the chappie quits of his own accord. You want to egg him on to overdoing the thing till he gets so that he says to himself, "Enough! Never again!" That was what was going to happen to Harold.

When you're going to do a thing, there's nothing like making a quick start. I wrote to Harold straight away, proposing myself for a visit; and Harold wrote back telling me to come right along.

Harold and Hilda lived alone in a large house on Long Island. I believe they did a good deal of entertaining at times, but on this occasion I was the only guest. The only other person of note in the place was Ponsonby, the butler, whom Harold had imported at great expense from England. It was a quiet little party, but it suited me all right.

OF COURSE, IF Harold had been an ordinary sort of chappie, what I had come to do would have been a pretty big order. I don't mind many things, but I do hesitate to dig into my host's most intimate private affairs. But Harold was such a simple-minded Johnnie, so grateful for a little sympathy and advice, that my job wasn't so very difficult.

It wasn't as if he minded talking about Amelia, which was his first wife's name. The difficulty was to get him to talk of anything else. I began to understand what Ann meant by saying it was tough on Hilda.

A child ought to have been able to see that it was beginning to jar on her; but dear old Harold was more like a child with water on the brain than anything else. He was pure chump, clean through. I have a pretty wide circle of friends, the majority of them more or less daffy, but good old Harold was unique in my experience.

As an instance of the sort of fellow he was: the first night I was down there, I was roused out of a refreshing sleep at about four o'clock or some such frightful hour, and found Harold standing by my bedside.

"Sh!" he said. "Don't make a noise. Come on!"

I was out of bed with an Indian club in one hand and a poker in the other before he could speak again. As we legged it through the house in our bare feet, I tried to keep in mind all I'd ever been told about burglars not shooting except as a last resort. We got on to the top floor, and up a ladder through a trap-door onto the roof, and I was just bracing myself for the conflict and hoping they were small burglars, when he grabbed me by the arm.

"Look!"

I jumped a foot, and looked where he pointed. I could not see anything.

"Isn't it wonderful?"

"Isn't what wonderful?"

"The dawn, man! Look at it! All pink!"

And then we went back to bed again.

That was Harold.

I'm bound to say the old boy was clay in my hands. People call me a chump, but Harold was a super-chump, and I did what I liked with him. The second morning of my visit, after breakfast, he grabbed me by the arm.

"This way, Reggie. I'm just going to show old Reggie Amelia's portrait, dear."

THERE WAS A LITTLE room all by itself on the top floor. He explained to me that it had been his studio. At one time Harold used to do a bit of painting in an amateur way.

"There!" he said, pointing at the portrait. "I did that myself, Reggie. It was away being cleaned when you were here last. It's like dear Amelia, isn't it?"

I suppose it was, in a way. At any rate, you could recognize the likeness when you were told who it was supposed to be.

He sat down in front of it, and gave it the thoughtful once over.

"Do you know, Reggie, old top, sometimes, when I sit here, I feel as if Amelia were back again."

"It would be a bit awkward for you if she was."

"How do you mean?"

"Well, old lad, you happen to be married to someone else."

A look of child-like enthusiasm came over his face.

"Reggie, I wouldn't talk about this to anyone else but you," he began. It's my experience that the fellows who begin by saying that are always the chappies who, if they couldn't get anyone else to tell their most intimate private affairs to, would rush out and buttonhole the traffic cop. I'm convinced that poor old Harold talked Amelia to everyone he got within speaking distance of. It wasn't his fault; it was just the way he was built. "But you are such an old pal," he went on, "that it's different with you. Reggie, I want to tell you how splendid Hilda is. Lots of other women might object to my still cherishing Amelia's memory, but Hilda has been so nice about it from the beginning. She understands so thoroughly."

I hadn't much breath left after that, but I used what I had to say: "She doesn't object?"

"Not a bit," said Harold. "It makes everything so pleasant."

When I had recovered a bit, I said, "What do you mean by everything?"

"Well," he said, "for instance, I come up here every evening at seven and—er—think for a few minutes."

"A few minutes!"

"What do you mean?"

"Well, a few minutes isn't long."

"But I always have my cocktail at a quarter past."

"You could postpone it."

"And Ponsonby likes us to start dinner at seven-thirty."

"What on earth has Ponsonby to do with it?"

"Well, he likes to get off by nine, you know. I think he goes off and plays bowls at the road-house. You see, Reggie, old man, we have to study Ponsonby a little. He's always on the verge of giving notice—in fact, it was only by coaxing him on one or two occasions that we got him to stay on—and he's such a treasure that I don't know what we should do if we lost him. But, if you think that I ought to stay longer—?"

"Certainly I do. You ought to do a thing like this properly, or not at all."

He sighed.

"It's a frightful risk, but in future we'll dine at eight."

So that was something accomplished. I knew Harold pretty well, and I had the feeling that, if this Amelia business could be made to inconvenience him, it wouldn't be long before he came to the conclusion that it was a trifle tough on Hilda. There's nothing like a little discomfort for injecting sense into the sort of fellow old Harold was.

It seemed to me that there was a suspicion of a cloud on Ponsonby's shining morning face, when the news was broken to him that for the future he couldn't unleash himself on the local bowling talent as early as usual, but he made no kick, and the new order of things began.

My next offensive movement I attribute to a flash of absolute genius.

I was glancing through a photograph album in the drawing-room before lunch, when I came upon a face which I vaguely remembered. It was one of those wide, flabby faces, with bulging eyes, and something about it struck me as familiar. I consulted Harold, who came in at that moment.

"That?" said Harold. "That's Percy."

He gave a slight shudder.

"Amelia's brother, you know. An awful fellow. I haven't seen him for years."

THEN I PLACED Percy. I had met him once or twice in the old days, and I had a brain-wave. Percy! He was the card to play. I remembered him well now: a stupendous blighter! Percy was everything that poor old Harold disliked most. He was hearty at breakfast, a confirmed back-slapper, a fellow whose only topic of conversation was baseball, a man who prodded you in the chest when he spoke to you. I recollected quite clearly that Harold had never been able to stand him at any price.

"You haven't seen him for years!" I said in a shocked voice.

"Thank heaven!" said Harold devoutly.

I put down the photograph-album, and looked at him in a deuced serious way.

"Then it's high time you asked him to come here."

Harold blanched.

"Reggie, old man, you don't know what you are saying. You can't remember Percy. I wish you wouldn't say these things, even in fun."

"I'm not saying it in fun. Of course, it's none of my business, but you have paid me the compliment of confiding in me about Amelia, and I feel justified in speaking. All I can say is that, if you cherish her memory as you say you do, you show it in a very strange way. How you can square your neglect of Percy with your alleged devotion to Amelia's memory, beats me. It seems to me that you have no choice. You must either drop the whole thing and admit that your love for her is dead, or else you must stop this infernal treatment of her favorite brother. You can't have it both ways."

He looked at me like a hunted stag. "But, Reggie, old man! Percy! He asks riddles at breakfast."

"I don't care."

"Hilda can't stand him."

"What of it?"

"The last time I saw him, he talked for nearly half an hour about somebody's home-run."

"It doesn't matter. You must invite him. It's not a case of what you like or dislike. It's your duty."

He struggled with his feelings for a bit.

"Very well," he said in a crushed sort of voice.

At dinner that night he said to Hilda:

"I'm going to ask Amelia's brother Percy down to spend a few days. It is so long since we have seen him."

Hilda didn't answer at once. She looked at him in rather a curious sort of way, I thought.

"Very well, dear," she said.

I was deuced sorry for the poor girl, but I felt like a surgeon. She would be glad later on, for I was convinced that in a very short while poor old Harold must crack under the strain, especially after I had put across the coup which I was meditating for the very next evening.

It was, so to speak, the culminating coup of my campaign. I had been watching Harold pretty closely, and I could see that the alteration in his schedule had not been without its effects. A man who has been in the habit for years of taking a cocktail at a quarter past seven suffers terribly if you suddenly deprive him of it. I speak from experience. When I used to go and stay with my uncle — the one who left me all his money — I never got a look at one. He was a teetotaller, and, if you wanted anything to put an edge on you before a meal, it had to be grape juice. So I could take a line through my own sufferings and arrive at a fairly close estimate of what Harold was feeling.

I had him weak. With my next move I hoped to administer the knock-out.

It was quite simple. Simple, that is to say, in its working, but a devilish brainy thing for a chappie to have thought out. If Ann had really meant what she had said at lunch that day, and was prepared to stick to her bargain and marry me as soon as I showed a burst of intelligence, she was mine. There wasn't a thing to it. I had only to think of it, and the air became heavy with the scent of orange blossoms, and invisible organs starting playing "The Voice That Breathed O'er Eden."

WHAT IT CAME TO WAS that, if dear old Harold enjoyed meditating in front of Amelia's portrait, he was jolly well going to have all the meditating he wanted, and a bit over, for my simple scheme was to lurk outside till he had gone into the little room on the top floor, and then, with the aid of one of those jolly little wedges which you use to keep windows from rattling, see to it that the old boy remained there till they sent out search-parties.

There wasn't a flaw in my reasoning. When Harold didn't roll in at the sound of the dinner-gong, Hilda would take it for granted that he was doing an extra bit of meditating that night, and her pride would stop her sending out a hurry-call for him. As for Harold, when he found that all was not well with the door, he would probably yell with considerable vim. But it was odds against any-one hearing him. As for me, you might think that I was going to suffer owing to the probable postponement of dinner. Not so, but far otherwise, for on the night I had selected for the coup I was dining out at the neighboring inn with my old college chum, Freddie Meadowes. It is true that Freddie wasn't going to be within fifty miles of the place on that particular night, but they weren't to know that.

Did I describe the peculiar isolation of that room on the top floor, where the portrait was? I don't think I did. It was, as a matter of fact, the only room in those parts, for, in the days when he did his amateur painting, old Harold was strong on the artistic seclusion business and hated noise, and his studio was the only room in use on that floor.

In short, to sum up, the thing was a cinch.

PUNCTUALLY AT TEN minutes to seven I was in readiness on the scene. There was a recess with a curtain in front of it a few yards from the door, and there I waited, fondling my little wedge, for Harold to walk up to allow the pro-ceedings to start. It was almost pitch-dark, and that made the time of waiting seem longer. Somehow it's always more of a job waiting in the dark. I didn't dare to strike a light and look at my watch, but I knew Harold was always on time, so there wasn't any necessity.

Presently—I seemed to have been there much longer than ten minutes—I heard steps approaching. They came past where I stood, and went on into the room. The door closed, and I hopped out and sprinted up to it, and the

next moment I had the good old wedge under the wood —
as neat a job as you could imagine. And then I strolled
downstairs, and toddled off to the inn.

I didn't hurry over my dinner, partly because the
browsing and sluicing at the inn was really astonishingly
good for a road-house and partly because I wanted to give
Harold plenty of time for meditation. I suppose it must
have been a couple of hours or more when I finally turned
in at the front door.

Somebody was playing the piano in the drawing-
room. I hesitated for a moment whether to go in or not. It
could only be Hilda who was playing, and I had doubts
as to whether Hilda wanted company just then — mine, at
any rate.

Eventually I decided to risk it, for I wanted to hear the
latest about dear old Harold, so in I went, and it wasn't
Hilda at all; it was Ann Selby.

"Hello," I said. "I didn't know you were coming down
here."

It seemed so odd, don't you know, as it hadn't been
more than ten days or so since her last visit.

"Good evening, Reggie," she said.

Have you ever noticed that, when things have been
happening, you can nearly always tell it in the way a person wishes you good evening or good morning? I remember once, when I was a kid, smashing a valuable Dresden
China figure in my uncle's study overnight. Next day,
when I came down to breakfast, he said, "Good morning,
Reginald!" and, if you'll believe me, I was out of the house
and up a tree before he had time even to touch the fringe
of the Dresden China topic. I knew, don't you know! It
was the same now — only the emotion I spotted in the

words wasn't wrath or resentment or whatever it is that makes an old gentleman weighing two hundred pounds leg it like a mustang of the prairie after a kid of ten and try to put one or two across him with an oak walking-stick; it was triumph. And what Ann had to be triumphant about I couldn't see.

"What's been happening?" I asked.

"How do you know anything has been happening?"

"I guessed it."

SHE PLAYED A BAR or two of "See the Conquering Hero Comes" with the soft pedal down, then swung round on the music stool and smiled happily.

"Well, you're quite right, as it happens, Reggie. A good deal has been happening."

She went to the door, and looked out, listening. Then she shut it, and came back.

"Hilda has revolted!"

"Revolted?"

"Yes, put her foot down—made a stand—refused to go on meekly putting up with Harold's insane behavior."

"I don't understand."

She gave me a look of pity.

"You always were so dense, Reggie. I will tell you the whole thing from the beginning. You remember what I spoke to you about, one day when we were lunching to-gether? Well, I don't suppose you have noticed it—I know what you are—but things have been getting steadily worse. For one thing Harold insisted on lengthening his visits to the top room, and naturally Ponsonby com-plained. Hilda tells me that she had to plead with him to induce him to stay on. Well, Hilda, poor girl, is so long-

suffering that she actually put up with that without a murmur. Then the climax came. I don't know if you recollect
Amelia's brother Percy? You must have met him when
she was alive—a perfectly unspeakable person with a
loud voice and overpowering manners. Suddenly, out of
a blue sky, Harold announced his intention of inviting
him to stay. It was the last straw. This afternoon I received
a telegram from poor Hilda, saying that she was leaving
Harold and coming to stay with me, and a few hours later
the poor child arrived at my apartment."

You mustn't suppose that I stood listening silently to
this speech. Every time she seemed to he going to stop for
breath I tried to horn in and tell her all these things which
had been happening were not mere flukes, as she seemed
to think, but parts of a deuced carefully-planned scheme
of my own. But you know how it is with girls—especially
if, like Ann, they're used to speaking in public. They don't
stop for breath; it doesn't seem to matter to them whether
they have any air in their lungs or not; they can keep on
talking by sheer will-power. Every time I tried to interrupt, Ann would wave me down, and carry on without so
much as a semi-colon.

But at this point I did manage to get a word in.

"I know, I know, I know! I did it all. It was I who suggested to old Harold that he should lengthen the meditations, and insisted on his inviting Percy to stay."

I HAD HARDLY GOT the words out, when I saw that they
were not making the hit I had anticipated. She looked at
me with an expression of absolute scorn, don't you know.

"Well, really, Reggie," she said at last. "I never had a
very high opinion of your intelligence, as you know, but

this is a revelation to me. What motive you can have had, unless you did it in a spirit of pure mischief—" She stopped, and there was a glare of undiluted repulsion in her eyes. "Reggie! I can't believe it! Of all the things I loathe most, a practical joker is the worst. Do you mean to tell me you did all this as a practical joke?"

"Great Scott, no! It was like this—"

I paused for a bare second to collect my thoughts, so as to put the thing clearly to her. I might have known what would happen. She dashed in and collared the conversation again.

"Well, never mind. As it happens there is no harm done. Quite the reverse, in fact. Hilda left a note for Harold, telling him what she had done and where she had gone and why she had gone, and Harold found it. The result was that, after Hilda had been with me for some time, in he came in a panic and absolutely grovelled before the dear child. It seems incredible, but he had apparently had no notion that his absurd behavior had met with anything but approval from Hilda. He went on as if he was mad. He was beside himself. He clutched his hair and stamped about the room, and then he jumped at the telephone and called this house up on the long distance, and got Ponsonby on the wire and told him to go straight to the little room on the top floor and take Amelia's portrait down. I thought that a little unnecessary myself, but he was in such a whirl of remorse that it was useless to try and get him to be rational. So Hilda was consoled, and he calmed down, and we all came down here in the automobile. So you see—"

At this moment the door opened, and in came Harold.

"I say—hello, Reggie, old man—I say, it's a funny thing, but we can't find Ponsonby anywhere."

THERE ARE MOMENTS in a chappie's life, don't you know, when Reason, so to speak, totters, as it were, on its bally throne. This was one of them. The situation seemed somehow to have got out of my grip. I suppose, strictly speaking, I ought, at this juncture, to have cleared my throat and said in an audible tone, "Harold, old top, I know where Ponsonby is." But somehow I couldn't. Something seemed to keep the words back. I just stood there and said nothing.

"Nobody seems to have seen anything of him," said Harold. "I wonder where he can have got to."

Hilda came in, looking so happy I hardly recognized her. I remember feeling how strange it was that anybody could be happy just then.

"I know," she said. "Of course! Doesn't he always go off to the inn and play bowls at this time?"

"Why, of course," said Harold. "So he does."

And he asked Ann to play something on the piano. And pretty soon we had settled down to a regular jolly musical evening.

I remember reading a story once of a chappie who murdered another chappie, and, not being quite decided what to do with the body, tied it under the dining-room table, and left it there pending his final decision. I had often wondered how he felt, especially as it happened that he had to give a dinner party in the room where the good old body was. Now I knew. He may have felt a trifle uncomfortable, but he hadn't anything on me.

Ann must have played a matter of two or three thousand tunes, when Harold got up.

"By the way," he said, "I suppose he did what I told him about the picture before he went out. Let's go and see."

"Oh, Harold, what does it matter?" asked Hilda.

"Don't be silly, Harold," said Ann.

I would have said the same, only I couldn't say anything.

Harold wasn't to be stopped. He led the way out of the room and upstairs, and we all trailed after him.

We had just reached the top floor, when Hilda stopped, and said "Hark!"

It was a voice.

"Hi!" it said. "Hi!"

Harold legged it to the door of the studio.

"Ponsonby!"

FROM WITHIN CAME the voice again, and I have never heard anything to touch the combined pathos, dignity, and indignation it managed to condense into two words.

"Yes, sir?"

"What on earth are you doing in there?"

"I came here, sir, in accordance with your instructions on the telephone, and—"

Harold rattled the door.

"The darned thing's stuck."

"Yes, sir."

"How on earth did that happen?"

"I could not say, sir."

"Kick the door, Ponsonby."

"Very good, sir."

A restrained kicking made itself heard.

"How can the door have stuck like this?" said Ann.

Somebody—I suppose it was me, though the voice didn't seem familiar—spoke.

"Perhaps there's a wedge under it," said this chappie.

"A wedge? What do you mean?"

"One of those little wedges you use to keep windows from rattling, don't you know."

"But why—? ... You're absolutely right, Reggie, old man, there is!

He yanked it out, and flung the door open, and out came Ponsonby, looking like Lady Macbeth.

"I wish to give notice, sir," he said, "and I should esteem it a favor if I might go to the pantry and procure some food, as I am extremely hungry."

And he passed from our midst, with Hilda after him, saying: "But, Ponsonby! Be reasonable, Ponsonby!"

Ann Selby turned on me with a swish.

"Reggie," she said, "did you shut Ponsonby in there?"

"Well, yes, as a matter of fact, I did."

"But why?" cried Harold.

"Oh, I don't know."

"But, heavens, man, you must have had a reason."

"Well, to be absolutely frank, old top, I thought it was you."

"You thought it was me? But why—what did you want to lock me in for?"

I hesitated. It was a delicate business telling him the idea. And, while I was hesitating, Ann jumped in.

"I can tell you why, Harold. It was because Reggie belongs to that sub-species of humanity known as practical jokers. This sort of thing is his idea of humor."

"Humor!" said Harold. "Losing us a priceless butler! If that's your idea of—"

Hilda came back, pale and anxious.

"Harold, dear, do come and help me reason with Ponsonby. He is in the pantry gnawing a cold chicken like a dog, and he only stops to say 'I give notice!' Do come and entreat him to take a broad view of the thing."

"Yes," said Ann. "Go, both of you. I wish to speak to Reggie alone."

That's how I came to lose Ann. At intervals during her remarks I tried to put my side of the case, but it was no good. She wouldn't listen. And presently something seemed to tell me that now was the time to go to my room and pack. Half an hour later I slid silently into the night.

Wasn't it Shakespeare or somebody who said that the road to Hell—or words to that effect—was paved with good intentions? If it was Shakespeare, it just goes to prove what they are always saying about him—that he knew a bit. Take it from one who knows, the old boy was absolutely right.

# Jeeves

REGINALD JEEVES AND HIS employer, Bertram Wooster, are two of literature's most beloved characters. Wodehouse published his first story featuring them in 1915, and his last completed novel, *Aunts Aren't Gentlemen* (1974), also stars Bertie and Jeeves. The intervening six decades found the two appearing in thirty-five short stories and eleven novels.

Among Wodehouse's earliest comic writings are three Sherlock Holmes parodies. The adventures of Jeeves and Bertie, though decidedly more light-hearted than those of Sherlock Holmes and Dr. Watson, bear more than a passing resemblance to those of Arthur Conan Doyle's duo. Wodehouse once noted, "Conan Doyle was my hero. Others might revere Hardy or Meredith. I was a Doyle man and I still am."

All but a few of the Jeeves and Bertie short stories can be found in the collections *My Man Jeeves* (1919), *The Inimitable Jeeves* (1923), *Carry On, Jeeves* (1925), and *Very Good, Jeeves* (1930).

# Leave It to Jeeves

Jeeves—my man, you know—is really a most extraordinary chap. So capable. Honestly, I shouldn't know what to do without him. On broader lines he's like those chappies who sit peering sadly over the marble battlements at the Pennsylvania Station in the place marked "Inquiries." You know the Johnnies I mean. You go up to them and say: "When's the next train for Melonsquashville, Tennessee?" and they reply, without stopping to think, "Two forty-three, track ten, change at San Francisco." And they're right every time. Well, Jeeves gives you just the same impression of omniscience.

As an instance of what I mean, I remember meeting Monty Byng in Bond Street one morning, looking the last word in a grey check suit, and I felt I should never be happy till I had one like it. I dug the address of the tailors out of him, and had them working on the thing inside the hour.

"Jeeves," I said that evening. "I'm getting a check suit like that one of Mr. Byng's."

"Injudicious, sir," he said firmly. "It will not become you."

"What absolute rot! It's the soundest thing I've struck for years."

"Unsuitable for you, sir."

Well, the long and the short of it was that the confounded thing came home, and I put it on, and when I caught sight of myself in the glass I nearly swooned. Jeeves was perfectly right. I looked a cross between a music-hall comedian and a cheap bookie. Yet Monty had looked fine in absolutely the same stuff. These things are just Life's mysteries, and that's all there is to it.

But it isn't only that Jeeves's judgment about clothes is infallible, though, of course, that's really the main thing. The man knows everything. There was the matter of that tip on the "Lincolnshire." I forget now how I got it, but it had the aspect of being the real, red-hot tabasco.

"Jeeves," I said, for I'm fond of the man, and like to do him a good turn when I can, "if you want to make a bit of money have something on Wonderchild for the 'Lincolnshire.'"

He shook his head.

"I'd rather not, sir."

"But it's the straight goods. I'm going to put my shirt on him."

"I do not recommend it, sir. The animal is not intended to win. Second place is what the stable is after."

Perfect piffle, I thought, of course. How the deuce could Jeeves know anything about it? Still, you know what happened. Wonderchild led till he was breathing on the wire, and then Banana Fritter came along and nosed him out. I went straight home and rang for Jeeves.

"After this," I said, "not another step for me without your advice. From now on consider yourself the brains of the establishment."

"Very good, sir. I shall endeavor to give satisfaction."

And he has, by Jove! I'm a bit short on brain myself; the old bean would appear to have been constructed more for ornament than for use, don't you know; but give me five minutes to talk the thing over with Jeeves, and I'm game to advise any one about anything. And that's why, when Bruce Corcoran came to me with his troubles, my first act was to ring the bell and put it up to the lad with the bulging forehead.

"Leave it to Jeeves," I said.

I first got to know Corky when I came to New York. He was a pal of my cousin Gussie, who was in with a lot of people down Washington Square way. I don't know if I ever told you about it, but the reason why I left England was because I was sent over by my Aunt Agatha to try to stop young Gussie marrying a girl on the vaudeville stage, and I got the whole thing so mixed up that I decided that it would be a sound scheme for me to stop on in America for a bit instead of going back and having long cozy chats about the thing with aunt. So I sent Jeeves out to find a decent apartment, and settled down for a bit of exile. I'm bound to say that New York's a topping place to be exiled in. Everybody was awfully good to me, and there seemed to be plenty of things going on, and I'm a wealthy bird, so everything was fine. Chappies introduced me to other chappies, and so on and so forth, and it wasn't long before I knew squads of the right sort, some who rolled in dollars in houses up by the Park, and others who lived with the gas turned down mostly around Washington Square — artists and writers and so forth. Brainy coves.

Corky was one of the artists. A portrait-painter, he called himself, but he hadn't painted any portraits. He was sitting on the side-lines with a blanket over his shoulders, waiting for a chance to get into the game. You see, the catch about portrait-painting—I've looked into the thing a bit—is that you can't start painting portraits till people come along and ask you to, and they won't come and ask you to until you've painted a lot first. This makes it kind of difficult for a chappie. Corky managed to get along by drawing an occasional picture for the comic papers—he had rather a gift for funny stuff when he got a good idea—and doing bedsteads and chairs and things for the advertisements. His principal source of income, however, was derived from biting the ear of a rich uncle — one Alexander Worple, who was in the jute business. I'm a bit foggy as to what jute is, but it's apparently something the populace is pretty keen on, for Mr. Worple had made quite an indecently large stack out of it.

Now, a great many fellows think that having a rich uncle is a pretty soft snap: but, according to Corky, such is not the case. Corky's uncle was a robust sort of cove, who looked like living for ever. He was fifty-one, and it seemed as if he might go to par. It was not this, however, that distressed poor old Corky, for he was not bigoted and had no objection to the man going on living. What Corky kicked at was the way the above Worple used to harry him.

Corky's uncle, you see, didn't want him to be an artist. He didn't think he had any talent in that direction. He was always urging him to chuck Art and go into the jute business and start at the bottom and work his way up. Jute had apparently become a sort of obsession with him. He seemed to attach almost a spiritual importance to it. And what Corky said was that, while he didn't know what they did at the bottom of the jute business, instinct told him that it was something too beastly for words. Corky, moreover, believed in his future as an artist. Some day, he said, he was going to make a hit. Meanwhile, by using the utmost tact and persuasiveness, he was inducing his uncle to cough up very grudgingly a small quarterly allowance.

He wouldn't have got this if his uncle hadn't had a hobby. Mr. Worple was peculiar in this respect. As a rule, from what I've observed, the American captain of industry doesn't do anything out of business hours. When he has put the cat out and locked up the office for the night, he just relapses into a state of coma from which he emerges only to start being a captain of industry again. But Mr. Worple in his spare time was what is known as an ornithologist. He had written a book called *American Birds*, and was writing another, to be called *More American Birds*. When he had finished that, the presumption was that he would begin a third, and keep on till the supply of American birds gave out. Corky used to go to him about once every three months and let him talk about American birds. Apparently you could do what you liked with old Worple if you gave him his head first on his pet subject, so these little chats used to make Corky's allowance all right for the time being. But it was pretty rotten for the poor chap. There was the frightful suspense, you see, and, apart from that, birds, except when broiled and in the society of a cold bottle, bored him stiff.

To complete the character-study of Mr. Worple, he was a man of extremely uncertain temper, and his general tendency was to think that Corky was a poor chump and that whatever step he took in any direction on his own account, was just another proof of his innate idiocy. I should imagine Jeeves feels very much the same about me.

So when Corky trickled into my apartment one afternoon, shooing a girl in front of him, and said, "Bertie, I want you to meet my fiancée, Miss Singer," the aspect of the matter which hit me first was precisely the one which he had come to consult me about. The very first words I spoke were, "Corky, how about your uncle?"

The poor chap gave one of those mirthless laughs. He was looking anxious and worried, like a man who has done the murder all right but can't think what the deuce to do with the body.

"We're so scared, Mr. Wooster," said the girl. "We were hoping that you might suggest a way of breaking it to him."

Muriel Singer was one of those very quiet, appealing girls who have a way of looking at you with their big eyes as if they thought you were the greatest thing on earth and wondered that you hadn't got on to it yet yourself. She sat there in a sort of shrinking way, looking at me as if she were saying to herself, "Oh, I do hope this great strong man isn't going to hurt me." She gave a fellow a protective kind of feeling, made him want to stroke her hand and say, "There, there, little one!" or words to that effect. She made me feel that there was nothing I wouldn't do for her. She was rather like one of those innocent-tasting American drinks which creep imperceptibly into your system so that, before you know what you're doing, you're starting out to reform the world by force if necessary and pausing on your way to tell the large man in the corner that, if he looks at you like that, you will knock his head off. What I

mean is, she made me feel alert and dashing, like a jolly
old knight-errant or something of that kind. I felt that I
was with her in this thing to the limit.

"I don't see why your uncle shouldn't be most awfully
bucked," I said to Corky. "He will think Miss Singer the
ideal wife for you."

Corky declined to cheer up.

"You don't know him. Even if he did like Muriel he
wouldn't admit it. That's the sort of pig-headed guy he is.
It would be a matter of principle with him to kick. All he
would consider would be that I had gone and taken an
important step without asking his advice, and he would
raise Cain automatically. He's always done it."

I strained the old bean to meet this emergency.

"You want to work it so that he makes Miss Singer's
acquaintance without knowing that you know her. Then
you come along—"

"But how can I work it that way?"

I saw his point. That was the catch.

"There's only one thing to do," I said.

"What's that?"

"Leave it to Jeeves."

And I rang the bell.

"Sir?" said Jeeves, kind of manifesting himself. One of
the rummy things about Jeeves is that, unless you watch
like a hawk, you very seldom see him come into a room.
He's like one of those weird chappies in India who dis-
solve themselves into thin air and nip through space in a
sort of disembodied way and assemble the parts again just
where they want them. I've got a cousin who's what they
call a Theosophist, and he says he's often nearly worked
the thing himself, but couldn't quite bring it off, probably

owing to having fed in his boyhood on the flesh of animals slain in anger and pie.

The moment I saw the man standing there, registering respectful attention, a weight seemed to roll off my mind. I felt like a lost child who spots his father in the offing. There was something about him that gave me confidence.

Jeeves is a tallish man, with one of those dark, shrewd faces. His eye gleams with the light of pure intelligence.

"Jeeves, we want your advice."

"Very good, sir."

I boiled down Corky's painful case into a few well-chosen words.

"So you see what it amount to, Jeeves. We want you to suggest some way by which Mr. Worple can make Miss Singer's acquaintance without getting on to the fact that Mr. Corcoran already knows her. Understand?"

"Perfectly, sir."

"Well, try to think of something."

"I have thought of something already, sir."

"You have!"

"The scheme I would suggest cannot fail of success, but it has what may seem to you a drawback, sir, in that it requires a certain financial outlay."

"He means," I translated to Corky, "that he has got a pippin of an idea, but it's going to cost a bit."

Naturally the poor chap's face dropped, for this seemed to dish the whole thing. But I was still under the influence of the girl's melting gaze, and I saw that this was where I started in as a knight-errant.

"You can count on me for all that sort of thing, Corky," I said. "Only too glad. Carry on, Jeeves."

"I would suggest, sir, that Mr. Corcoran take advantage of Mr. Worple's attachment to ornithology."

"How on earth did you know that he was fond of birds?"

"It is the way these New York apartments are constructed, sir. Quite unlike our London houses. The partitions between the rooms are of the flimsiest nature. With no wish to overhear, I have sometimes heard Mr. Corcoran expressing himself with a generous strength on the subject I have mentioned."

"Oh! Well?"

"Why should not the young lady write a small volume, to be entitled—let us say—*The Children's Book of American Birds*, and dedicate it to Mr. Worple! A limited edition could be published at your expense, sir, and a great deal of the book would, of course, be given over to eulogistic remarks concerning Mr. Worple's own larger treatise on the same subject. I should recommend the dispatching of a presentation copy to Mr. Worple, immediately on publication, accompanied by a letter in which the young lady asks to be allowed to make the acquaintance of one to whom she owes so much. This would, I fancy, produce the desired result, but as I say, the expense involved would be considerable."

I felt like the proprietor of a performing dog on the vaudeville stage when the tyke has just pulled off his trick without a hitch. I had betted on Jeeves all along, and I had known that he wouldn't let me down. It beats me sometimes why a man with his genius is satisfied to hang around pressing my clothes and what-not. If I had half Jeeves's brain, I should have a stab at being Prime Minister or something.

"Jeeves," I said, "that is absolutely ripping! One of your very best efforts."

"Thank you, sir."

The girl made an objection.

"But I'm sure I couldn't write a book about anything. I can't even write good letters."

"Muriel's talents," said Corky, with a little cough "lie more in the direction of the drama, Bertie. I didn't mention it before, but one of our reasons for being a trifle nervous as to how Uncle Alexander will receive the news is that Muriel is in the chorus of that show *Choose Your Exit* at the Manhattan. It's absurdly unreasonable, but we both feel that that fact might increase Uncle Alexander's natural tendency to kick like a steer."

I saw what he meant. Goodness knows there was fuss enough in our family when I tried to marry into musical comedy a few years ago. And the recollection of my Aunt Agatha's attitude in the matter of Gussie and the vaudeville girl was still fresh in my mind. I don't know why it is—one of these psychology sharps could explain it, I suppose—but uncles and aunts, as a class, are always dead against the drama, legitimate or otherwise. They don't seem able to stick it at any price.

But Jeeves had a solution, of course.

"I fancy it would be a simple matter, sir, to find some impecunious author who would be glad to do the actual composition of the volume for a small fee. It is only necessary that the young lady's name should appear on the title page."

"That's true," said Corky. "Sam Patterson would do it for a hundred dollars. He writes a novelette, three short stories, and ten thousand words of a serial for one of the all-fiction magazines under different names every month. A little thing like this would be nothing to him. I'll get after him right away."

"Fine!"

"Will that be all, sir?" said Jeeves. "Very good, sir. Thank you, sir."

I ALWAYS USED TO THINK that publishers had to be devilish intelligent fellows, loaded down with the grey matter; but I've got their number now. All a publisher has to do is to write checks at intervals, while a lot of deserving and industrious chappies rally round and do the real work. I know, because I've been one myself. I simply sat tight in the old apartment with a fountain-pen, and in due season a topping, shiny book came along.

I happened to be down at Corky's place when the first copies of *The Children's Book of American Birds* bobbed up. Muriel Singer was there, and we were talking of things in general when there was a bang at the door and the parcel was delivered.

It was certainly some book. It had a red cover with a fowl of some species on it, and underneath the girl's name in gold letters. I opened a copy at random.

"Often of a spring morning," it said at the top of page twenty-one, "as you wander through the fields, you will hear the sweet-toned, carelessly flowing warble of the purple finch linnet. When you are older you must read all about him in Mr. Alexander Worple's wonderful book — *American Birds*."

You see. A boost for the uncle right away. And only a few pages later there he was in the limelight again in connection with the yellow-billed cuckoo. It was great stuff.

The more I read, the more I admired the chap who had written it and Jeeves's genius in putting us on to the wheeze. I didn't see how the uncle could fail to drop. You can't call a chap the world's greatest authority on the yellow-billed cuckoo without rousing a certain disposition towards chumminess in him.

"It's a cert!" I said.

"An absolute cinch!" said Corky.

And a day or two later he meandered up the Avenue to my apartment to tell me that all was well. The uncle had written Muriel a letter so dripping with the milk of human kindness that if he hadn't known Mr. Worple's handwriting Corky would have refused to believe him the author of it. Any time it suited Miss Singer to call, said the uncle, he would be delighted to make her acquaintance.

SHORTLY AFTER THIS I had to go out of town. Divers sound sportsmen had invited me to pay visits to their country places, and it wasn't for several months that I settled down in the city again. I had been wondering a lot, of course, about Corky, whether it all turned out right, and so forth, and my first evening in New York, happening to pop into a quiet sort of little restaurant which I go to when I don't feel inclined for the bright lights, I found Muriel Singer there, sitting by herself at a table near the door. Corky, I took it, was out telephoning. I went up and passed the time of day.

"Well, well, well, what?" I said.

"Why, Mr. Wooster! How do you do?"

"Corky around?"

"I beg your pardon?"

"You're waiting for Corky, aren't you?"

"Oh, I didn't understand. No, I'm not waiting for him."

It seemed to me that there was a sort of something in her voice, a kind of thingummy, you know.

"I say, you haven't had a row with Corky, have you?"

"A row?"

"A spat, don't you know—little misunderstanding—faults on both sides—er—and all that sort of thing."

"Why, whatever makes you think that?"

"Oh, well, as it were, what? What I mean is—I thought you usually dined with him before you went to the theatre."

"I've left the stage now."

Suddenly the whole thing dawned on me. I had forgotten what a long time I had been away.

"Why, of course, I see now! You're married!"

"Yes."

"How perfectly topping! I wish you all kinds of happiness."

"Thank you, so much. Oh Alexander," she said, looking past me, "this is a friend of mine—Mr. Wooster."

I spun round. A chappie with a lot of stiff grey hair and a red sort of healthy face was standing there. Rather a formidable Johnnie, he looked, though quite peaceful at the moment.

"I want you to meet my husband, Mr. Wooster. Mr. Wooster is a friend of Bruce's, Alexander."

The old boy grasped my hand warmly, and that was all that kept me from hitting the floor in a heap. The place was rocking. Absolutely.

"So you know my nephew, Mr. Wooster," I heard him say. "I wish you would try to knock a little sense into him and make him quit this playing at painting. But I have an idea that he is steadying down. I noticed it first that night he came to dinner with us, my dear, to be introduced to you. He seemed altogether quieter and more serious. Something seemed to have sobered him. Perhaps you will give us the pleasure of your company at dinner tonight, Mr. Wooster? Or have you dined?"

I said I had. What I needed then was air, not dinner. I felt that I wanted to get into the open and think this thing out.

When I reached my apartment I heard Jeeves moving about in his lair. I called him.

"Jeeves," I said, "now is the time for all good men to come to the aid of the party. A stiff b.-and-s. first of all, and then I've a bit of news for you."

He came back with a tray and a long glass.

"Better have one yourself, Jeeves. You'll need it."

"Later on, perhaps, thank you, sir."

"All right. Please yourself. But you're going to get a shock. You remember my friend, Mr. Corcoran?"

"Yes, sir."

"And the girl who was to slide gracefully into his uncle's esteem by writing the book on birds?"

"Perfectly, sir."

"Well, she's slid. She's married the uncle."

He took it without blinking. You can't rattle Jeeves.

"That was always a development to be feared, sir."

"You don't mean to tell me that you were expecting it?"

"It crossed my mind as a possibility."

"Did it, by Jove! Well, I think, you might have warned us!"

"I hardly liked to take the liberty, sir."

Of course, as I saw after I had had a bite to eat and was in a calmer frame of mind, what had happened wasn't my fault, if you come down to it. I couldn't be expected to foresee that the scheme, in itself a cracker-jack, would skid into the ditch as it had done; but all the same I'm bound to admit that I didn't relish the idea of meeting Corky again until time, the great healer, had been able to get in a bit of soothing work. I cut Washington Square out absolutely for the next few months. I gave it the complete miss-in-baulk. And then, just when I was beginning to think I might safely pop down in that direction and gather up the dropped threads, so to speak, time, instead of working the healing wheeze, went and pulled the most awful bone and put the lid on it. Opening the paper one morning, I read that Mrs. Alexander Worple had presented her husband with a son and heir.

I was so darned sorry for poor old Corky that I hadn't the heart to touch my breakfast. I told Jeeves to drink it himself. I was bowled over. Absolutely. It was the limit.

I hardly knew what to do. I wanted, of course, to rush down to Washington Square and grip the poor blighter silently by the hand; and then, thinking it over, I hadn't the nerve. Absent treatment seemed the touch. I gave it him in waves.

But after a month or so I began to hesitate again. It struck me that it was playing it a bit low-down on the poor chap, avoiding him like this just when he probably wanted his pals to surge round him most. I pictured him sitting in his lonely studio with no company but his bitter thoughts, and the pathos of it got me to such an extent that I bounded straight into a taxi and told the driver to go all out for the studio.

I rushed in, and there was Corky, hunched up at the easel, painting away, while on the model throne sat a severe-looking female of middle age, holding a baby.

A fellow has to be ready for that sort of thing.

"Oh, ah!" I said, and started to back out.

Corky looked over his shoulder.

"Halloa, Bertie. Don't go. We're just finishing for the day. That will be all this afternoon," he said to the nurse, who got up with the baby and decanted it into a perambulator which was standing in the fairway.

"At the same hour tomorrow, Mr. Corcoran?"

"Yes, please."

"Good afternoon."

"Good afternoon."

Corky stood there, looking at the door, and then he turned to me and began to get it off his chest. Fortunately, he seemed to take it for granted that I knew all about what had happened, so it wasn't as awkward as it might have been.

"It's my uncle's idea," he said. "Muriel doesn't know about it yet. The portrait's to be a surprise for her on her birthday. The nurse takes the kid out ostensibly to get a breather, and they beat it down here. If you want an instance of the irony of fate, Bertie, get acquainted with this. Here's the first commission I have ever had to paint a portrait, and the sitter is that human poached egg that has butted in and bounced me out of my inheritance. Can you beat it! I call it rubbing the thing in to expect me to spend my afternoons gazing into the ugly face of a little brat who to all intents and purposes has hit me behind the ear with a blackjack and swiped all I possess. I can't refuse to paint the portrait because if I did my uncle would stop my allowance; yet every time I look up and catch that kid's vacant eye, I suffer agonies. I tell you, Bertie, sometimes when he gives me a patronizing glance and then turns away and is sick, as if it revolted him to look at me, I come within an ace of occupying the entire front page of the evening papers as the latest murder sensation. There are moments when I can almost see the headlines: 'Promising Young Artist Beans Baby With Axe.'"

I patted his shoulder silently. My sympathy for the poor old scout was too deep for words.

I kept away from the studio for some time after that, because it didn't seem right to me to intrude on the poor chappie's sorrow. Besides, I'm bound to say that nurse intimidated me. She reminded me so infernally of Aunt Agatha. She was the same gimlet-eyed type.

But one afternoon Corky called me on the 'phone.

"Bertie."

"Halloa?"

"Are you doing anything this afternoon?"

"Nothing special."

"You couldn't come down here, could you?"

"What's the trouble? Anything up?"

"I've finished the portrait."

"Good boy! Stout work!"

"Yes." His voice sounded rather doubtful. "The fact is, Bertie, it doesn't look quite right to me. There's something about it… My uncle's coming in half an hour to inspect it, and … I don't know why it is, but I kind of feel I'd like your moral support!"

I began to see that I was letting myself in for something. The sympathetic co-operation of Jeeves seemed to me to be indicated.

"You think he'll cut up rough?"

"He may."

I threw my mind back to the red-faced chappie I had met at the restaurant, and tried to picture him cutting up rough. It was only too easy. I spoke to Corky firmly on the telephone.

"I'll come," I said.

"Good!"

"But only if I may bring Jeeves!"

"Why Jeeves? What's Jeeves got to do with it? Who wants Jeeves? Jeeves is the fool who suggested the scheme that has led —"

"Listen, Corky, old top! If you think I am going to face that uncle of yours without Jeeves's support, you're mistaken. I'd sooner go into a den of wild beasts and bite a lion on the back of the neck."

"Oh, all right," said Corky. Not cordially, but he said it; so I rang for Jeeves, and explained the situation.

"Very good, sir," said Jeeves.

That's the sort of chap he is. You can't rattle him.

WE FOUND CORKY NEAR the door, looking at the picture, with one hand up in a defensive sort of way, as if he thought it might swing on him.

"Stand right where you are, Bertie," he said, without moving. "Now, tell me honestly, how does it strike you?"

The light from the big window fell right on the picture. I took a good look at it. Then I shifted a bit nearer and took another look. Then I went back to where I had been at first, because it hadn't seemed quite so bad from there.

"Well?" said Corky, anxiously.

I hesitated a bit.

"Of course, old man, I only saw the kid once, and then only for a moment, but—but it was an ugly sort of kid, wasn't it, if I remember rightly?"

"As ugly as that?"

I looked again, and honesty compelled me to be frank.

"I don't see how it could have been, old chap."

Poor old Corky ran his fingers through his hair in a temperamental sort of way. He groaned.

"You're right quite, Bertie. Something's gone wrong with the darned thing. My private impression is that, without knowing it, I've worked that stunt that Sargent and those fellows pull—painting the soul of the sitter. I've got through the mere outward appearance, and have put the child's soul on canvas."

"But could a child of that age have a soul like that? I don't see how he could have managed it in the time. What do you think, Jeeves?"

"I doubt it, sir."

"It—it sorts of leers at you, doesn't it?"

"You've noticed that, too?" said Corky.

"I don't see how one could help noticing."

"All I tried to do was to give the little brute a cheerful expression. But, as it worked out, he looks positively dissipated."

"Just what I was going to suggest, old man. He looks as if he were in the middle of a colossal spree, and enjoying every minute of it. Don't you think so, Jeeves?"

"He has a decidedly inebriated air, sir."

Corky was starting to say something when the door opened, and the uncle came in.

For about three seconds all was joy, jollity, and good-will. The old boy shook hands with me, slapped Corky on the back, said that he didn't think he had ever seen such a fine day, and whacked his leg with his stick. Jeeves had projected himself into the background, and he didn't notice him.

"Well, Bruce, my boy; so the portrait is really finished, is it—really finished? Well, bring it out. Let's have a look at it. This will be a wonderful surprise for your aunt. Where is it? Let's—"

And then he got it—suddenly, when he wasn't set for the punch; and he rocked back on his heels.

"Oosh!" he exclaimed. And for perhaps a minute there was one of the scaliest silences I've ever run up against.

"Is this a practical joke?" he said at last, in a way that set about sixteen draughts cutting through the room at once.

I thought it was up to me to rally round old Corky.

"You want to stand a bit farther away from it," I said.

"You're perfectly right!" he snorted. "I do! I want to stand so far away from it that I can't see the thing with a telescope!" He turned on Corky like an untamed tiger of the jungle who has just located a chunk of meat. "And this—this—is what you have been wasting your time and my money for all these years! A painter! I wouldn't let you paint a house of mine! I gave you this commission, thinking that you were a competent worker, and this—this—this extract from a comic colored supplement is the result!" He swung towards the door, lashing his tail and growling to himself. "This ends it! If you wish to continue this foolery of pretending to be an artist because you want an excuse for idleness, please yourself. But let me tell you this. Unless you report at my office on Monday morning, prepared to abandon all this idiocy and start in at the bottom of the business to work your way up, as you should have done half a dozen years ago, not another cent—not another cent—not another—Boosh!"

Then the door closed, and he was no longer with us. And I crawled out of the bombproof shelter.

"Corky, old top!" I whispered faintly.

Corky was standing staring at the picture. His face was set. There was a hunted look in his eye.

"Well, that finishes it!" he muttered brokenly.

"What are you going to do?"

"Do? What can I do? I can't stick on here if he cuts off supplies. You heard what he said. I shall have to go to the office on Monday."

I couldn't think of a thing to say. I knew exactly how he felt about the office. I don't know when I've been so infernally uncomfortable. It was like hanging round trying to make conversation to a pal who's just been sentenced to twenty years in quod.

And then a soothing voice broke the silence.

"If I might make a suggestion, sir!"

It was Jeeves. He had slid from the shadows and was gazing gravely at the picture. Upon my word, I can't give you a better idea of the shattering effect of Corky's uncle Alexander when in action than by saying that he had absolutely made me forget for the moment that Jeeves was there.

"I wonder if I have ever happened to mention to you, sir, a Mr. Digby Thistleton, with whom I was once in service? Perhaps you have met him? He was a financier. He is now Lord Bridgnorth. It was a favourite saying of his that there is always a way. The first time I heard him use the expression was after the failure of a patent depilatory which he promoted."

"Jeeves," I said, "what on earth are you talking about?"

"I mentioned Mr. Thistleton, sir, because his was in some respects a parallel case to the present one. His depilatory failed, but he did not despair. He put it on the market again under the name of Hair-o, guaranteed to produce a full crop of hair in a few months. It was advertised, if you remember, sir, by a humorous picture of a billiard-ball, before and after taking, and made such a substantial fortune that Mr. Thistleton was soon afterwards elevated to the peerage for services to his Party. It seems to me that, if Mr. Corcoran looks into the matter, he will find, like Mr. Thistleton, that there is always a way. Mr. Worple himself suggested the solution of the difficulty. In the heat of the moment he compared the portrait to an extract from a colored comic supplement. I consider the suggestion a very valuable one, sir. Mr. Corcoran's portrait may not have pleased Mr. Worple as a likeness of his only child, but I have no doubt that editors would gladly consider it as a foundation for a series of humorous drawings. If Mr. Corcoran will allow me to make the suggestion, his talent has always been for the humorous. There is something about this picture—something bold and vigorous, which arrests the attention. I feel sure it would be highly popular."

Corky was glaring at the picture, and making a sort of dry, sucking noise with his mouth. He seemed completely overwrought.

And then suddenly he began to laugh in a wild way.

"Corky, old man!" I said, massaging him tenderly. I feared the poor blighter was hysterical.

He began to stagger about all over the floor.

"He's right! The man's absolutely right! Jeeves, you're a life-saver! You've hit on the greatest idea of the age! Report at the office on Monday! Start at the bottom of the business! I'll buy the business if I feel like it. I know the man who runs the comic section of the Sunday Star. He'll eat this thing. He was telling me only the other day how hard it was to get a good new series. He'll give me anything I ask for a real winner like this. I've got a gold-mine. Where's my hat? I've got an income for life! Where's that confounded hat? Lend me a fiver, Bertie. I want to take a taxi down to Park Row!"

Jeeves smiled paternally. Or, rather, he had a kind of paternal muscular spasm about the mouth, which is the nearest he ever gets to smiling.

"If I might make the suggestion, Mr. Corcoran—for a title of the series which you have in mind—'The Adventures of Baby Blobbs.'"

Corky and I looked at the picture, then at each other in an awed way. Jeeves was right. There could be no other title.

"JEEVES," I SAID. IT WAS a few weeks later, and I had just finished looking at the comic section of the Sunday Star. "I'm an optimist. I always have been. The older I get, the more I agree with Shakespeare and those poet Johnnies about it always being darkest before the dawn and there's a silver lining and what you lose on the swings you make up on the roundabouts. Look at Mr. Corcoran, for instance. There was a fellow, one would have said, clear up to the eyebrows in the soup. To all appearances he had got it right in the neck. Yet look at him now. Have you seen these pictures?"

"I took the liberty of glancing at them before bringing them to you, sir. Extremely diverting."

"They have made a big hit, you know."

"I anticipated it, sir."

I leaned back against the pillows.

"You know, Jeeves, you're a genius. You ought to be drawing a commission on these things."

"I have nothing to complain of in that respect, sir. Mr. Corcoran has been most generous. I am putting out the brown suit, sir."

"No, I think I'll wear the blue with the faint red stripe."

"Not the blue with the faint red stripe, sir."

"But I rather fancy myself.in it."

"Not the blue with the faint red stripe, sir."

"Oh, all right, have it your own way."

"Very good, sir. Thank you, sir."

Of course, I know it's as bad as being henpecked; but then Jeeves is always right. You've got to consider that, you know. What?

# The Aunt and the Sluggard

NOW THAT IT'S ALL OVER, I may as well admit that there was a time during the rather funny affair of Rockmetteller Todd when I thought that Jeeves was going to let me down. The man had the appearance of being baffled.

Jeeves is my man, you know. Officially he pulls in his weekly wages for pressing my clothes and all that sort of thing; but actually he's more like what the poet Johnnie called some bird of his acquaintance who was apt to rally round him in times of need—a guide, don't you know; philosopher, if I remember rightly, and—I rather fancy— friend. I rely on him at every turn.

So naturally, when Rocky Todd told me about his aunt, I didn't hesitate. Jeeves was in on the thing from the start.

The affair of Rocky Todd broke loose early one morning of spring. I was in bed, restoring the good old tissues with about nine hours of the dreamless, when the door flew open and somebody prodded me in the lower ribs and began to shake the bedclothes. After blinking a bit and generally pulling myself together, I located Rocky, and my first impression was that it was some horrid dream.

Rocky, you see, lived down on Long Island somewhere, miles away from New York; and not only that, but he had told me himself more than once that he never got up before twelve, and seldom earlier than one. Constitutionally the laziest young devil in America, he had hit on a walk in life which enabled him to go the limit in that direction. He was a poet. At least, he wrote poems when he did anything; but most of his time, as far as I could make out, he spent in a sort of trance. He told me once that he could sit on a fence, watching a worm and wondering what on earth it was up to, for hours at a stretch.

He had his scheme of life worked out to a fine point. About once a month he would take three days writing a few poems; the other three hundred and twenty-nine days of the year he rested. I didn't know there was enough money in poetry to support a chappie, even in the way in which Rocky lived; but it seems that, if you stick to exhortations to young men to lead the strenuous life and don't shove in any rhymes, American editors fight for the stuff. Rocky showed me one of his things once. It began:

> *Be!*
> *Be!*
> > *The past is dead.*
> > *Tomorrow is not born.*
> > > *Be today!*
> > *Today!*
> > > *Be with every nerve,*
> > > *With every muscle,*
> > > *With every drop of your red blood!*
> *Be!*

It was printed opposite the frontispiece of a magazine with a sort of scroll round it, and a picture in the middle of a fairly-nude chappie, with bulging muscles, giving the rising sun the glad eye. Rocky said they gave him a hundred dollars for it, and he stayed in bed till four in the afternoon for over a month.

As regarded the future he was pretty solid, owing to the fact that he had a moneyed aunt tucked away somewhere in Illinois; and, as he had been named Rockmetteller after her, and was her only nephew, his position was pretty sound. He told me that when he did come into the money he meant to do no work at all, except perhaps an occasional poem recommending the young man with life opening out before him, with all its splendid possibilities, to light a pipe and shove his feet upon the mantelpiece.

And this was the man who was prodding me in the ribs in the grey dawn!

"Read this, Bertie!" I could just see that he was waving a letter or something equally foul in my face. "Wake up and read this!"

I can't read before I've had my morning tea and a cigarette. I groped for the bell.

Jeeves came in looking as fresh as a dewy violet. It's a mystery to me how he does it.

"Tea, Jeeves."

"Very good, sir."

He flowed silently out of the room—he always gives you the impression of being some liquid substance when he moves; and I found that Rocky was surging round with his beastly letter again.

"What is it?" I said. "What on earth's the matter?"

"Read it!"

"I can't. I haven't had my tea."

"Well, listen then."

"Who's it from?"

"My aunt."

At this point I fell asleep again. I woke to hear him saying:

"So what on earth am I to do?"

Jeeves trickled in with the tray, like some silent stream meandering over its mossy bed; and I saw daylight.

"Read it again, Rocky, old top," I said. "I want Jeeves to hear it. Mr. Todd's aunt has written him a rather rummy letter, Jeeves, and we want your advice."

"Very good, sir."

He stood in the middle of the room, registering devotion to the cause, and Rocky started again:

"MY DEAR ROCKMETTELLER.—I have been thinking things over for a long while, and I have come to the conclusion that I have been very thoughtless to wait so long before doing what I have made up my mind to do now."

"What do you make of that, Jeeves?"

"It seems a little obscure at present, sir, but no doubt it becomes cleared at a later point in the communication."

"It becomes as clear as mud!" said Rocky.

"Proceed, old scout," I said, champing my bread and butter.

"You know how all my life I have longed to visit New York and see for myself the wonderful gay life of which I have read so much. I fear that now it will be impossible for me to fulfil my dream. I am old and worn out. I seem to have no strength left in me."

"Sad, Jeeves, what?"

"Extremely, sir."

"Sad nothing!" said Rocky. "It's sheer laziness. I went to see her last Christmas and she was bursting with health. Her doctor told me himself that there was nothing wrong with her whatever. But she will insist that she's a hopeless invalid, so he has to agree with her. She's got a fixed idea that the trip to New York would kill her; so, though it's been her ambition all her life to come here, she stays where she is."

"Rather like the chappie whose heart was 'in the Highlands a-chasing of the deer,' Jeeves?"

"The cases are in some respects parallel, sir."

"Carry on, Rocky, dear boy."

"So I have decided that, if I cannot enjoy all the marvels of the city myself, I can at least enjoy them through you. I suddenly thought of this yesterday after reading a beautiful poem in the Sunday paper about a young man who had longed all his life for a certain thing and won it in the end only when he was too old to enjoy it. It was very sad, and it touched me."

"A thing," interpolated Rocky bitterly, "that I've not been able to do in ten years."

"As you know, you will have my money when I am gone; but until now I have never been able to see my way to giving you an allowance. I have now decided to do so — on one condition. I have written to a firm of lawyers in New York, giving them instructions to pay you quite a substantial sum each month. My one condition is that you live in New York and enjoy yourself as I have always wished to do. I want you to be my representative, to spend this money for me as I should do myself. I want you to plunge into the gay, prismatic life of New York. I want you to be the life and soul of brilliant supper parties.

"Above all, I want you — indeed, I insist on this — to write me letters at least once a week giving me a full description of all you are doing and all that is going on in the city, so that I may enjoy at second-hand what my wretched health prevents my enjoying for myself. Remember that I shall expect full details, and that no detail is too trivial to interest.—Your affectionate Aunt,

"Isabel Rockmetteller."

"What about it?" said Rocky.

"What about it?" I said.

"Yes. What on earth am I going to do?"

It was only then that I really got on to the extremely rummy attitude of the chappie, in view of the fact that a quite unexpected mess of the right stuff had suddenly descended on him from a blue sky. To my mind it was an occasion for the beaming smile and the joyous whoop; yet here the man was, looking and talking as if Fate had swung on his solar plexus. It amazed me.

"Aren't you bucked?" I said.

"Bucked!"

"If I were in your place I should be frightfully braced. I consider this pretty soft for you."

He gave a kind of yelp, stared at me for a moment, and then began to talk of New York in a way that reminded me of Jimmy Mundy, the reformer chappie. Jimmy had just come to New York on a hit-the-trail campaign, and I had popped in at the Garden a couple of days before, for half an hour or so, to hear him. He had certainly told New York some pretty straight things about itself, having apparently taken a dislike to the place, but, by Jove, you know, dear old Rocky made him look like a publicity agent for the old metrop!

"Pretty soft!" he cried. "To have to come and live in New York! To have to leave my little cottage and take a stuffy, smelly, over-heated hole of an apartment in this

Heaven-forsaken, festering Gehenna. To have to mix night after night with a mob who think that life is a sort of St. Vitus's dance, and imagine that they're having a good time because they're making enough noise for six and drinking too much for ten. I loathe New York, Bertie. I wouldn't come near the place if I hadn't got to see editors occasionally. There's a blight on it. It's got moral delirium tremens. It's the limit. The very thought of staying more than a day in it makes me sick. And you call this thing pretty soft for me!"

I felt rather like Lot's friends must have done when they dropped in for a quiet chat and their genial host began to criticize the Cities of the Plain. I had no idea old Rocky could be so eloquent.

"It would kill me to have to live in New York," he went on. "To have to share the air with six million people! To have to wear stiff collars and decent clothes all the time! To—" He started. "Good Lord! I suppose I should have to dress for dinner in the evenings. What a ghastly notion!"

I was shocked, absolutely shocked.

"My dear chap!" I said reproachfully.

"Do you dress for dinner every night, Bertie?"

"Jeeves," I said coldly. The man was still standing like a statue by the door. "How many suits of evening clothes have I?"

"We have three suits full of evening dress, sir; two dinner jackets—"

"Three."

"For practical purposes two only, sir. If you remember we cannot wear the third. We have also seven white waistcoats."

"And shirts?"

"Four dozen, sir."

"And white ties?"

"The first two shallow shelves in the chest of drawers are completely filled with our white ties, sir."

I turned to Rocky.

"You see?"

The chappie writhed like an electric fan.

"I won't do it! I can't do it! I'll be hanged if I'll do it! How on earth can I dress up like that? Do you realize that most days I don't get out of my pyjamas till five in the afternoon, and then I just put on an old sweater?"

I saw Jeeves wince, poor chap! This sort of revelation shocked his finest feelings.

"Then, what are you going to do about it?" I said.

"That's what I want to know."

"You might write and explain to your aunt."

"I might—if I wanted her to get round to her lawyer's in two rapid leaps and cut me out of her will."

I saw his point.

"What do you suggest, Jeeves?" I said.

Jeeves cleared his throat respectfully.

"The crux of the matter would appear to be, sir, that Mr. Todd is obliged by the conditions under which the money is delivered into his possession to write Miss Rockmetteller long and detailed letters relating to his movements, and the only method by which this can be accomplished, if Mr. Todd adheres to his expressed intention of remaining in the country, is for Mr. Todd to induce some second party to gather the actual experiences which Miss Rockmetteller wishes reported to her, and to convey these to him in the shape of a careful report, on which it would be possible for him, with the aid of his imagination, to base the suggested correspondence."

Having got which off the old diaphragm, Jeeves was silent. Rocky looked at me in a helpless sort of way. He hasn't been brought up on Jeeves as I have, and he isn't on to his curves.

"Could he put it a little clearer, Bertie?" he said. "I thought at the start it was going to make sense, but it kind of flickered. What's the idea?"

"My dear old man, perfectly simple. I knew we could stand on Jeeves. All you've got to do is to get somebody to go round the town for you and take a few notes, and then you work the notes up into letters. That's it, isn't it, Jeeves?"

"Precisely, sir."

The light of hope gleamed in Rocky's eyes. He looked at Jeeves in a startled way, dazed by the man's vast intellect.

"But who would do it?" he said. "It would have to be a pretty smart sort of man, a man who would notice things."

"Jeeves!" I said. "Let Jeeves do it."

"But would he?"

"You would do it, wouldn't you, Jeeves?"

For the first time in our long connection I observed Jeeves almost smile. The corner of his mouth curved quite a quarter of an inch, and for a moment his eye ceased to look like a meditative fish's.

"I should be delighted to oblige, sir. As a matter of fact, I have already visited some of New York's places of interest on my evening out, and it would be most enjoyable to make a practice of the pursuit."

"Fine! I know exactly what your aunt wants to hear about, Rocky. She wants an earful of cabaret stuff. The place you ought to go to first, Jeeves, is Reigelheimer's. It's on Forty-second Street. Anybody will show you the way."

Jeeves shook his head.

"Pardon me, sir. People are no longer going to Reigelheimer's. The place at the moment is Frolics on the Roof."

"You see?" I said to Rocky. "Leave it to Jeeves. He knows."

IT ISN'T OFTEN THAT you find an entire group of your fellow-humans happy in this world; but our little circle was certainly an example of the fact that it can be done. We were all full of beans. Everything went absolutely right from the start.

Jeeves was happy, partly because he loves to exercise his giant brain, and partly because he was having a corking time among the bright lights. I saw him one night at the Midnight Revels. He was sitting at a table on the edge of the dancing floor, doing himself remarkably well with a fat cigar and a bottle of the best. I'd never imagined he could look so nearly human. His face wore an expression of austere benevolence, and he was making notes in a small book.

As for the rest of us, I was feeling pretty good, because I was fond of old Rocky and glad to be able to do him a good turn. Rocky was perfectly contented, because he was still able to sit on fences in his pyjamas and watch worms. And, as for the aunt, she seemed tickled to death. She was getting Broadway at pretty long range, but it seemed to be hitting her just right. I read one of her letters to Rocky, and it was full of life.

But then Rocky's letters, based on Jeeves's notes, were enough to buck anybody up. It was rummy when you came to think of it. There was I, loving the life, while the mere mention of it gave Rocky a tired feeling; yet here is a letter I wrote to a pal of mine in London:

"DEAR FREDDIE—Well, here I am in New York. It's not a bad place. I'm not having a bad time. Everything's pretty all right. The cabarets aren't bad. Don't know when I shall be back. How's everybody? Cheer-o!—Yours,

"Bertie.

"PS.—Seen old Ted lately?"

Not that I cared about Ted; but if I hadn't dragged him in I couldn't have got the confounded thing on to the second page.

Now here's old Rocky on exactly the same subject:

"DEAREST AUNT ISABEL—How can I ever thank you enough for giving me the opportunity to live in this astounding city! New York seems more wonderful every day.

"Fifth Avenue is at its best, of course, just now. The dresses are magnificent!"

Wads of stuff about the dresses. I didn't know Jeeves was such an authority.

"I was out with some of the crowd at the Midnight Revels the other night. We took in a show first, after a little dinner at a new place on Forty-third Street. We were quite a gay party. Georgie Cohan looked in about midnight and got off a good one about Willie Collier. Fred Stone could only stay a minute, but Doug. Fairbanks did all sorts of stunts and made us roar. Diamond Jim Brady was there, as usual, and Laurette Taylor showed up with a party. The show at the Revels is quite good. I am enclosing a program.

"Last night a few of us went round to Frolics on the Roof—"

And so on and so forth, yards of it. I suppose it's the artistic temperament or something. What I mean is, it's easier for a chappie who's used to writing poems and that sort of tosh to put a bit of a punch into a letter than it is for a chappie like me. Anyway, there's no doubt that Rocky's correspondence was hot stuff. I called Jeeves in and congratulated him.

"Jeeves, you're a wonder!"

"Thank you, sir."

"How you notice everything at these places beats me. I couldn't tell you a thing about them, except that I've had a good time."

"It's just a knack, sir."

"Well, Mr. Todd's letters ought to brace Miss Rockmetteller all right, what?"

"Undoubtedly, sir," agreed Jeeves.

And, by Jove, they did! They certainly did, by George! What I mean to say is, I was sitting in the apartment one afternoon, about a month after the thing had started, smoking a cigarette and resting the old bean, when the door opened and the voice of Jeeves burst the silence like a bomb.

It wasn't that he spoke loud. He has one of those soft, soothing voices that slide through the atmosphere like the note of a far-off sheep. It was what he said made me leap like a young gazelle.

"Miss Rockmetteller!"

And in came a large, solid female.

The situation floored me. I'm not denying it. Hamlet must have felt much as I did when his father's ghost bobbed up in the fairway. I'd come to look on Rocky's aunt as such a permanency at her own home that it didn't seem possible that she could really be here in New York. I stared at her. Then I looked at Jeeves. He was standing there in an attitude of dignified detachment, the chump, when, if ever he should have been rallying round the young master, it was now.

Rocky's aunt looked less like an invalid than any one I've ever seen, except my Aunt Agatha. She had a good deal of Aunt Agatha about her, as a matter of fact. She looked as if she might be deucedly dangerous if put upon; and something seemed to tell me that she would certainly regard herself as put upon if she ever found out the game which poor old Rocky had been pulling on her.

"Good afternoon," I managed to say.

"How do you do?" she said. "Mr. Cohan?"

"Er—no."

"Mr. Fred Stone?"

"Not absolutely. As a matter of fact, my name's Wooster—Bertie Wooster."

She seemed disappointed. The fine old name of Wooster appeared to mean nothing in her life.

"Isn't Rockmetteller home?" she said. "Where is he?"

She had me with the first shot. I couldn't think of anything to say. I couldn't tell her that Rocky was down in the country, watching worms.

There was the faintest flutter of sound in the background. It was the respectful cough with which Jeeves announces that he is about to speak without having been spoken to.

"If you remember, sir, Mr. Todd went out in the automobile with a party in the afternoon."

"So he did, Jeeves; so he did," I said, looking at my watch. "Did he say when he would be back?"

"He gave me to understand, sir, that he would be somewhat late in returning."

He vanished; and the aunt took the chair which I'd forgotten to offer her. She looked at me in rather a rummy way. It was a nasty look. It made me feel as if I were something the dog had brought in and intended to bury later on, when he had time. My own Aunt Agatha, back in England, has looked at me in exactly the same way many a time, and it never fails to make my spine curl.

"You seem very much at home here, young man. Are you a great friend of Rockmetteller's?"

"Oh, yes, rather!"

She frowned as if she had expected better things of old Rocky.

"Well, you need to be," she said, "the way you treat his flat as your own!"

I give you my word, this quite unforeseen slam simply robbed me of the power of speech. I'd been looking on myself in the light of the dashing host, and suddenly to be treated as an intruder jarred me. It wasn't, mark you, as if she had spoken in a way to suggest that she considered my presence in the place as an ordinary social call. She obviously looked on me as a cross between a burglar and the plumber's man come to fix the leak in the bathroom. It hurt her—my being there.

At this juncture, with the conversation showing every sign of being about to die in awful agonies, an idea came to me. Tea—the good old stand-by.

"Would you care for a cup of tea?" I said.

"Tea?"

She spoke as if she had never heard of the stuff.

"Nothing like a cup after a journey," I said. "Bucks you up! Puts a bit of zip into you. What I mean is, restores you, and so on, don't you know. I'll go and tell Jeeves."

I tottered down the passage to Jeeves's lair. The man was reading the evening paper as if he hadn't a care in the world.

"Jeeves," I said, "we want some tea."

"Very good, sir."

"I say, Jeeves, this is a bit thick, what?"

I wanted sympathy, don't you know—sympathy and kindness. The old nerve centers had had the deuce of a shock.

"She's got the idea this place belongs to Mr. Todd. What on earth put that into her head?"

Jeeves filled the kettle with a restrained dignity.

"No doubt because of Mr. Todd's letters, sir," he said. "It was my suggestion, sir, if you remember, that they should be addressed from this apartment in order that Mr. Todd should appear to possess a good central residence in the city."

I remembered. We had thought it a brainy scheme at the time.

"Well, it's bally awkward, you know, Jeeves. She looks on me as an intruder. By Jove! I suppose she thinks I'm someone who hangs about here, touching Mr. Todd for free meals and borrowing his shirts."

"Yes, sir."

"It's pretty rotten, you know."

"Most disturbing, sir."

"And there's another thing: What are we to do about Mr. Todd? We've got to get him up here as soon as ever we can. When you have brought the tea you had better go out and send him a telegram, telling him to come up by the next train."

"I have already done so, sir. I took the liberty of writing the message and dispatching it by the lift attendant."

"By Jove, you think of everything, Jeeves!"

"Thank you, sir. A little buttered toast with the tea? Just so, sir. Thank you."

I went back to the sitting-room. She hadn't moved an inch. She was still bolt upright on the edge of her chair, gripping her umbrella like a hammer-thrower. She gave me another of those looks as I came in. There was no doubt about it; for some reason she had taken a dislike to me. I suppose because I wasn't George M. Cohan. It was a bit hard on a chap.

"This is a surprise, what?" I said, after about five minutes' restful silence, trying to crank the conversation up again.

"What is a surprise?"

"Your coming here, don't you know, and so on."

She raised her eyebrows and drank me in a bit more through her glasses.

"Why is it surprising that I should visit my only nephew?" she said.

Put like that, of course, it did seem reasonable.

"Oh, rather," I said. "Of course! Certainly. What I mean is—"

Jeeves projected himself into the room with the tea. I was jolly glad to see him. There's nothing like having a bit of business arranged for one when one isn't certain of one's lines. With the teapot to fool about with I felt happier.

"Tea, tea, tea—what? What?" I said.

It wasn't what I had meant to say. My idea had been to be a good deal more formal, and so on. Still, it covered the situation. I poured her out a cup. She sipped it and put the cup down with a shudder.

"Do you mean to say, young man," she said frostily, "that you expect me to drink this stuff?"

"Rather! Bucks you up, you know."

"What do you mean by the expression 'Bucks you up'?"

"Well, makes you full of beans, you know. Makes you fizz."

"I don't understand a word you say. You're English, aren't you?"

I admitted it. She didn't say a word. And somehow she did it in a way that made it worse than if she had spoken for hours. Somehow it was brought home to me that she didn't like Englishmen, and that if she had had to meet an Englishman, I was the one she'd have chosen last.

Conversation languished again after that.

Then I tried again. I was becoming more convinced every moment that you can't make a real lively salon with a couple of people, especially if one of them lets it go a word at a time.

"Are you comfortable at your hotel?" I said.

"At which hotel?"

"The hotel you're staying at."

"I am not staying at a hotel."

"Stopping with friends—what?"

"I am naturally stopping with my nephew."

I didn't get it for the moment; then it hit me.

"What! Here?" I gurgled.

"Certainly! Where else should I go?"

The full horror of the situation rolled over me like a wave. I couldn't see what on earth I was to do. I couldn't explain that this wasn't Rocky's flat without giving the poor old chap away hopelessly, because she would then ask me where he did live, and then he would be right in the soup. I was trying to induce the old bean to recover from the shock and produce some results when she spoke again.

"Will you kindly tell my nephew's man-servant to prepare my room? I wish to lie down."

"Your nephew's man-servant?"

"The man you call Jeeves. If Rockmetteller has gone for an automobile ride, there is no need for you to wait for him. He will naturally wish to be alone with me when he returns."

I found myself tottering out of the room. The thing was too much for me. I crept into Jeeves's den.

"Jeeves!" I whispered.

"Sir?"

"Mix me a b.-and-s., Jeeves. I feel weak."

"Very good, sir."

"This is getting thicker every minute, Jeeves."

"Sir?"

"She thinks you're Mr. Todd's man. She thinks the whole place is his, and everything in it. I don't see what you're to do, except stay on and keep it up. We can't say anything or she'll get on to the whole thing, and I don't want to let Mr. Todd down. By the way, Jeeves, she wants you to prepare her bed."

He looked wounded.

"It is hardly my place, sir—"

"I know—I know. But do it as a personal favor to me. If you come to that, it's hardly my place to be flung out of the flat like this and have to go to a hotel, what?"

"Is it your intention to go to a hotel, sir? What will you do for clothes?"

"Good Lord! I hadn't thought of that. Can you put a few things in a bag when she isn't looking, and sneak them down to me at the St. Aurea?"

"I will endeavor to do so, sir."

"Well, I don't think there's anything more, is there? Tell Mr. Todd where I am when he gets here."

"Very good, sir."

I looked round the place. The moment of parting had come. I felt sad. The whole thing reminded me of one of those melodramas where they drive chappies out of the old homestead into the snow.

"Good-bye, Jeeves," I said.

"Good-bye, sir."

And I staggered out.

YOU KNOW, I RATHER think I agree with those poet-and-philosopher Johnnies who insist that a fellow ought to be devilish pleased if he has a bit of trouble. All that stuff about being refined by suffering, you know. Suffering does give a chap a sort of broader and more sympathetic outlook. It helps you to understand other people's misfortunes if you've been through the same thing yourself.

As I stood in my lonely bedroom at the hotel, trying to tie my white tie myself, it struck me for the first time that there must be whole squads of chappies in the world who had to get along without a man to look after them. I'd always thought of Jeeves as a kind of natural phenomenon; but, by Jove! of course, when you come to think of it, there must be quite a lot of fellows who have to press their own clothes themselves and haven't got anybody to bring them tea in the morning, and so on. It was rather a solemn thought, don't you know. I mean to say, ever since then I've been able to appreciate the frightful privations the poor have to stick.

I got dressed somehow. Jeeves hadn't forgotten a thing in his packing. Everything was there, down to the final stud. I'm not sure this didn't make me feel worse. It kind of deepened the pathos. It was like what somebody or other wrote about the touch of a vanished hand.

I had a bit of dinner somewhere and went to a show of some kind; but nothing seemed to make any difference. I simply hadn't the heart to go on to supper anywhere. I just sucked down a whisky-and-soda in the hotel smoking-room and went straight up to bed. I don't know when I've felt so rotten. Somehow I found myself moving about the room softly, as if there had been a death in the family. If I had anybody to talk to I should have talked in a whisper; in fact, when the telephone-bell rang I answered in such a sad, hushed voice that the fellow at the other end of the wire said "Halloa!" five times, thinking he hadn't got me.

It was Rocky. The poor old scout was deeply agitated.

"Bertie! Is that you, Bertie! Oh, gosh? I'm having a time!"

"Where are you speaking from?"

"The Midnight Revels. We've been here an hour, and I think we're a fixture for the night. I've told Aunt Isabel I've gone out to call up a friend to join us. She's glued to a chair, with this-is-the-life written all over her, taking it in through the pores. She loves it, and I'm nearly crazy."

"Tell me all, old top," I said.

"A little more of this," he said, "and I shall sneak quietly off to the river and end it all. Do you mean to say you go through this sort of thing every night, Bertie, and enjoy it? It's simply infernal! I was just snatching a wink of sleep behind the bill of fare just now when about a million yelling girls swooped down, with toy balloons. There are two orchestras here, each trying to see if it can't play louder than the other. I'm a mental and physical wreck. When your telegram arrived I was just lying down for a quiet pipe, with a sense of absolute peace stealing over me. I had to get dressed and sprint two miles to catch the train. It nearly gave me heart-failure; and on top of that I almost got brain fever inventing lies to tell Aunt Isabel. And then I had to cram myself into these confounded evening clothes of yours."

I gave a sharp wail of agony. It hadn't struck me till then that Rocky was depending on my wardrobe to see him through.

"You'll ruin them!"

"I hope so," said Rocky, in the most unpleasant way. His troubles seemed to have had the worst effect on his character. "I should like to get back at them somehow;

they've given me a bad enough time. They're about three sizes too small, and something's apt to give at any moment. I wish to goodness it would, and give me a chance to breathe. I haven't breathed since half-past seven. Thank Heaven, Jeeves managed to get out and buy me a collar that fitted, or I should be a strangled corpse by now! It was touch and go till the stud broke. Bertie, this is pure Hades! Aunt Isabel keeps on urging me to dance. How on earth can I dance when I don't know a soul to dance with? And how the deuce could I, even if I knew every girl in the place? It's taking big chances even to move in these trousers. I had to tell her I've hurt my ankle. She keeps asking me when Cohan and Stone are going to turn up; and it's simply a question of time before she discovers that Stone is sitting two tables away. Something's got to be done, Bertie! You've got to think up some way of getting me out of this mess. It was you who got me into it."

"Me! What do you mean?"

"Well, Jeeves, then. It's all the same. It was you who suggested leaving it to Jeeves. It was those letters I wrote from his notes that did the mischief. I made them too good! My aunt's just been telling me about it. She says she had resigned herself to ending her life where she was, and then my letters began to arrive, describing the joys of New York; and they stimulated her to such an extent that she pulled herself together and made the trip. She seems to think she's had some miraculous kind of faith cure. I tell you I can't stand it, Bertie! It's got to end!"

"Can't Jeeves think of anything?"

"No. He just hangs round saying: 'Most disturbing, sir!' A fat lot of help that is!"

"Well, old lad," I said, "after all, it's far worse for me than it is for you. You've got a comfortable home and Jeeves. And you're saving a lot of money."

"Saving money? What do you mean—saving money?"

"Why, the allowance your aunt was giving you. I suppose she's paying all the expenses now, isn't she?"

"Certainly she is; but she's stopped the allowance. She wrote the lawyers tonight. She says that, now she's in New York, there is no necessity for it to go on, as we shall always be together, and it's simpler for her to look after that end of it. I tell you, Bertie, I've examined the darned cloud with a microscope, and if it's got a silver lining it's some little dissembler!"

"But, Rocky, old top, it's too bally awful! You've no notion of what I'm going through in this beastly hotel, without Jeeves. I must get back to the flat."

"Don't come near the flat."

"But it's my own flat."

"I can't help that. Aunt Isabel doesn't like you. She asked me what you did for a living. And when I told her you didn't do anything she said she thought as much, and that you were a typical specimen of a useless and decaying aristocracy. So if you think you have made a hit, forget it. Now I must be going back, or she'll be coming out here after me. Good-bye."

Next morning Jeeves came round. It was all so homelike when he floated noiselessly into the room that I nearly broke down.

"Good morning, sir," he said. "I have brought a few more of your personal belongings."

He began to unstrap the suit-case he was carrying.

"Did you have any trouble sneaking them away?"

"It was not easy, sir. I had to watch my chance. Miss Rockmetteller is a remarkably alert lady."

"You know, Jeeves, say what you like—this is a bit thick, isn't it?"

"The situation is certainly one that has never before come under my notice, sir. I have brought the heather-mixture suit, as the climatic conditions are congenial. To-morrow, if not prevented, I will endeavor to add the brown lounge with the faint green twill."

"It can't go on—this sort of thing—Jeeves."

"We must hope for the best, sir."

"Can't you think of anything to do?"

"I have been giving the matter considerable thought, sir, but so far without success. I am placing three silk shirts—the dove-colored, the light blue, and the mauve—in the first long drawer, sir."

"You don't mean to say you can't think of anything, Jeeves?"

"For the moment, sir, no. You will find a dozen hand-kerchiefs and the tan socks in the upper drawer on the left." He strapped the suit-case and put it on a chair. "A curious lady, Miss Rockmetteller, sir."

"You understate it, Jeeves."

He gazed meditatively out of the window.

"In many ways, sir, Miss Rockmetteller reminds me of an aunt of mine who resides in the south-east portion of London. Their temperaments are much alike. My aunt has the same taste for the pleasures of the great city. It is a passion with her to ride in hansom cabs, sir. Whenever the family take their eyes off her she escapes from the house and spends the day riding about in cabs. On several occasions she has broken into the children's savings bank to secure the means to enable her to gratify this desire."

"I love to have these little chats with you about your female relatives, Jeeves," I said coldly, for I felt that the man had let me down, and I was fed up with him. "But I don't see what all this has got to do with my trouble."

"I beg your pardon, sir. I am leaving a small assortment of neckties on the mantelpiece, sir, for you to select according to your preference. I should recommend the blue with the red domino pattern, sir."

Then he streamed imperceptibly toward the door and flowed silently out.

I'VE OFTEN HEARD THAT chappies, after some great shock or loss, have a habit, after they've been on the floor for a while wondering what hit them, of picking themselves up and piecing themselves together, and sort of taking a whirl at beginning a new life. Time, the great healer, and Nature, adjusting itself, and so on and so forth. There's a lot in it. I know, because in my own case, after a day or two of what you might call prostration, I began to recover. The frightful loss of Jeeves made any thought of pleasure more or less a mockery, but at least I found that I was able to have a dash at enjoying life again. What I mean is, I was braced up to the extent of going round the cabarets once more, so as to try to forget, if only for the moment.

New York's a small place when it comes to the part of it that wakes up just as the rest is going to bed, and it wasn't long before my tracks began to cross old Rocky's. I saw him once at Peale's, and again at Frolics on the roof. There wasn't anybody with him either time except the aunt, and, though he was trying to look as if he had struck the ideal life, it wasn't difficult for me, knowing the circumstances, to see that beneath the mask the poor chap was suffering. My heart bled for the fellow. At least, what there was of it that wasn't bleeding for myself bled for him. He had the air of one who was about to crack under the strain.

It seemed to me that the aunt was looking slightly upset also. I took it that she was beginning to wonder when the celebrities were going to surge round, and what had suddenly become of all those wild, careless spirits Rocky used to mix with in his letters. I didn't blame her. I had only read a couple of his letters, but they certainly gave the impression that poor old Rocky was by way of being the hub of New York night life, and that, if by any chance he failed to show up at a cabaret, the management said: "What's the use?" and put up the shutters.

The next two nights I didn't come across them, but the night after that I was sitting by myself at the Maison Pierre when somebody tapped me on the shoulder-blade, and I found Rocky standing beside me, with a sort of mixed expression of wistfulness and apoplexy on his face. How the chappie had contrived to wear my evening clothes so many times without disaster was a mystery to me. He confided later that early in the proceedings he had slit the waistcoat up the back and that that had helped a bit.

For a moment I had the idea that he had managed to get away from his aunt for the evening; but, looking past him, I saw that she was in again. She was at a table over by the wall, looking at me as if I were something the management ought to be complained to about.

"Bertie, old scout," said Rocky, in a quiet, sort of crushed voice, "we've always been pals, haven't we? I mean, you know I'd do you a good turn if you asked me?"

"My dear old lad," I said. The man had moved me.

"Then, for Heaven's sake, come over and sit at our table for the rest of the evening."

Well, you know, there are limits to the sacred claims of friendship.

"My dear chap," I said, "you know I'd do anything in reason; but—"

"You must come, Bertie. You've got to. Something's got to be done to divert her mind. She's brooding about something. She's been like that for the last two days. I think she's beginning to suspect. She can't understand why we never seem to meet anyone I know at these joints. A few nights ago I happened to run into two newspaper men I used to know fairly well. That kept me going for a while. I introduced them to Aunt Isabel as David Belasco and Jim Corbett, and it went well. But the effect has worn off now, and she's beginning to wonder again. Something's got to be done, or she will find out everything, and if she does I'd take a nickel for my chance of getting a cent from her later on. So, for the love of Mike, come across to our table and help things along."

I went along. One has to rally round a pal in distress. Aunt Isabel was sitting bolt upright, as usual. It certainly did seem as if she had lost a bit of the zest with which she had started out to explore Broadway. She looked as if she had been thinking a good deal about rather unpleasant things.

"You've met Bertie Wooster, Aunt Isabel?" said Rocky.

"I have."

There was something in her eye that seemed to say:

"Out of a city of six million people, why did you pick on me?"

"Take a seat, Bertie. What'll you have?" said Rocky.

And so the merry party began. It was one of those jolly, happy, bread-crumbling parties where you cough twice before you speak, and then decide not to say it after all. After we had had an hour of this wild dissipation, Aunt Isabel said she wanted to go home. In the light of what Rocky had been telling me, this struck me as sinister. I had gathered that at the beginning of her visit she had had to be dragged home with ropes.

It must have hit Rocky the same way, for he gave me a pleading look.

"You'll come along, won't you, Bertie, and have a drink at the flat?"

I had a feeling that this wasn't in the contract, but there wasn't anything to be done. It seemed brutal to leave the poor chap alone with the woman, so I went along.

Right from the start, from the moment we stepped into the taxi, the feeling began to grow that something was about to break loose. A massive silence prevailed in the corner where the aunt sat, and, though Rocky, balancing himself on the little seat in front, did his best to supply dialogue, we weren't a chatty party.

I had a glimpse of Jeeves as we went into the flat, sitting in his lair, and I wished I could have called to him to rally round. Something told me that I was about to need him.

The stuff was on the table in the sitting-room. Rocky took up the decanter.

"Say when, Bertie."

"Stop!" barked the aunt, and he dropped it.

I caught Rocky's eye as he stooped to pick up the ruins. It was the eye of one who sees it coming.

"Leave it there, Rockmetteller!" said Aunt Isabel; and Rocky left it there.

"The time has come to speak," she said. "I cannot stand idly by and see a young man going to perdition!"

Poor old Rocky gave a sort of gurgle, a kind of sound rather like the whisky had made running out of the decanter on to my carpet.

"Eh?" he said, blinking.

The aunt proceeded.

"The fault," she said, "was mine. I had not then seen the light. But now my eyes are open. I see the hideous mistake I have made. I shudder at the thought of the wrong I did you, Rockmetteller, by urging you into contact with this wicked city."

I saw Rocky grope feebly for the table. His fingers touched it, and a look of relief came into the poor chappie's face. I understood his feelings.

"But when I wrote you that letter, Rockmetteller, instructing you to go to the city and live its life, I had not had the privilege of hearing Mr. Mundy speak on the subject of New York."

"Jimmy Mundy!" I cried.

You know how it is sometimes when everything seems all mixed up and you suddenly get a clue. When she mentioned Jimmy Mundy I began to understand more or less what had happened. I'd seen it happen before. I remember, back in England, the man I had before Jeeves sneaked off to a meeting on his evening out and came back and denounced me in front of a crowd of chappies I was giving a bit of supper to as a moral leper.

The aunt gave me a withering up and down.

"Yes; Jimmy Mundy!" she said. "I am surprised at a man of your stamp having heard of him. There is no music, there are no drunken, dancing men, no shameless, flaunting women at his meetings; so for you they would have no attraction. But for others, less dead in sin, he has his message. He has come to save New York from itself; to force it—in his picturesque phrase—to hit the trail. It was three days ago, Rockmetteller, that I first heard him. It was an accident that took me to his meeting. How often in this life a mere accident may shape our whole future!

"You had been called away by that telephone message from Mr. Belasco; so you could not take me to the Hippodrome, as we had arranged. I asked your man-servant, Jeeves, to take me there. The man has very little intelligence. He seems to have misunderstood me. I am thankful that he did. He took me to what I subsequently learned was Madison Square Garden, where Mr. Mundy is holding his meetings. He escorted me to a seat and then left me. And it was not till the meeting had begun that I discovered the mistake which had been made. My seat was in the middle of a row. I could not leave without inconveniencing a great many people, so I remained."

She gulped.

"Rockmetteller, I have never been so thankful for anything else. Mr. Mundy was wonderful! He was like some prophet of old, scourging the sins of the people. He leaped about in a frenzy of inspiration till I feared he would do himself an injury. Sometimes he expressed himself in a somewhat odd manner, but every word carried conviction. He showed me New York in its true colours. He showed me the vanity and wickedness of sitting in gilded haunts of vice, eating lobster when decent people should be in bed.

"He said that the tango and the fox-trot were devices of the devil to drag people down into the Bottomless Pit. He said that there was more sin in ten minutes with a negro banjo orchestra than in all the ancient revels of Nineveh and Babylon. And when he stood on one leg and pointed right at where I was sitting and shouted, 'This means you!' I could have sunk through the floor. I came away a changed woman. Surely you must have noticed the change in me, Rockmetteller? You must have seen that I was no longer the careless, thoughtless person who had urged you to dance in those places of wickedness?"

Rocky was holding on to the table as if it was his only friend.

"Y-yes," he stammered; "I—I thought something was wrong."

"Wrong? Something was right! Everything was right! Rockmetteller, it is not too late for you to be saved. You have only sipped of the evil cup. You have not drained it. It will be hard at first, but you will find that you can do it if you fight with a stout heart against the glamour and fascination of this dreadful city. Won't you, for my sake, try, Rockmetteller? Won't you go back to the country tomorrow and begin the struggle? Little by little, if you use your will—"

I can't help thinking it must have been that word "will" that roused dear old Rocky like a trumpet call. It must have brought home to him the realisation that a miracle had come off and saved him from being cut out of Aunt Isabel's. At any rate, as she said it he perked up, let go of the table, and faced her with gleaming eyes.

"Do you want me to go back to the country, Aunt Isabel?"

"Yes."

"Not to live in the country?"

"Yes, Rockmetteller."

"Stay in the country all the time, do you mean? Never come to New York?"

"Yes, Rockmetteller; I mean just that. It is the only way. Only there can you be safe from temptation. Will you do it, Rockmetteller? Will you—for my sake?"

Rocky grabbed the table again. He seemed to draw a lot of encouragement from that table.

"I will!" he said.

"JEEVES," I SAID. IT WAS next day, and I was back in the old flat, lying in the old arm-chair, with my feet upon the good old table. I had just come from seeing dear old Rocky off to his country cottage, and an hour before he had seen his aunt off to whatever hamlet it was that she was the curse of; so we were alone at last. "Jeeves, there's no place like home—what?"

"Very true, sir."

"The jolly old roof-tree, and all that sort of thing—what?"

"Precisely, sir."

I lit another cigarette.

"Jeeves."

"Sir?"

"Do you know, at one point in the business I really thought you were baffled."

"Indeed, sir?"

"When did you get the idea of taking Miss Rockmetteller to the meeting? It was pure genius!"

"Thank you, sir. It came to me a little suddenly, one morning when I was thinking of my aunt, sir."

"Your aunt? The hansom cab one?"

"Yes, sir. I recollected that, whenever we observed one of her attacks coming on, we used to send for the clergyman of the parish. We always found that if he talked to her a while of higher things it diverted her mind from hansom cabs. It occurred to me that the same treatment might prove efficacious in the case of Miss Rockmetteller."

I was stunned by the man's resource.

"It's brain," I said; "pure brain! What do you do to get like that, Jeeves? I believe you must eat a lot of fish, or something. Do you eat a lot of fish, Jeeves?"

"No, sir."

"Oh, well, then, it's just a gift, I take it; and if you aren't born that way there's no use worrying."

"Precisely, sir," said Jeeves. "If I might make the suggestion, sir, I should not continue to wear your present tie. The green shade gives you a slightly bilious air. I should strongly advocate the blue with the red domino pattern instead, sir."

"All right, Jeeves." I said humbly. "You know!"

# Jeeves and the Chump Cyril

YOU KNOW, THE LONGER I live, the more clearly I see that half the trouble in this bally world is caused by the light-hearted and thoughtless way in which chappies dash off letters of introduction and hand them to other chappies to deliver to chappies of the third part. It's one of those things that make you wish you were living in the Stone Age. What I mean to say is, if a fellow in those days wanted to give anyone a letter of introduction, he had to spend a month or so carving it on a large-sized boulder, and the chances were that the other chappie got so sick of lugging the thing round in the hot sun that he dropped it after the first mile. But nowadays it's so easy to write letters of introduction that everybody does it without a second thought, with the result that some perfectly harmless cove like myself gets in the soup.

Mark you, all the above is what you might call the result of my riper experience. I don't mind admitting that in the first flush of the thing, so, to speak, when Jeeves told me—this would be about three weeks after I'd landed in America—that a blighter called Cyril Bassington-Bassington had arrived and I found that he had brought a letter of introduction to me from Aunt Agatha ... where was I? Oh, yes ... I don't mind admitting, I was saying, that just at first I was rather bucked. You see, after the painful events which had resulted in my leaving England I hadn't expected to get any sort of letter from Aunt Agatha which would pass the censor, so to speak. And it was a pleasant surprise to open this one and find it almost civil. Chilly, perhaps, in parts, but on the whole quite tolerably polite. I looked on the thing as a hopeful sign. Sort of olive-branch, you know. Or do I mean orange blossom? What I'm getting at is that the fact that Aunt Agatha was writing to me without calling me names seemed, more or less, like a step in the direction of peace.

And I was all for peace, and that right speedily. I'm not saying a word against New York, mind you. I liked the place, and was having quite a ripe time there. But the fact remains that a fellow who's been used to London all his life does get a trifle homesick on a foreign strand, and I wanted to pop back to the cozy old flat in Berkeley Street—which could only be done when Aunt Agatha had simmered down and got over the Glossop episode. I know that London is a biggish city, but, believe me, it isn't half big enough for any fellow to live in with Aunt Agatha when she's after him with the old hatchet. And so I'm bound to say I looked on this chump Bassington-Bassington, when he arrived, more or less as a Dove of Peace, and was all for him.

He would seem from contemporary accounts to have blown in one morning at seven-forty-five, that being the ghastly sort of hour they shoot you off the liner in New York. He was given the respectful raspberry by Jeeves, and told to try again about three hours later, when there would be a sporting chance of my having sprung from my bed with a glad cry to welcome another day and all that sort of thing. Which was rather decent of Jeeves, by the way, for it so happened that there was a slight estrangement, a touch of coldness, a bit of a row in other words, between us at the moment because of some rather priceless purple socks which I was wearing against his wishes: and a lesser man might easily have snatched at the chance of getting back at me a bit by loosing Cyril into my bedchamber at a moment when I couldn't have stood a two-minutes' conversation with my dearest pal. For until I have had my early cup of tea and have brooded on life for a bit absolutely undisturbed, I'm not much of a lad for the merry chit-chat.

So Jeeves very sportingly shot Cyril out into the crisp morning air, and didn't let me know of his existence till he brought his card in with the Bohea.

"And what might all this be, Jeeves?" I said, giving the thing the glassy gaze.

"The gentleman has arrived from England, I understand, sir. He called to see you earlier in the day."

"Good Lord, Jeeves! You don't mean to say the day starts earlier than this?"

"He desired me to say he would return later, sir."

"I've never heard of him. Have you ever heard of him, Jeeves?"

"I am familiar with the name Bassington-Bassington, sir. There are three branches of the Bassington-Bassington family: the Shropshire Bassington-Bassingtons, the Hampshire Bassington-Bassingtons, and the Kent Bassington-Bassingtons."

"England seems pretty well stocked up with Bassington-Bassingtons."

"Tolerably so, sir."

"No chance of a sudden shortage, I mean, what?"

"Presumably not, sir."

"And what sort of a specimen is this one?"

"I could not say, sir, on such short acquaintance."

"Will you give me a sporting two to one, Jeeves, judging from what you have seen of him, that this chappie is not a blighter or an excrescence?"

"No, sir. I should not care to venture such liberal odds."

"I knew it. Well, the only thing that remains to be discovered is what kind of a blighter he is."

"Time will tell, sir. The gentleman brought a letter for you, sir."

"Oh, he did, did he?" I said, and grasped the communication. And then I recognized the handwriting. "I say, Jeeves, this is from my Aunt Agatha!"

"Indeed, sir?"

"Don't dismiss it in that light way. Don't you see what this means? She says she wants me to look after this excrescence while he's in New York. By Jove, Jeeves, if I only fawn on him a bit, so that he sends back a favorable report to head-quarters, I may yet be able to get back to England in time for Goodwood. Now is certainly the time for all good men to come to the aid of the party, Jeeves. We must rally round and cosset this cove in no uncertain manner."

"Yes, sir."

"He isn't going to stay in New York long," I said, taking another look at the letter. "He's headed for Washington. Going to give the nibs there the once-over, apparently, before taking a whirl at the Diplomatic Service. I should say that we can win this lad's esteem and affection with a lunch and a couple of dinners, what?"

"I fancy that should be entirely adequate, sir."

"This is the jolliest thing that's happened since we left England. It looks to me as if the sun were breaking through the clouds."

"Very possibly, sir."

He started to put out my things, and there was an awkward sort of silence.

"Not those socks, Jeeves," I said, gulping a bit but having a dash at the careless, off-hand tone. "Give me the purple ones."

"I beg your pardon, sir?"

"Those jolly purple ones."

"Very good, sir."

He lugged them out of the drawer as if he were a vegetarian fishing a caterpillar out of the salad. You could see he was feeling deeply. Deuced painful and all that, this sort of thing, but a chappie has got to assert himself every now and then. Absolutely.

I WAS LOOKING FOR CYRIL to show up again any time after breakfast, but he didn't appear: so towards one o'clock I trickled out to the Lambs Clùb, where I had an appointment to feed the Wooster face with a cove of the name of Caffyn I'd got pally with since my arrival—George Caffyn, a fellow who wrote plays and what not. I'd made a lot of friends during my stay in New York, the city being crammed with bonhomous lads who one and all extended a welcoming hand to the stranger in their midst.

Caffyn was a bit late, but bobbed up finally, saying that he had been kept at a rehearsal of his new musical comedy, "Ask Dad"; and we started in. We had just reached the coffee, when the waiter came up and said that Jeeves wanted to see me.

Jeeves was in the waiting-room. He gave the socks one pained look as I came in, then averted his eyes.

"Mr. Bassington-Bassington has just telephoned, sir."

"Oh?"

"Yes, sir."

"Where is he?"

"In prison, sir."

I reeled against the wallpaper. A nice thing to happen to Aunt Agatha's nominee on his first morning under my wing, I did not think!

"In prison!"

"Yes, sir. He said on the telephone that he had been arrested and would be glad if you could step round and bail him out."

"Arrested! What for?"

"He did not favour me with his confidence in that respect, sir."

"This is a bit thick, Jeeves."

"Precisely, sir."

I collected old George, who very decently volunteered to stagger along with me, and we hopped into a taxi. We sat around at the police-station for a bit on a wooden bench in a sort of ante-room, and presently a policeman appeared, leading in Cyril.

"Halloa! Halloa! Halloa!" I said. "What?"

My experience is that a fellow never really looks his best just after he's come out of a cell. When I was up at Oxford, I used to have a regular job bailing out a pal of mine who never failed to get pinched every Boat-Race night, and he always looked like something that had been dug up by the roots. Cyril was in pretty much the same sort of shape. He had a black eye and a torn collar, and altogether was nothing to write home about—especially if one was writing to Aunt Agatha. He was a thin, tall chappie with a lot of light hair and pale-blue goggly eyes which made him look like one of the rarer kinds of fish.

"I got your message," I said.

"Oh, are you Bertie Wooster?"

"Absolutely. And this is my pal George Caffyn. Writes plays and what not, don't you know."

We all shook hands, and the policeman, having retrieved a piece of chewing-gum from the underside of a chair, where he had parked it against a rainy day, went off into a corner and began to contemplate the infinite.

"This is a rotten country," said Cyril.

"Oh, I don't know, you know, don't you know!" I said.

"We do our best," said George.

"Old George is an American," I explained. "Writes plays, don't you know, and what not."

"Of course, I didn't invent the country," said George. "That was Columbus. But I shall be delighted to consider any improvements you may suggest and lay them before the proper authorities."

"Well, why don't the policemen in New York dress properly?"

George took a look at the chewing officer across the room.

"I don't see anything missing," he said.

"I mean to say, why don't they wear helmets like they do in London? Why do they look like postmen? It isn't fair on a fellow. Makes it dashed confusing. I was simply standing on the pavement, looking at things, when a fellow who looked like a postman prodded me in the ribs with a club. I didn't see why I should have postmen prodding me. Why the dickens should a fellow come three thousand miles to be prodded by postmen?"

"The point is well taken," said George. "What did you do?"

"I gave him a shove, you know. I've got a frightfully hasty temper, you know. All the Bassington-Bassingtons have got frightfully hasty tempers, don't you know! And then he biffed me in the eye and lugged me off to this beastly place."

"I'll fix it, old son," I said. And I hauled out the bank-roll and went off to open negotiations, leaving Cyril to talk to George. I don't mind admitting that I was a bit perturbed. There were furrows in the old brow, and I had a kind of foreboding feeling. As long as this chump stayed in New York, I was responsible for him: and he didn't give me the impression of being the species of cove a reasonable chappie would care to be responsible for for more than about three minutes.

I mused with a considerable amount of tensity over Cyril that night, when I had got home and Jeeves had brought me the final whisky. I couldn't help feeling that this visit of his to America was going to be one of those times that try men's souls and what not. I hauled out Aunt Agatha's letter of introduction and re-read it, and there was no getting away from the fact that she undoubtedly appeared to be somewhat wrapped up in this blighter and to consider it my mission in life to shield him from harm while on the premises. I was deuced thankful that he had taken such a liking for George Caffyn, old George being a steady sort of cove. After I had got him out of his dungeon-cell, he and old George had gone off together, as chummy as brothers, to watch the afternoon rehearsal of "Ask Dad." There was some talk, I gathered, of their dining together. I felt pretty easy in my mind while George had his eye on him.

I had got about as far as this in my meditations, when Jeeves came in with a telegram. At least, it wasn't a telegram: it was a cable—from Aunt Agatha, and this is what it said:

*Has Cyril Bassington-Bassington called yet? On no account introduce him into theatrical circles. Vitally important. Letter follows.*

I read it a couple of times.

"This is rummy, Jeeves!"

"Yes, sir?"

"Very rummy and dashed disturbing!"

"Will there be anything further tonight, sir?"

Of course, if he was going to be as bally unsympathetic as that there was nothing to be done. My idea had been to show him the cable and ask his advice. But if he was letting those purple socks rankle to that extent, the good old noblesse oblige of the Woosters couldn't lower itself to the extent of pleading with the man. Absolutely not. So I gave it a miss.

"Nothing more, thanks."

"Good night, sir."

"Good night."

He floated away, and I sat down to think the thing over. I had been directing the best efforts of the old bean to the problem for a matter of half an hour, when there was a ring at the bell. I went to the door, and there was Cyril, looking pretty festive.

"I'll come in for a bit if I may," he said. "Got something rather priceless to tell you."

He curveted past me into the sitting-room, and when I got there after shutting the front door I found him reading Aunt Agatha's cable and giggling in a rummy sort of manner. "Oughtn't to have looked at this, I suppose. Caught sight of my name and read it without thinking. I say, Wooster, old friend of my youth, this is rather funny. Do you mind if I have a drink? Thanks awfully and all that sort of rot. Yes, it's rather funny, considering what I came to tell you. Jolly old Caffyn has given me a small part in that musical comedy of his, 'Ask Dad.' Only a bit, you know, but quite tolerably ripe. I'm feeling frightfully braced, don't you know!"

He drank his drink, and went on. He didn't seem to notice that I wasn't jumping about the room, yapping with joy.

"You know, I've always wanted to go on the stage, you know," he said. "But my jolly old guv'nor wouldn't stick it at any price. Put the old Waukeesi down with a bang, and turned bright purple whenever the subject was mentioned. That's the real reason why I came over here, if you want to know. I knew there wasn't a chance of my being able to work this stage wheeze in London without somebody getting on to it and tipping off the guv'nor, so I rather brainily sprang the scheme of popping over to Washington to broaden my mind. There's nobody to interfere on this side, you see, so I can go right ahead!"

I tried to reason with the poor chump.

"But your guv'nor will have to know some time."

"That'll be all right. I shall be the jolly old star by then, and he won't have a leg to stand on."

"It seems to me he'll have one leg to stand on while he kicks me with the other."

"Why, where do you come in? What have you got to do with it?"

"I introduced you to George Caffyn."

"So you did, old top, so you did. I'd quite forgotten. I ought to have thanked you before. Well, so long. There's an early rehearsal of 'Ask Dad' tomorrow morning, and I must be toddling. Rummy the thing should be called 'Ask Dad,' when that's just what I'm not going to do. See what I mean, what, what? Well, pip-pip!"

"Toodle-oo!" I said sadly, and the blighter scudded off. I dived for the phone and called up George Caffyn.

"I say, George, what's all this about Cyril Bassington-Bassington?"

"What about him?"

"He tells me you've given him a part in your show."

"Oh, yes. Just a few lines."

"But I've just had fifty-seven cables from home telling me on no account to let him go on the stage."

"I'm sorry. But Cyril is just the type I need for that part. He's simply got to be himself."

"It's pretty tough on me, George, old man. My Aunt Agatha sent this blighter over with a letter of introduction to me, and she will hold me responsible."

"She'll cut you out of her will?"

"It isn't a question of money. But—of course, you've never met my Aunt Agatha, so it's rather hard to explain. But she's a sort of human vampire-bat, and she'll make things most fearfully unpleasant for me when I go back to England. She's the kind of woman who comes and rags you before breakfast, don't you know."

"Well, don't go back to England, then. Stick here and become President."

"But, George, old top—!"

"Good night!"

"But, I say, George, old man!"

"You didn't get my last remark. It was 'Good night!' You Idle Rich may not need any sleep, but I've got to be bright and fresh in the morning. God bless you!"

I felt as if I hadn't a friend in the world. I was so jolly well worked up that I went and banged on Jeeves's door. It wasn't a thing I'd have cared to do as a rule, but it seemed to me that now was the time for all good men to come to the aid of the party, so to speak, and that it was up to Jeeves to rally round the young master, even if it broke up his beauty-sleep.

Jeeves emerged in a brown dressing-gown.

"Sir?"

"Deuced sorry to wake you up, Jeeves, and what not, but all sorts of dashed disturbing things have been happening."

"I was not asleep. It is my practice, on retiring, to read a few pages of some instructive book."

"That's good! What I mean to say is, if you've just finished exercising the old bean, it's probably in mid-season form for tackling problems. Jeeves, Mr. Bassington-Bassington is going on the stage!"

"Indeed, sir?"

"Ah! The thing doesn't hit you! You don't get it properly! Here's the point. All his family are most fearfully dead against his going on the stage. There's going to be no end of trouble if he isn't headed off. And, what's worse, my Aunt Agatha will blame me, you see."

"I see, sir."

"Well, can't you think of some way of stopping him?"

"Not, I confess, at the moment, sir."

"Well, have a stab at it."

"I will give the matter my best consideration, sir. Will there be anything further tonight?"

"I hope not! I've had all I can stand already."

"Very good, sir."

He popped off.

THE PART WHICH OLD George had written for the chump Cyril took up about two pages of typescript; but it might have been Hamlet, the way that poor, misguided pinhead worked himself to the bone over it. I suppose, if I heard him his lines once, I did it a dozen times in the first couple of days. He seemed to think that my only feeling about the whole affair was one of enthusiastic admiration, and that he could rely on my support and sympathy. What with trying to imagine how Aunt Agatha was going to take this thing, and being woken up out of the dreamless in the small hours every other night to give my opinion of some new bit of business which Cyril had invented, I became more or less the good old shadow. And all the time Jeeves remained still pretty cold and distant about the purple socks. It's this sort of thing that ages a chappie, don't you know, and makes his youthful *joie-de-vivre* go a bit groggy at the knees.

In the middle of it Aunt Agatha's letter arrived. It took her about six pages to do justice to Cyril's father's feelings in regard to his going on the stage and about six more to give me a kind of sketch of what she would say, think, and do if I didn't keep him clear of injurious influences while he was in America. The letter came by the afternoon mail, and left me with a pretty firm conviction that it wasn't a thing I ought to keep to myself. I didn't even wait to ring the bell: I whizzed for the kitchen, bleating for Jeeves, and butted into the middle of a regular tea-party of sorts. Seated at the table were a depressed-looking cove who might have been a valet or something, and a boy in a Norfolk suit. The valet-chappie was drinking a whisky and soda, and the boy was being tolerably rough with some jam and cake.

"Oh, I say, Jeeves!" I said. "Sorry to interrupt the feast of reason and flow of soul and so forth, but—"

At this juncture the small boy's eye hit me like a bullet and stopped me in my tracks. It was one of those cold, clammy, accusing sort of eyes—the kind that makes you reach up to see if your tie is straight: and he looked at me as if I were some sort of unnecessary product which Cuthbert the Cat had brought in after a ramble among the local ash-cans. He was a stoutish infant with a lot of freckles and a good deal of jam on his face.

"Hallo! Hallo! Hallo!" I said. "What?" There didn't seem much else to say.

The stripling stared at me in a nasty sort of way through the jam. He may have loved me at first sight, but the impression he gave me was that he didn't think a lot of me and wasn't betting much that I would improve a great deal on acquaintance. I had a kind of feeling that I was about as popular with him as a cold Welsh rabbit.

"What's your name?" he asked.

"My name? Oh, Wooster, don't you know, and what not."

"My pop's richer than you are!"

That seemed to be all about me. The child having said his say, started in on the jam again. I turned to Jeeves.

"I say, Jeeves, can you spare a moment? I want to show you something."

"Very good, sir." We toddled into the sitting-room.

"Who is your little friend, Sidney the Sunbeam, Jeeves?"

"The young gentleman, sir?"

"It's a loose way of describing him, but I know what you mean."

"I trust I was not taking a liberty in entertaining him, sir?"

"Not a bit. If that's your idea of a large afternoon, go ahead."

"I happened to meet the young gentleman taking a walk with his father's valet, sir, whom I used to know somewhat intimately in London, and I ventured to invite them both to join me here."

"Well, never mind about him, Jeeves. Read this letter."

He gave it the up-and-down.

"Very disturbing, sir!" was all he could find to say.

"What are we going to do about it?"

"Time may provide a solution, sir."

"On the other hand, it mayn't, what?"

"Extremely true, sir."

We'd got as far as this, when there was a ring at the door. Jeeves shimmered off, and Cyril blew in, full of good cheer and blitheringness.

"I say, Wooster, old thing," he said, "I want your advice. You know this jolly old part of mine. How ought I to dress it? What I mean is, the first act scene is laid in a hotel of sorts, at about three in the afternoon. What ought I to wear, do you think?"

I wasn't feeling fit for a discussion of gent's suitings.

"You'd better consult Jeeves," I said.

"A hot and by no means unripe idea! Where is he?"

"Gone back to the kitchen, I suppose."

"I'll smite the good old bell, shall I? Yes. No?"

"Right-o!"

Jeeves poured silently in.

"Oh, I say, Jeeves," began Cyril, "I just wanted to have a syllable or two with you. It's this way—Hallo, who's this?"

I then perceived that the stout stripling had trickled into the room after Jeeves. He was standing near the door looking at Cyril as if his worst fears had been realized. There was a bit of a silence. The child remained there, drinking Cyril in for about half a minute; then he gave his verdict:

"Fish-face!"

"Eh? What?" said Cyril.

The child, who had evidently been taught at his mother's knee to speak the truth, made his meaning a trifle clearer.

"You've a face like a fish!"

He spoke as if Cyril was more to be pitied than censured, which I am bound to say I thought rather decent and broad-minded of him. I don't mind admitting that, whenever I looked at Cyril's face, I always had a feeling that he couldn't have got that way without its being mostly his own fault. I found myself warming to this child. Absolutely, don't you know. I liked his conversation.

It seemed to take Cyril a moment or two really to grasp the thing, and then you could hear the blood of the Bassington-Bassingtons begin to sizzle.

"Well, I'm dashed!" he said. "I'm dashed if I'm not!"

"I wouldn't have a face like that," proceeded the child, with a good deal of earnestness, "not if you gave me a million dollars." He thought for a moment, then corrected himself. "Two million dollars!" he added.

Just what occurred then I couldn't exactly say, but the next few minutes were a bit exciting. I take it that Cyril must have made a dive for the infant. Anyway, the air seemed pretty well congested with arms and legs and things. Something bumped into the Wooster waistcoat just around the third button, and I collapsed on to the settee and rather lost interest in things for the moment. When I had unscrambled myself, I found that Jeeves and the child had retired and Cyril was standing in the middle of the room snorting a bit.

"Who's that frightful little brute, Wooster?"

"I don't know. I never saw him before today."

"I gave him a couple of tolerably juicy buffets before he legged it. I say, Wooster, that kid said a dashed odd thing. He yelled out something about Jeeves promising him a dollar if he called me—er—what he said."

It sounded pretty unlikely to me.

"What would Jeeves do that for?"

"It struck me as rummy, too."

"Where would be the sense of it?"

"That's what I can't see."

"I mean to say, it's nothing to Jeeves what sort of a face you have!"

"No!" said Cyril. He spoke a little coldly, I fancied. I don't know why. "Well, I'll be popping. Toodle-oo!"

"Pip-pip!"

It must have been about a week after this rummy little episode that George Caffyn called me up and asked me if I would care to go and see a run-through of his show. "Ask Dad," it seemed, was to open out of town in Schenectady on the following Monday, and this was to be a sort of preliminary dress-rehearsal. A preliminary dress-rehearsal, old George explained, was the same as a regular dress-rehearsal inasmuch as it was apt to look like nothing on earth and last into the small hours, but more exciting because they wouldn't be timing the piece and consequently all the blighters who on these occasions let their angry passions rise would have plenty of scope for interruptions, with the result that a pleasant time would be had by all.

The thing was billed to start at eight o'clock, so I rolled up at ten-fifteen, so as not to have too long to wait before they began. The dress-parade was still going on. George was on the stage, talking to a cove in shirt-sleeves and an absolutely round chappie with big spectacles and a practically hairless dome. I had seen George with the latter merchant once or twice at the club, and I knew that he was Blumenfield, the manager. I waved to George, and slid into a seat at the back of the house, so as to be out of the way when the fighting started. Presently George hopped down off the stage and came and joined me, and fairly soon after that the curtain went down. The chappie at the piano whacked out a well-meant bar or two, and the curtain went up again.

I can't quite recall what the plot of "Ask Dad" was about, but I do know that it seemed able to jog along all right without much help from Cyril. I was rather puzzled at first. What I mean is, through brooding on Cyril and hearing him in his part and listening to his views on what ought and what ought not to be done, I suppose I had got a sort of impression rooted in the old bean that he was pretty well the backbone of the show, and that the rest of the company didn't do much except go on and fill in when he happened to be off the stage. I sat there for nearly half an hour, waiting for him to make his entrance, until I suddenly discovered he had been on from the start. He was, in fact, the rummy-looking plug-ugly who was now leaning against a potted palm a couple of feet from the O.P. side, trying to appear intelligent while the heroine sang a song about Love being like something which for the moment has slipped my memory. After the second refrain he began to dance in company with a dozen other equally weird birds. A painful spectacle for one who could see a vision of Aunt Agatha reaching for the hatchet and old Bassington-Bassington senior putting on his strongest pair of hob-nailed boots. Absolutely!

The dance had just finished, and Cyril and his pals had shuffled off into the wings when a voice spoke from the darkness on my right.

"Pop!"

Old Blumenfield clapped his hands, and the hero, who had just been about to get the next line off his diaphragm, cheesed it. I peered into the shadows. Who should it be but Jeeves's little playmate with the freckles! He was now strolling down the aisle with his hands in his pockets as if the place belonged to him. An air of respectful attention seemed to pervade the building.

"Pop," said the stripling, "that number's no good." Old Blumenfield beamed over his shoulder.

"Don't you like it, darling?"

"It gives me a pain."

"You're dead right."

"You want something zippy there. Something with a bit of jazz to it!"

"Quite right, my boy. I'll make a note of it. All right. Go on!"

I turned to George, who was muttering to himself in rather an overwrought way.

"I say, George, old man, who the dickens is that kid?"

Old George groaned a bit hollowly, as if things were a trifle thick.

"I didn't know he had crawled in! It's Blumenfield's son. Now we're going to have a Hades of a time!"

"Does he always run things like this?"

"Always!"

"But why does old Blumenfield listen to him?"

"Nobody seems to know. It may be pure fatherly love, or he may regard him as a mascot. My own idea is that he thinks the kid has exactly the amount of intelligence of the average member of the audience, and that what makes a hit with him will please the general public. While, conversely, what he doesn't like will be too rotten for anyone. The kid is a pest, a wart, and a pot of poison, and should be strangled!"

The rehearsal went on. The hero got off his line. There was a slight outburst of frightfulness between the stage-manager and a Voice named Bill that came from some-where near the roof, the subject under discussion being where the devil Bill's "ambers" were at that particular juncture. Then things went on again until the moment arrived for Cyril's big scene.

I was still a trifle hazy about the plot, but I had got on to the fact that Cyril was some sort of an English peer who had come over to America doubtless for the best reasons. So far he had only had two lines to say. One was "Oh, I say!" and the other was "Yes, by Jove!"; but I seemed to recollect, from hearing him read his part, that pretty soon he was due rather to spread himself. I sat back in my chair and waited for him to bob up.

He bobbed up about five minutes later. Things had got a bit stormy by that time. The Voice and the stage-director had had another of their love-feasts—this time something to do with why Bill's "blues" weren't on the job or some-thing. And, almost as soon as that was over, there was a bit of unpleasantness because a flower-pot fell off a win-dow-ledge and nearly brained the hero. The atmosphere was consequently more or less hotted up when Cyril, who had been hanging about at the back of the stage, breezed down center and toed the mark for his most substantial chunk of entertainment. The heroine had been saying something—I forget what—and all the chorus, with Cyril at their head, had begun to surge round her in the restless sort of way those chappies always do when there's a num-ber coming along.

Cyril's first line was, "Oh, I say, you know, you mustn't say that, really!" and it seemed to me he passed it over the larynx with a goodish deal of vim and *je-ne-sais-quoi*. But, by Jove, before the heroine had time for the come-back, our little friend with the freckles had risen to lodge a protest.

"Pop!"

"Yes, darling?"

"That one's no good!"

"Which one, darling?"

"The one with a face like a fish."

"But they all have faces like fish, darling."

The child seemed to see the justice of this objection. He became more definite.

"The ugly one."

"Which ugly one? That one?" said old Blumenfield, pointing to Cyril.

"Yep! He's rotten!"

"I thought so myself."

"He's a pill!"

"You're dead right, my boy. I've noticed it for some time."

Cyril had been gaping a bit while these few remarks were in progress. He now shot down to the footlights. Even from where I was sitting, I could see that these harsh words had hit the old Bassington-Bassington family pride a frightful wallop. He started to get pink in the ears, and then in the nose, and then in the cheeks, till in about a quarter of a minute he looked pretty much like an explosion in a tomato cannery on a sunset evening.

"What the deuce do you mean?"

"What the deuce do *you* mean?" shouted old Blumenfield. "Don't yell at me across the footlights!"

"I've a dashed good mind to come down and spank that little brute!"

"What!"

"A dashed good mind!"

Old Blumenfield swelled like a pumped-up tyre. He got rounder than ever.

"See here, mister—I don't know your darn name—!"

"My name's Bassington-Bassington, and the jolly old Bassington-Bassingtons—I mean the Bassington-Bassingtons aren't accustomed—"

Old Blumenfield told him in a few brief words pretty much what he thought of the Bassington-Bassingtons and what they weren't accustomed to. The whole strength of the company rallied round to enjoy his remarks. You could see them jutting out from the wings and protruding from behind trees.

"You got to work good for my pop!" said the stout child, waggling his head reprovingly at Cyril.

"I don't want any bally cheek from you!" said Cyril, gurgling a bit.

"What's that?" barked old Blumenfield. "Do you understand that this boy is my son?"

"Yes, I do," said Cyril. "And you both have my sympathy!"

"You're fired!" bellowed old Blumenfield, swelling a good bit more. "Get out of my theatre!"

ABOUT HALF-PAST TEN next morning, just after I had finished lubricating the good old interior with a soothing cup of Oolong, Jeeves filtered into my bedroom, and said that Cyril was waiting to see me in the sitting-room.

"How does he look, Jeeves?"

"Sir?"

"What does Mr. Bassington-Bassington look like?"

"It is hardly my place, sir, to criticise the facial peculiarities of your friends."

"I don't mean that. I mean, does he appear peeved and what not?"

"Not noticeably, sir. His manner is tranquil."

"That's rum!"

"Sir?"

"Nothing. Show him in, will you?"

I'm bound to say I had expected to see Cyril showing a few more traces of last night's battle. I was looking for a bit of the overwrought soul and the quivering ganglions, if you know what I mean. He seemed pretty ordinary and quite fairly cheerful.

"Hallo, Wooster, old thing!"

"Cheero!"

"I just looked in to say good-bye."

"Good-bye?"

"Yes. I'm off to Washington in an hour." He sat down on the bed. "You know, Wooster, old top," he went on, "I've been thinking it all over, and really it doesn't seem quite fair to the jolly old guv'nor, my going on the stage and so forth. What do you think?"

"I see what you mean."

"I mean to say, he sent me over here to broaden my jolly old mind and words to that effect, don't you know, and I can't help thinking it would be a bit of a jar for the old boy if I gave him the bird and went on the stage instead. I don't know if you understand me, but what I mean to say is, it's a sort of question of conscience."

"Can you leave the show without upsetting everything?"

"Oh, that's all right. I've explained everything to old Blumenfield, and he quite sees my position. Of course, he's sorry to lose me—said he didn't see how he could fill my place and all that sort of thing—but, after all, even if it does land him in a bit of a hole, I think I'm right in resigning my part, don't you?"

"Oh, absolutely."

"I thought you'd agree with me. Well, I ought to be shifting. Awfully glad to have seen something of you, and all that sort of rot. Pip-pip!"

"Toodle-oo!"

He sallied forth, having told all those bally lies with the clear, blue, pop-eyed gaze of a young child. I rang for Jeeves. You know, ever since last night I had been exercising the old bean to some extent, and a good deal of light had dawned upon me.

"Jeeves!"

"Sir?"

"Did you put that pie-faced infant up to bally-ragging Mr. Bassington-Bassington?"

"Sir?"

"Oh, you know what I mean. Did you tell him to get Mr. Bassington-Bassington sacked from the 'Ask Dad' company?"

"I would not take such a liberty, sir." He started to put out my clothes. "It is possible that young Master Blumenfield may have gathered from casual remarks of mine that I did not consider the stage altogether a suitable sphere for Mr. Bassington-Bassington."

"I say, Jeeves, you know, you're a bit of a marvel."

"I endeavour to give satisfaction, sir."

"And I'm frightfully obliged, if you know what I mean. Aunt Agatha would have had sixteen or seventeen fits if you hadn't headed him off."

"I fancy there might have been some little friction and unpleasantness, sir. I am laying out the blue suit with the thin red stripe, sir. I fancy the effect will be pleasing."

IT'S A RUMMY THING, but I had finished breakfast and gone out and got as far as the lift before I remembered what it was that I had meant to do to reward Jeeves for his really sporting behavior in this matter of the chump Cyril. It cut me to the heart to do it, but I had decided to give him his way and let those purple socks pass out of my life. After all, there are times when a cove must make sacrifices. I was just going to nip back and break the glad news to him, when the lift came up, so I thought I would leave it till I got home.

The colored chappie in charge of the lift looked at me, as I hopped in, with a good deal of quiet devotion and what not.

"I wish to thank yo', suh," he said, "for yo' kindness."

"Eh? What?"

"Misto' Jeeves done give me them purple socks, as you told him. Thank yo' very much, suh!"

I looked down. The blighter was a blaze of mauve from the ankle-bone southward. I don't know when I've seen anything so dressy.

"Oh, ah! Not at all! Right-o! Glad you like them!" I said.

Well, I mean to say, what? Absolutely!

# Jeeves in the Springtime

"MORNING, JEEVES," I said.

"Good morning, sir," said Jeeves. He put the good old cup of tea softly on the table by my bed, and I took a refreshing sip. Just right, as usual. Not too hot, not too sweet, not too weak, not too strong, not too much milk, and not a drop spilled in the saucer. A most amazing cove, Jeeves. So dashed competent in every respect. I've said it before, and I'll say it again. I mean to say, take just one small instance. Every other valet I've ever had used to barge into my room in the morning while I was still asleep, causing much misery: but Jeeves seems to know when I'm awake by a sort of telepathy. He always floats in with the cup exactly two minutes after I come to life. Makes a deuce of a lot of difference to a fellow's day.

"How's the weather, Jeeves?"

"Exceptionally clement, sir."

"Anything in the papers?"

"Some slight friction threatening in the Balkans, sir. Otherwise, nothing."

"I say, Jeeves, a man I met at the club last night told me to put my shirt on Privateer for the two o'clock race this afternoon. How about it?"

"I should not advocate it, sir. The stable is not sanguine."

That was enough for me. Jeeves knows. How, I couldn't say, but he knows. There was a time when I would laugh lightly, and go ahead, and lose my little all against his advice, but not now.

"Talking of shirts," I said, "have those mauve ones I ordered arrived yet?"

"Yes, sir. I sent them back."

"Sent them back?"

"Yes, sir. They would not have become you."

Well, I must say I'd thought fairly highly of those shirtings, but I bowed to superior knowledge. Weak? I don't know. Most fellows, no doubt, are all for having their valets confine their activities to creasing trousers and what not without trying to run the home; but it's different with Jeeves. Right from the first day he came to me, I have looked on him as a sort of guide, philosopher, and friend.

"Mr. Little rang up on the telephone a few moments ago, sir. I informed him that you were not yet awake."

"Did he leave a message?"

"No, sir. He mentioned that he had a matter of importance to discuss with you, but confided no details."

"Oh, well, I expect I shall be seeing him at the club."

"No doubt, sir."

I wasn't what you might call in a fever of impatience. Bingo Little is a chap I was at school with, and we see a lot of each other still. He's the nephew of old Mortimer Little, who retired from business recently with a goodish pile. (You've probably heard of Little's Liniment—It Limbers Up the Legs.) Bingo biffs about London on a pretty comfortable allowance given him by his uncle, and leads on the whole a fairly unclouded life. It wasn't likely that anything which he described as a matter of importance would turn out to be really so frightfully important. I took it that he had discovered some new brand of cigarette which he wanted me to try, or something like that, and didn't spoil my breakfast by worrying.

After breakfast I lit a cigarette and went to the open window to inspect the day. It certainly was one of the best and brightest.

"Jeeves," I said.

"Sir?" said Jeeves. He had been clearing away the breakfast things, but at the sound of the young master's voice cheesed it courteously.

"You were absolutely right about the weather. It is a juicy morning."

"Decidedly, sir."

"Spring and all that."

"Yes, sir."

"In the spring, Jeeves, a livelier iris gleams upon the burnished dove."

"So I have been informed, sir."

"Right ho! Then bring me my whangee, my yellowest shoes, and the old green Homburg. I'm going into the Park to do pastoral dances."

I don't know if you know that sort of feeling you get on these days round about the end of April and the beginning of May, when the sky's a light blue, with cotton-wool clouds, and there's a bit of a breeze blowing from the west? Kind of uplifted feeling. Romantic, if you know what I mean. I'm not much of a ladies' man, but on this particular morning it seemed to me that what I really wanted was some charming girl to buzz up and ask me to save her from assassins or something. So that it was a bit of an anti-climax when I merely ran into young Bingo Little, looking perfectly foul in a crimson satin tie decorated with horseshoes.

"Hallo, Bertie," said Bingo.

"My God, man!" I gargled. "The cravat! The gent's neckwear! Why? For what reason?"

"Oh, the tie?" He blushed. "I—er—I was given it."

He seemed embarrassed, so I dropped the subject. We toddled along a bit, and sat down on a couple of chairs by the Serpentine.

"Jeeves tells me you want to talk to me about something," I said.

"Eh?" said Bingo, with a start. "Oh yes, yes. Yes."

I waited for him to unleash the topic of the day, but he didn't seem to want to get going. Conversation languished. He stared straight ahead of him in a glassy sort of manner.

"I say, Bertie," he said, after a pause of about an hour and a quarter.

"Hallo!"

"Do you like the name Mabel?"

"No."

"No?"

"No."

"You don't think there's a kind of music in the word, like the wind rustling gently through the tree-tops?"

"No."

He seemed disappointed for a moment; then cheered up.

"Of course, you wouldn't. You always were a fatheaded worm without any soul, weren't you?"

"Just as you say. Who is she? Tell me all."

For I realized now that poor old Bingo was going through it once again. Ever since I have known him — and we were at school together — he has been perpetually falling in love with someone, generally in the spring, which seems to act on him like magic. At school he had the finest collection of actresses' photographs of anyone of his time; and at Oxford his romantic nature was a byword.

"You'd better come along and meet her at lunch," he said, looking at his watch.

"A ripe suggestion," I said. "Where are you meeting her? At the Ritz?"

"Near the Ritz."

He was geographically accurate. About fifty yards east of the Ritz there is one of those blighted tea-and-bun shops you see dotted about all over London, and into this, if you'll believe me, young Bingo dived like a homing rabbit; and before I had time to say a word we were wedged in at a table, on the brink of a silent pool of coffee left there by an early luncher.

I'm bound to say I couldn't quite follow the development of the scenario. Bingo, while not absolutely rolling in the stuff, has always had a fair amount of the ready. Apart from what he got from his uncle, I knew that he had finished up the jumping season well on the right side of the ledger. Why, then, was he lunching the girl at this Godforsaken eatery? It couldn't be because he was hard up.

Just then the waitress arrived. Rather a pretty girl.

"Aren't we going to wait—?" I started to say to Bingo, thinking it somewhat thick that, in addition to asking a girl to lunch with him in a place like this, he should fling himself on the foodstuffs before she turned up, when I caught sight of his face, and stopped.

The man was goggling. His entire map was suffused with a rich blush. He looked like the Soul's Awakening done in pink.

"Hallo, Mabel!" he said, with a sort of gulp.

"Hallo!" said the girl.

"Mabel," said Bingo, "this is Bertie Wooster, a pal of mine."

"Pleased to meet you," she said. "Nice morning."

"Fine," I said.

"You see I'm wearing the tie," said Bingo.

"It suits you beautiful," said the girl.

Personally, if anyone had told me that a tie like that suited me, I should have risen and struck them on the mazzard, regardless of their age and sex; but poor old Bingo simply got all flustered with gratification, and smirked in the most gruesome manner.

"Well, what's it going to be today?" asked the girl, introducing the business touch into the conversation.

Bingo studied the menu devoutly.

"I'll have a cup of cocoa, cold veal and ham pie, slice of fruit cake, and a macaroon. Same for you, Bertie?"

I gazed at the man, revolted. That he could have been a pal of mine all these years and think me capable of insulting the old tum with this sort of stuff cut me to the quick.

"Or how about a bit of hot steak-pudding, with a sparkling limado to wash it down?" said Bingo.

You know, the way love can change a fellow is really frightful to contemplate. This chappie before me, who spoke in that absolutely careless way of macaroons and limado, was the man I had seen in happier days telling the head-waiter at Claridge's exactly how he wanted the chef to prepare the sole *frite au gourmet aux champignons*, and saying he would jolly well sling it back if it wasn't just right. Ghastly! Ghastly!

A roll and butter and a small coffee seemed the only things on the list that hadn't been specially prepared by the nastier-minded members of the Borgia family for people they had a particular grudge against, so I chose them, and Mabel hopped it.

"Well?" said Bingo rapturously.

I took it that he wanted my opinion of the female poisoner who had just left us.

"Very nice," I said.

He seemed dissatisfied.

"You don't think she's the most wonderful girl you ever saw?" he said wistfully.

"Oh, absolutely!" I said, to appease the blighter. "Where did you meet her?"

"At a subscription dance at Camberwell."

"What on earth were you doing at a subscription dance at Camberwell?"

"Your man Jeeves asked me if I would buy a couple of tickets. It was in aid of some charity or other."

"Jeeves? I didn't know he went in for that sort of thing."

"Well, I suppose he has to relax a bit every now and then. Anyway, he was there, swinging a dashed efficient shoe. I hadn't meant to go at first, but I turned up for a lark. Oh, Bertie, think what I might have missed!"

"What might you have missed?" I asked, the old lemon being slightly clouded.

"Mabel, you chump. If I hadn't gone I shouldn't have met Mabel."

"Oh, ah!"

At this point Bingo fell into a species of trance, and only came out of it to wrap himself round the pie and macaroon.

"Bertie," he said, "I want your advice."

"Carry on."

"At least, not your advice, because that wouldn't be much good to anybody. I mean, you're a pretty consummate old ass, aren't you? Not that I want to hurt your feelings, of course."

"No, no, I see that."

"What I wish you would do is to put the whole thing to that fellow Jeeves of yours, and see what he suggests. You've often told me that he has helped other pals of yours out of messes. From what you tell me, he's by way of being the brains of the family."

"He's never let me down yet."

"Then put my case to him."

"What case?"

"My problem."

"What problem?"

"Why, you poor fish, my uncle, of course. What do you think my uncle's going to say to all this? If I sprang it on him cold, he'd tie himself in knots on the hearthrug."

"One of these emotional johnnies, eh?"

"Somehow or other his mind has got to be prepared to receive the news. But how?"

"Ah!"

"That's a lot of help, that 'ah'! You see, I'm pretty well dependent on the old boy. If he cut off my allowance, I should be very much in the soup. So you put the whole binge to Jeeves and see if he can't scare up a happy ending somehow. Tell him my future is in his hands, and that, if the wedding bells ring out, he can rely on me, even unto half my kingdom. Well, call it ten quid. Jeeves would exert himself with ten quid on the horizon, what?"

"Undoubtedly," I said.

I wasn't in the least surprised at Bingo wanting to lug Jeeves into his private affairs like this. It was the first thing I would have thought of doing myself if I had been in any hole of any description. As I have frequently had occasion to observe, he is a bird of the ripest intellect, full of bright ideas. If anybody could fix things for poor old Bingo, he could.

I stated the case to him that night after dinner.

"Jeeves."

"Sir?"

"Are you busy just now?"

"No, sir."

"I mean, not doing anything in particular?"

"No, sir. It is my practice at this hour to read some improving book; but, if you desire my services, this can easily be postponed, or, indeed, abandoned altogether."

"Well, I want your advice. It's about Mr. Little."

"Young Mr. Little, sir, or the elder Mr. Little, his uncle, who lives in Pounceby Gardens?"

Jeeves seemed to know everything. Most amazing thing. I'd been pally with Bingo practically all my life, and yet I didn't remember ever having heard that his uncle lived anywhere is particular.

"How did you know he lived in Pounceby Gardens?" I said.

"I am on terms of some intimacy with the elder Mr. Little's cook, sir. In fact, there is an understanding."

I'm bound to say that this gave me a bit of a start. Somehow I'd never thought of Jeeves going in for that sort of thing.

"Do you mean you're engaged?"

"It may be said to amount to that, sir."

"Well, well!"

"She is a remarkably excellent cook, sir," said Jeeves, as though he felt called on to give some explanation. "What was it you wished to ask me about Mr. Little?"

I sprang the details on him.

"And that's how the matter stands, Jeeves," I said. "I think we ought to rally round a trifle and help poor old Bingo put the thing through. Tell me about old Mr. Little. What sort of a chap is he?"

"A somewhat curious character, sir. Since retiring from business he has become a great recluse, and now devotes himself almost entirely to the pleasures of the table."

"Greedy hog, you mean?"

"I would not, perhaps, take the liberty of describing him in precisely those terms, sir. He is what is usually called a gourmet. Very particular about what he eats, and for that reason sets a high value on Miss Watson's services."

"The cook?"

"Yes, sir."

"Well, it looks to me as though our best plan would be to shoot young Bingo in on him after dinner one night. Melting mood, I mean to say, and all that."

"The difficulty is, sir, that at the moment Mr. Little is on a diet, owing to an attack of gout."

"Things begin to look wobbly."

"No, sir, I fancy that the elder Mr. Little's misfortune may be turned to the younger Mr. Little's advantage. I was speaking only the other day to Mr. Little's valet, and he was telling me that it has become his principal duty to read to Mr. Little in the evenings. If I were in your place, sir, I should send young Mr. Little to read to his uncle."

"Nephew's devotion, you mean? Old man touched by kindly action, what?"

"Partly that, sir. But I would rely more on young Mr. Little's choice of literature."

"That's no good. Jolly old Bingo has a kind face, but when it comes to literature he stops at the *Sporting Times*."

"That difficulty may be overcome. I would be happy to select books for Mr. Little to read. Perhaps I might explain my idea further?"

"I can't say I quite grasp it yet."

"The method which I advocate is what, I believe, the advertisers call Direct Suggestion, sir, consisting as it does of driving an idea home by constant repetition. You may have had experience of the system?"

"You mean they keep on telling you that some soap or other is the best, and after a bit you come under the influence and charge round the corner and buy a cake?"

"Exactly, sir. The same method was the basis of all the most valuable propaganda during the recent war. I see no reason why it should not be adopted to bring about the desired result with regard to the subject's views on class distinctions. If young Mr. Little were to read day after day to his uncle a series of narratives in which marriage with young persons of an inferior social status was held up as both feasible and admirable, I fancy it would prepare the elder Mr. Little's mind for the reception of the information that his nephew wishes to marry a waitress in a tea-shop."

"Are there any books of that sort nowadays? The only ones I ever see mentioned in the papers are about married couples who find life grey, and can't stick each other at any price."

"Yes, sir, there are a great many, neglected by the reviewers but widely read. You have never encountered *All for Love*, by Rosie M. Banks?"

"No."

"Nor *A Red, Red Summer Rose*, by the same author?"

"No."

"I have an aunt, sir, who owns an almost complete set of Rosie M. Banks. I could easily borrow as many volumes as young Mr. Little might require. They make very light, attractive reading."

"Well, it's worth trying."

"I should certainly recommend the scheme, sir."

"All right, then. Toddle round to your aunt's tomorrow and grab a couple of the fruitiest. We can but have a dash at it."

"Precisely, sir."

BINGO REPORTED THREE days later that Rosie M. Banks was the goods and beyond a question the stuff to give the troops. Old Little had jibbed somewhat at first at the proposed change of literary diet, he not being much of a lad for fiction and having stuck hitherto exclusively to the heavier monthly reviews; but Bingo had got chapter one of *All for Love* past his guard before he knew what was happening, and after that there was nothing to it. Since then they had finished *A Red, Red Summer Rose, Madcap*

*Myrtle* and *Only a Factory Girl*, and were half-way through *The Courtship of Lord Strathmorlick*.

Bingo told me all this in a husky voice over an egg beaten up in sherry. The only blot on the thing from his point of view was that it wasn't doing a bit of good to the old vocal cords, which were beginning to show signs of cracking under the strain. He had been looking his symptoms up in a medical dictionary, and he thought he had got "clergyman's throat." But against this you had to set the fact that he was making an undoubted hit in the right quarter, and also that after the evening's reading he always stayed on to dinner; and, from what he told me, the dinners turned out by old Little's cook had to be tasted to be believed. There were tears in the old blighter's eyes as he got on the subject of the clear soup. I suppose to a fellow who for weeks had been tackling macaroons and limado it must have been like Heaven.

Old Little wasn't able to give any practical assistance at these banquets, but Bingo said that he came to the table and had his whack of arrowroot, and sniffed the dishes, and told stories of entrées he had had in the past, and sketched out scenarios of what he was going to do to the bill of fare in the future, when the doctor put him in shape; so I suppose he enjoyed himself, too, in a way. Anyhow, things seemed to be buzzing along quite satisfactorily, and Bingo said he had got an idea which, he thought, was going to clinch the thing. He wouldn't tell me what it was, but he said it was a pippin.

"We make progress, Jeeves," I said.

"That is very satisfactory, sir."

"Mr. Little tells me that when he came to the big scene in *Only a Factory Girl,* his uncle gulped like a stricken bullpup."

"Indeed, sir?"

"Where Lord Claude takes the girl in his arms, you know, and says—"

"I am familiar with the passage, sir. It is distinctly moving. It was a great favorite of my aunt's."

"I think we're on the right track."

"It would seem so, sir."

"In fact, this looks like being another of your successes. I've always said, and I always shall say, that for sheer brain, Jeeves, you stand alone. All the other great thinkers of the age are simply in the crowd, watching you go by."

"Thank you very much, sir. I endeavor to give satisfaction."

ABOUT A WEEK AFTER this, Bingo blew in with the news that his uncle's gout had ceased to trouble him, and that on the morrow he would be back at the old stand working away with knife and fork as before.

"And, by the way," said Bingo, "he wants you to lunch with him tomorrow."

"Me? Why me? He doesn't know I exist."

"Oh, yes, he does. I've told him about you."

"What have you told him?"

"Oh, various things. Anyhow, he wants to meet you. And take my tip, laddie—you go! I should think lunch tomorrow would be something special."

I don't know why it was, but even then it struck me that there was something dashed odd—almost sinister, if you know what I mean—about young Bingo's manner.

The old egg had the air of one who has something up his sleeve.

"There is more in this than meets the eye," I said. "Why should your uncle ask a fellow to lunch whom he's never seen?"

"My dear old fathead, haven't I just said that I've been telling him all about you—that you're my best pal—at school together, and all that sort of thing?"

"But even then—and another thing. Why are you so dashed keen on my going?"

Bingo hesitated for a moment.

"Well, I told you I'd got an idea. This is it. I want you to spring the news on him. I haven't the nerve myself."

"What! I'm hanged if I do!"

"And you call yourself a pal of mine!"

"Yes, I know; but there are limits."

"Bertie," said Bingo reproachfully, "I saved your life once."

"When?"

"Didn't I? It must have been some other fellow, then. Well, anyway, we were boys together and all that. You can't let me down."

"Oh, all right," I said. "But, when you say you haven't nerve enough for any dashed thing in the world, you misjudge yourself. A fellow who—"

"Cheerio!" said young Bingo. "One-thirty tomorrow. Don't be late."

I'M BOUND TO SAY that the more I contemplated the binge, the less I liked it. It was all very well for Bingo to say that I was slated for a magnificent lunch; but what good is the best possible lunch to a fellow if he is slung out into the street on his ear during the soup course? However, the word of a Wooster is his bond and all that sort of rot, so at one-thirty next day I tottered up the steps of No. 16, Pounceby Gardens, and punched the bell. And half a minute later I was up in the drawing-room, shaking hands with the fattest man I have ever seen in my life.

The motto of the Little family was evidently "variety." Young Bingo is long and thin and hasn't had a superfluous ounce on him since we first met; but the uncle restored the average and a bit over. The hand which grasped mine wrapped it round and enfolded it till I began to wonder if I'd ever get it out without excavating machinery.

"Mr. Wooster, I am gratified—I am proud—I am honored."

It seemed to me that young Bingo must have boosted me to some purpose.

"Oh, ah!" I said.

He stepped back a bit, still hanging on to the good right hand.

"You are very young to have accomplished so much!"

I couldn't follow the train of thought. The family, especially my Aunt Agatha, who has savaged me incessantly from childhood up, have always rather made a point of the fact that mine is a wasted life, and that, since I won the prize at my first school for the best collection of wild flowers made during the summer holidays, I haven't done a dam' thing to land me on the nation's scroll of fame. I was wondering if he couldn't have got me mixed up with someone else, when the telephone-bell rang outside in the hall, and the maid came in to say that I was wanted. I buzzed down, and found it was young Bingo.

"Hallo!" said young Bingo. "So you've got there? Good man! I knew I could rely on you. I say, old crumpet, did my uncle seem pleased to see you?"

"Absolutely all over me. I can't make it out."

"Oh, that's all right. I just rang up to explain. The fact is, old man, I know you won't mind, but I told him that you were the author of those books I've been reading to him."

"What!"

"Yes, I said that 'Rosie M. Banks' was your pen-name, and you didn't want it generally known, because you were a modest, retiring sort of chap. He'll listen to you now. Absolutely hang on your words. A brightish idea, what? I doubt if Jeeves in person could have thought up a better one than that. Well, pitch it strong, old lad, and keep steadily before you the fact that I must have my allowance raised. I can't possibly marry on what I've got now. If this film is to end with the slow fade-out on the embrace, at least double is indicated. Well, that's that. Cheerio!"

And he rang off. At that moment the gong sounded, and the genial host came tumbling downstairs like the delivery of a ton of coals.

I ALWAYS LOOK BACK to that lunch with a sort of aching regret. It was the lunch of a lifetime, and I wasn't in a fit state to appreciate it. Subconsciously, if you know what I mean, I could see it was pretty special, but I had got the wind up to such a frightful extent over the ghastly situation in which young Bingo had landed me that its deeper meaning never really penetrated. Most of the time I might have been eating sawdust for all the good it did me.

Old Little struck the literary note right from the start.

"My nephew has probably told you that I have been making a close study of your books of late?" he began.

"Yes. He did mention it. How—er—how did you like the bally things?"

He gazed reverently at me.

"Mr. Wooster, I am not ashamed to say that the tears came into my eyes as I listened to them. It amazes me that a man as young as you can have been able to plumb human nature so surely to its depths; to play with so unerring a hand on the quivering heart-strings of your reader; to write novels so true, so human, so moving, so vital!"

"Oh, it's just a knack," I said.

The good old persp was bedewing my forehead by this time in a pretty lavish manner. I don't know when I've been so rattled.

"Do you find the room a trifle warm?"

"Oh, no, no, rather not. Just right."

"Then it's the pepper. If my cook has a fault—which I am not prepared to admit—it is that she is inclined to stress the pepper a trifle in her made dishes. By the way, do you like her cooking?"

I was so relieved that we had got off the subject of my literary output that I shouted approval in a ringing baritone.

"I am delighted to hear it, Mr. Wooster. I may be prejudiced, but to my mind that woman is a genius."

"Absolutely!" I said.

"She has been with me seven years, and in all that time I have not known her guilty of a single lapse from the highest standard. Except once, in the winter of 1917, when a purist might have condemned a certain mayonnaise of hers as lacking in creaminess. But one must make allowances. There had been several air-raids about that time, and no doubt the poor woman was shaken. But nothing is perfect in this world, Mr. Wooster, and I have had my cross to bear. For seven years I have lived in constant apprehension lest some evilly-disposed person might lure her from my employment. To my certain knowledge she has received offers, lucrative offers, to accept service elsewhere. You may judge of my dismay, Mr. Wooster, when only this morning the bolt fell. She gave notice!"

"Good Lord!"

"Your consternation does credit, if I may say so, to the heart of the author of *A Red, Red Summer Rose*. But I am thankful to say the worst has not happened. The matter has been adjusted. Jane is not leaving me."

"Good egg!"

"Good egg, indeed—though the expression is not familiar to me. I do not remember having come across it in your books. And, speaking of your books, may I say that what has impressed me about them even more than the moving poignancy of the actual narrative, is your philosophy of life. If there were more men like you, Mr. Wooster, London would be a better place."

This was dead opposite to my Aunt Agatha's philosophy of life, she having always rather given me to understand that it is the presence in it of chappies like me that makes London more or less of a plague spot; but I let it go.

"Let me tell you, Mr. Wooster, that I appreciate your splendid defiance of the outworn fetishes of a purblind social system. I appreciate it! You are big enough to see that rank is but the guinea stamp and that, in the magnificent words of Lord Bletchmore in *Only a Factory Girl*, 'Be her origin ne'er so humble, a good woman is the equal of the finest lady on earth!'"

I sat up.

"I say! Do you think that?"

"I do, Mr. Wooster. I am ashamed to say that there was a time when I was like other men, a slave to the idiotic convention which we call Class Distinction. But, since I read your books—"

I might have known it. Jeeves had done it again.

"You think it's all right for a chappie in what you might call a certain social position to marry a girl of what you might describe as the lower classes?"

"Most assuredly I do, Mr. Wooster."

I took a deep breath, and slipped him the good news.

"Young Bingo—your nephew, you know—wants to marry a waitress," I said.

"I honor him for it," said old Little.

"You don't object?"

"On the contrary."

I took another deep breath and shifted to the sordid side of the business.

"I hope you won't think I'm butting in, don't you know," I said, "but—er—well, how about it?"

"I fear I do not quite follow you."

"Well, I mean to say, his allowance and all that. The money you're good enough to give him. He was rather hoping that you might see your way to jerking up the total a bit."

Old Little shook his head regretfully.

"I fear that can hardly be managed. You see, a man in my position is compelled to save every penny. I will gladly continue my nephew's existing allowance, but beyond that I cannot go. It would not be fair to my wife."

"What! But you're not married?"

"Not yet. But I propose to enter upon that holy state almost immediately. The lady who for years has cooked so well for me honored me by accepting my hand this very morning." A cold gleam of triumph came into his eye. "Now let 'em try to get her away from me!" he muttered, defiantly.

"YOUNG MR. LITTLE HAS been trying frequently during the afternoon to reach you on the telephone, sir," said Jeeves that night, when I got home.

"I'll bet he has," I said. I had sent poor old Bingo an outline of the situation by messenger-boy shortly after lunch.

"He seemed a trifle agitated."

"I don't wonder. Jeeves," I said, "so brace up and bite the bullet. I'm afraid I've bad news for you."

"That scheme of yours—reading those books to old Mr. Little and all that—has blown out a fuse."

"They did not soften him?"

"They did. That's the whole bally trouble. Jeeves, I'm sorry to say that fiancée of yours—Miss Watson, you know—the cook, you know—well, the long and the short of it is that she's chosen riches instead of honest worth, if you know what I mean."

"Sir?"

"She's handed you the mitten and gone and got engaged to old Mr. Little!"

"Indeed, sir?"

"You don't seem much upset."

"The fact is, sir, I had anticipated some such outcome."

I stared at him. "Then what on earth did you suggest the scheme for?"

"To tell you the truth, sir, I was not wholly averse from a severance of my relations with Miss Watson. In fact, I greatly desired it. I respect Miss Watson exceedingly, but I have seen for a long time that we were not suited. Now, the other young person with whom I have an understanding—"

"Great Scott, Jeeves! There isn't another?"

"Yes, sir."

"How long has this been going on?"

"For some weeks, sir. I was greatly attracted by her when I first met her at a subscription dance at Camberwell."

"My sainted aunt! Not—"

Jeeves inclined his head gravely.

"Yes, sir. By an odd coincidence it is the same young person that young Mr. Little— I have placed the cigarettes on the small table. Good night, sir."

# Sir Roderick Comes to Lunch

THE BLOW FELL PRECISELY at one forty-five (summer time). Spenser, Aunt Agatha's butler, was offering me the fried potatoes at the moment, and such was my emotion that I lofted six of them on to the sideboard with the spoon. Shaken to the core, if you know what I mean.

Mark you, I was in a pretty enfeebled condition already. I had been engaged to Honoria Glossop nearly two weeks, and during all that time not a day had passed without her putting in some heavy work in the direction of what Aunt Agatha had called "molding" me. I had read solid literature till my eyes bubbled; we had legged it together through miles of picture-galleries; and I had been compelled to undergo classical concerts to an extent you would hardly believe. All in all, therefore, I was in no fit state to receive shocks, especially shocks like this. Honoria had lugged me round to lunch at Aunt Agatha's, and I had just been saying to myself, "Death, where is thy jolly old sting?" when she hove the bomb.

"Bertie," she said, suddenly, as if she had just remembered it, "what is the name of that man of yours—your valet?"

"Eh? Oh, Jeeves."

"I think he's a bad influence for you," said Honoria. "When we are married, you must get rid of Jeeves."

It was at this point that I jerked the spoon and sent six of the best and crispest sailing on to the sideboard, with Spenser gambolling after them like a dignified old retriever.

"Get rid of Jeeves!" I gasped.

"Yes. I don't like him."

"I don't like him," said Aunt Agatha.

"But I can't. I mean—why, I couldn't carry on for a day without Jeeves."

"You will have to," said Honoria. "I don't like him at all."

"I don't like him at all," said Aunt Agatha. "I never did."

Ghastly, what? I'd always had an idea that marriage was a bit of a wash-out, but I'd never dreamed that it demanded such frightful sacrifices from a fellow. I passed the rest of the meal in a sort of stupor.

The scheme had been, if I remember, that after lunch I should go off and caddy for Honoria on a shopping tour down Regent Street; but when she got up and started collecting me and the rest of her things, Aunt Agatha stopped her.

"You run along, dear," she said. "I want to say a few words to Bertie."

So Honoria legged it, and Aunt Agatha drew up her chair and started in.

"Bertie," she said, "dear Honoria does not know it, but a little difficulty has arisen about your marriage."

"By Jove! not really?" I said, hope starting to dawn.

"Oh, it's nothing at all, of course. It is only a little exasperating. The fact is, Sir Roderick is being rather troublesome."

"Thinks I'm not a good bet? Wants to scratch the fixture? Well, perhaps he's right."

"Pray do not be so absurd, Bertie. It is nothing so serious as that. But the nature of Sir Roderick's profession unfortunately makes him — over-cautious."

I didn't get it.

"Over-cautious?"

"Yes. I suppose it is inevitable. A nerve specialist with his extensive practice can hardly help taking a rather warped view of humanity."

I got what she was driving at now. Sir Roderick Glossop, Honoria's father, is always called a nerve specialist, because it sounds better, but everybody knows that he's really a sort of janitor to the looney-bin. I mean to say, when your uncle the Duke begins to feel the strain a bit and you find him in the blue drawing-room sticking straws in his hair, old Glossop is the first person you send for. He toddles round, gives the patient the once-over, talks about over-excited nervous systems, and recommends complete rest and seclusion and all that sort of thing. Practically every posh family in the country has called him in at one time or another, and I suppose that, being in that position — I mean constantly having to sit on people's heads while their nearest and dearest phone to the asylum to send round the wagon — does tend to make a chappie take what you might call a warped view of humanity.

"You mean he thinks I may be a looney, and he doesn't want a looney son-in-law?" I said.

Aunt Agatha seemed rather peeved than otherwise at my ready intelligence.

"Of course, he does not think anything so ridiculous. I told you he was simply exceedingly cautious. He wants to satisfy himself that you are perfectly normal." Here she paused, for Spenser had come in with the coffee. When he had gone, she went on: "He appears to have got hold of some extraordinary story about your having pushed his son Oswald into the lake at Ditteredge Hall. Incredible, of course. Even you would hardly do a thing like that."

"Well, I did sort of lean against him, you know, and he shot off the bridge."

"Oswald definitely accuses you of having pushed him into the water. That has disturbed Sir Roderick, and unfortunately it has caused him to make inquiries, and he has heard about your poor Uncle Henry."

She eyed me with a good deal of solemnity, and I took a grave sip of coffee. We were peeping into the family cupboard and having a look at the good old skeleton. My late Uncle Henry, you see, was by way of being the blot on the Wooster escutcheon. An extremely decent chappie personally, and one who had always endeared himself to me by tipping me with considerable lavishness when I was at school; but there's no doubt he did at times do rather rummy things, notably keeping eleven pet rabbits in his bedroom; and I suppose a purist might have considered him more or less off his onion. In fact, to be perfectly frank, he wound up his career, happy to the last and completely surrounded by rabbits, in some sort of a home.

"It is very absurd, of course," continued Aunt Agatha. "If any of the family had inherited poor Henry's eccentricity—and it was nothing more—it would have been Claude and Eustace, and there could not be two brighter boys."

Claude and Eustace were twins, and had been kids at school with me in my last summer term. Casting my mind back, it seemed to me that "bright" just about described them. The whole of that term, as I remembered it, had been spent in getting them out of a series of frightful rows.

"Look how well they are doing at Oxford. Your Aunt Emily had a letter from Claude only the other day saying that they hoped to be elected shortly to a very important college club, called The Seekers."

"Seekers?" I couldn't recall any club of the name in my time at Oxford. "What do they seek?"

"Claude did not say. Truth or knowledge, I should imagine. It is evidently a very desirable club to belong to, for Claude added that Lord Rainsby, the Earl of Datchet's son, was one of his fellow-candidates. However, we are wandering from the point, which is that Sir Roderick wants to have a quiet talk with you quite alone. Now I rely on you, Bertie, to be—I won't say intelligent, but at least sensible. Don't giggle nervously: try to keep that horrible glassy expression out of your eyes: don't yawn or fidget; and remember that Sir Roderick is the president of the West London branch of the anti-gambling league, so please do not talk about horse-racing. He will lunch with you at your flat tomorrow at one-thirty. Please remember that he drinks no wine, strongly disapproves of smoking, and can only eat the simplest food, owing to an impaired digestion. Do not offer him coffee, for he considers it the root of half the nerve-trouble in the world."

"I should think a dog-biscuit and a glass of water would about meet the case, what?"

"Bertie!"

"Oh, all right. Merely persiflage."

"Now it is precisely that sort of remark that would be calculated to arouse Sir Roderick's worst suspicions. Do please try to refrain from any misguided flippancy when you are with him. He is a very serious-minded man. …Are you going? Well, please remember all I have said. I rely on you, and, if anything goes wrong, I shall never forgive you."

"Right-o!" I said.

And so home, with a jolly day to look forward to.

I BREAKFASTED PRETTY late next morning and went for a stroll afterwards. It seemed to me that anything I could do to clear the old lemon ought to be done, and a bit of fresh air generally relieves that rather foggy feeling that comes over a fellow early in the day. I had taken a stroll in the park, and got back as far as Hyde Park Corner, when some blighter sloshed me between the shoulder-blades. It was young Eustace, my cousin. He was arm-in-arm with two other fellows, the one on the outside being my cousin Claude and the one in the middle a pink-faced chappie with light hair and an apologetic sort of look.

"Bertie, old egg!" said young Eustace affably.

"Hallo!" I said, not frightfully chirpily.

"Fancy running into you, the one man in London who can support us in the style we are accustomed to! By the way, you've never met old Dog-Face, have you? Dog-Face, this is my cousin Bertie. Lord Rainsby—Mr. Wooster. We've just been round to your flat, Bertie. Bitterly disappointed that you were out, but were hospitably entertained by old Jeeves. That man's a corker, Bertie. Stick to him."

"What are you doing in London?" I asked.

"Oh, buzzing round. We're just up for the day. Flying visit, strictly unofficial. We oil back on the three-ten. And now, touching that lunch you very decently volunteered to stand us, which shall it be? Ritz? Savoy? Carlton? Or, if you're a member of Ciro's or the Embassy, that would do just as well."

"I can't give you lunch. I've got an engagement myself. And, by Jove," I said, taking a look at my watch, "I'm late." I hailed a taxi. "Sorry."

"As man to man, then," said Eustace, "lend us a fiver."

I hadn't time to stop and argue. I unbelted the fiver and hopped into the cab. It was twenty to two when I got to the flat. I bounded into the sitting-room, but it was empty.

Jeeves shimmied in.

"Sir Roderick has not yet arrived, sir."

"Good egg!" I said. "I thought I should find him smashing up the furniture." My experience is that the less you want a fellow, the more punctual he's bound to be, and I had had a vision of the old lad pacing the rug in my sitting-room, saying "He cometh not!" and generally hotting up. "Is everything in order?"

"I fancy you will find the arrangements quite satisfactory, sir."

"What are you giving us?"

"Cold consommé, a cutlet, and a savory, sir. With lemon-squash, iced."

"Well, I don't see how that can hurt him. Don't go getting carried away by the excitement of the thing and start bringing in coffee."

"No, sir."

"And don't let your eyes get glassy, because, if you do, you're apt to find yourself in a padded cell before you know where you are."

"Very good, sir."

There was a ring at the bell.

"Stand by, Jeeves," I said. "We're off!"

I HAD MET SIR RODERICK Glossop before, of course, but only when I was with Honoria; and there is something about Honoria which makes almost anybody you meet in the same room seem sort of under-sized and trivial by comparison. I had never realized till this moment what an extraordinarily formidable old bird he was. He had a pair of shaggy eyebrows which gave his eyes a piercing look which was not at all the sort of thing a fellow wanted to encounter on an empty stomach. He was fairly tall and fairly broad, and he had the most enormous head, with practically no hair on it, which made it seem bigger and much more like the dome of St. Paul's. I suppose he must have taken about a nine or something in hats. Shows what a rotten thing it is to let your brain develop too much.

"What ho! What ho! What ho!" I said, trying to strike the genial note, and then had a sudden feeling that that was just the sort of thing I had been warned not to say. Dashed difficult it is to start things going properly on an occasion like this. A fellow living in a London flat is so handicapped. I mean to say, if I had been the young squire greeting the visitor in the country, I could have said, "Welcome to Meadowsweet Hall!" or something zippy like that. It sounds silly to say "Welcome to Number 6A, Crichton Mansions, Berkeley Street, W."

"I am afraid I am a little late," he said, as we sat down. "I was detained at my club by Lord Alastair Hungerford, the Duke of Ramfurline's son. His Grace, he informed me, had exhibited a renewal of the symptoms which have been causing the family so much concern. I could not leave him immediately. Hence my unpunctuality, which I trust has not discommoded you."

"Oh, not at all. So the Duke is off his rocker, what?"

"The expression which you use is not precisely the one I should have employed myself with reference to the head of perhaps the noblest family in England, but there is no doubt that cerebral excitement does, as you suggest, exist in no small degree." He sighed as well as he could with his mouth full of cutlet. "A profession like mine is a great strain, a great strain."

"Must be."

"Sometimes I am appalled at what I see around me." He stopped suddenly and sort of stiffened. "Do you keep a cat, Mr. Wooster?"

"Eh? What? Cat? No, no cat."

"I was conscious of a distinct impression that I had heard a cat mewing either in the room or very near to where we are sitting."

"Probably a taxi or something in the street."

"I fear I do not follow you."

"I mean to say, taxis squawk, you know. Rather like cats in a sort of way."

"I had not observed the resemblance," he said, rather coldly.

"Have some lemon-squash," I said. The conversation seemed to be getting rather difficult.

"Thank you. Half a glassful, if I may." The hell-brew appeared to buck him up, for he resumed in a slightly more pally manner. "I have a particular dislike for cats. But I was saying—Oh, yes. Sometimes I am positively appalled at what I see around me. It is not only the cases which come under my professional notice, painful as many of those are. It is what I see as I go about London. Sometimes it seems to me that the whole world is mentally unbalanced. This very morning, for example, a most singular and distressing occurrence took place as I was driving from my house to the club. The day being clement, I had instructed my chauffeur to open my landaulette, and I was leaning back, deriving no little pleasure from the sunshine, when our progress was arrested in the middle of the thoroughfare by one of those blocks in the traffic which are inevitable in so congested a system as that of London."

I suppose I had been letting my mind wander a bit, for when he stopped and took a sip of lemon-squash I had a feeling that I was listening to a lecture and was expected to say something.

"Hear, hear!" I said.

"I beg your pardon?"

"Nothing, nothing. You were saying—"

"The vehicles proceeding in the opposite direction had also been temporarily arrested, but after a moment they were permitted to proceed. I had fallen into a meditation, when suddenly the most extraordinary thing took place. My hat was snatched abruptly from my head! And as I looked back I perceived it being waved in a kind of feverish triumph from the interior of a taxicab, which, even as

I looked, disappeared through a gap in the traffic and was lost to sight."

I didn't laugh, but I distinctly heard a couple of my floating ribs part from their moorings under the strain.

"Must have been meant for a practical joke," I said. "What?"

This suggestion didn't seem to please the old boy.

"I trust," he said, "I am not deficient in an appreciation of the humorous, but I confess that I am at a loss to detect anything akin to pleasantry in the outrage. The action was beyond all question that of a mentally unbalanced subject. These mental lesions may express themselves in almost any form. The Duke of Ramfurline, to whom I had occasion to allude just now, is under the impression—this is in the strictest confidence—that he is a canary; and his seizure today, which so perturbed Lord Alastair, was due to the fact that a careless footman had neglected to bring him his morning lump of sugar. Cases are common, again, of men waylaying women and cutting off portions of their hair. It is from a branch of this latter form of mania that I should be disposed to imagine that my assailant was suffering. I can only trust that he will be placed under proper control before he— Mr. Wooster, there is a cat close at hand! It is not in the street! The mewing appears to come from the adjoining room."

THIS TIME I HAD TO admit there was no doubt about it. There was a distinct sound of mewing coming from the next room. I punched the bell for Jeeves, who drifted in and stood waiting with an air of respectful devotion.

"Sir?"

"Oh, Jeeves," I said. "Cats! What about it? Are there any cats in the flat?"

"Only the three in your bedroom, sir."

"What!"

"Cats in his bedroom!" I heard Sir Roderick whisper in a kind of stricken way, and his eyes hit me amidships like a couple of bullets.

"What do you mean," I said, "only the three in my bedroom?"

"The black one, the tabby and the small lemon-colored animal, sir."

"What on earth?—"

I charged round the table in the direction of the door. Unfortunately, Sir Roderick had just decided to edge in that direction himself, with the result that we collided in the doorway with a good deal of force, and staggered out into the hall together. He came smartly out of the clinch and grabbed an umbrella from the rack.

"Stand back!" he shouted, waving it overhead. "Stand back, sir! I am armed!"

It seemed to me that the moment had come to be soothing.

"Awfully sorry I barged into you," I said. "Wouldn't have had it happen for worlds. I was just dashing out to have a look into things."

He appeared a trifle reassured, and lowered the umbrella. But just then the most frightful shindy started in the bedroom. It sounded as though all the cats in London, assisted by delegates from outlying suburbs, had got together to settle their differences once for all. A sort of augmented orchestra of cats.

"This noise is unendurable," yelled Sir Roderick. "I cannot hear myself speak."

"I fancy, sir," said Jeeves respectfully, "that the animals may have become somewhat exhilarated as the result of having discovered the fish under Mr. Wooster's bed."

The old boy tottered.

"Fish! Did I hear you rightly?"

"Sir?"

"Did you say that there was a fish under Mr. Wooster's bed?"

"Yes, sir."

Sir Roderick gave a low moan, and reached for his hat and stick.

"You aren't going?" I said.

"Mr. Wooster, I am going! I prefer to spend my leisure time in less eccentric society."

"But I say. Here, I must come with you. I'm sure the whole business can be explained. Jeeves, my hat."

Jeeves rallied round. I took the hat from him and shoved it on my head.

"Good heavens!"

Beastly shock it was! The bally thing had absolutely engulfed me, if you know what I mean. Even as I was putting it on I got a sort of impression that it was a trifle roomy; and no sooner had I let go of it than it settled down over my ears like a kind of extinguisher.

"I say! This isn't my hat!"

"It is my hat!" said Sir Roderick in about the coldest, nastiest voice I'd ever heard. "The hat which was stolen from me this morning as I drove in my car."

"But—"

I suppose Napoleon or somebody like that would have been equal to the situation, but I'm bound to say it was too much for me. I just stood there goggling in a sort of coma, while the old boy lifted the hat off me and turned to Jeeves.

"I should be glad, my man," he said, "if you would accompany me a few yards down the street. I wish to ask you some questions."

"Very good, sir."

"Here, but, I say —!" I began, but he left me standing. He stalked out, followed by Jeeves. And at that moment the row in the bedroom started again, louder than ever.

I was about fed up with the whole thing. I mean, cats in your bedroom — a bit thick, what? I didn't know how the dickens they had got in, but I was jolly well resolved that they weren't going to stay picknicking there any longer. I flung open the door. I got a momentary flash of about a hundred and fifteen cats of all sizes and colors scrapping in the middle of the room, and then they all shot past me with a rush and out of the front door; and all that was left of the mob-scene was the head of a whacking big fish, lying on the carpet and staring up at me in a rather austere sort of way, as if it wanted a written explanation and apology.

There was something about the thing's expression that absolutely chilled me, and I withdrew on tiptoe and shut the door. And, as I did so, I bumped into someone.

"Oh, sorry!" he said.

I spun round. It was the pink-faced chappie, Lord Something or other, the fellow I had met with Claude and Eustace.

"I say," he said apologetically, "awfully sorry to bother you, but those weren't my cats I met just now legging it downstairs, were they? They looked like my cats."

"They came out of my bedroom."

"Then they were my cats!" he said sadly. "Oh, dash it!"

"Did you put cats in my bedroom?"

"Your man, what's-his-name, did. He rather decently said I could keep them there till my train went. I'd just come to fetch them. And now they've gone! Oh, well, it can't be helped, I suppose. I'll take the hat and the fish, anyway."

I was beginning to dislike this chappie.

"Did you put that bally fish there, too?"

"No, that was Eustace's. The hat was Claude's."

I sank limply into a chair.

"I say, you couldn't explain this, could you?" I said. The chappie gazed at me in mild surprise.

"Why, don't you know all about it? I say!" He blushed profusely. "Why, if you don't know about it, I shouldn't wonder if the whole thing didn't seem rummy to you."

"Rummy is the word."

"It was for The Seekers, you know."

"The Seekers?"

"Rather a blood club, you know, up at Oxford, which your cousins and I are rather keen on getting into. You have to pinch something, you know, to get elected. Some sort of a souvenir, you know. A policeman's helmet, you know, or a door-knocker or something, you know. The room's decorated with the things at the annual dinner, and everybody makes speeches and all that sort of thing. Rather jolly! Well, we wanted rather to make a sort of special effort and do the thing in style, if you understand, so we came up to London to see if we couldn't pick up something here that would be a bit out of the ordinary. And we had the most amazing luck right from the start. Your cousin Claude managed to collect a quite decent top-hat out of a passing car, and your cousin Eustace got away with a really goodish salmon or something from Harrods, and I snaffled three excellent cats all in the first hour. We were fearfully braced, I can tell you. And then the difficulty was to know where to park the things till our train went. You look so beastly conspicuous, you know, tooling about London with a fish and a lot of cats. And then Eustace remembered you, and we all came on here in a cab. You were out, but your man said it would be all right. When we met you, you were in such a hurry that we hadn't time to explain. Well, I think I'll be taking the hat, if you don't mind."

"It's gone."

"Gone?"

"The fellow you pinched it from happened to be the man who was lunching here. He took it away with him."

"Oh, I say! Poor old Claude will be upset. Well, how about the goodish salmon or something?"

"Would you care to view the remains?" He seemed all broken up when he saw the wreckage.

"I doubt if the committee would accept that," he said sadly. "There isn't a frightful lot of it left, what?"

"The cats ate the rest."

He sighed deeply.

"No cats, no fish, no hat. We've had all our trouble for nothing. I do call that hard! And on top of that—I say, I hate to ask you, but you couldn't lend me a tenner, could you?"

"A tenner? What for?"

"Well, the fact is, I've got to pop round and bail Claude and Eustace out. They've been arrested."

"Arrested!"

"Yes. You see, what with the excitement of collaring the hat and the salmon or something, added to the fact that we had rather a festive lunch, they got a bit above themselves, poor chaps, and tried to pinch a motor-lorry. Silly, of course, because I don't see how they could have got the thing to Oxford and shown it to the committee. Still, there wasn't any reasoning with them, and when the driver started making a fuss, there was a bit of a mix-up, and Claude and Eustace are more or less languishing in Vine Street police-station till I pop round and bail them out. So if you could manage a tenner—Oh, thanks, that's fearfully good of you. It would have been too bad to leave them there, what? I mean, they're both such frightfully good chaps, you know. Everybody likes them up at the 'Varsity. They're fearfully popular."

"I bet they are!" I said.

WHEN JEEVES CAME BACK, I was waiting for him on the mat. I wanted speech with the blighter.

"Well?" I said.

"Sir Roderick asked me a number of questions, sir, respecting your habits and mode of life, to which I replied guardedly."

"I don't care about that. What I want to know is why you didn't explain the whole thing to him right at the start? A word from you would have put everything clear."

"Yes, sir."

"Now he's gone off thinking me a looney."

"I should not be surprised, from his conversation with me, sir, if some such idea had not entered his head."

I was just starting in to speak, when the telephone bell rang. Jeeves answered it.

"No, madam, Mr. Wooster is not in. No, madam, I do not know when he will return, No, madam, he left no message. Yes, madam, I will inform him." He put back the receiver. "Mrs. Gregson, sir."

Aunt Agatha! I had been expecting it. Ever since the luncheon-party had blown out a fuse, her shadow had been hanging over me, so to speak.

"Does she know? Already?"

"I gather that Sir Roderick has been speaking to her on the telephone, sir, and—"

"No wedding bells for me, what?"

Jeeves coughed.

"Mrs. Gregson did not actually confide in me, sir, but I fancy that some such thing may have occurred. She seemed decidedly agitated, sir."

It's a rummy thing, but I'd been so snootered by the old boy and the cats and the fish and the hat and the pink-faced chappie and all the rest of it that the bright side simply hadn't occurred to me till now. By Jove, it was like a bally weight rolling off my chest! I gave a yelp of pure relief.

"Jeeves!" I said, "I believe you worked the whole thing!"

"Sir?"

"I believe you had the jolly old situation in hand right from the start."

"Well, sir, Spenser, Mrs. Gregson's butler, who inadvertently chanced to overhear something of your conversation when you were lunching at the house, did mention certain of the details to me; and I confess that, though it may be a liberty to say so, I entertained hopes that something might occur to prevent the match. I doubt if the young lady was entirely suitable to you, sir."

"And she would have shot you out on your ear five minutes after the ceremony."

"Yes, sir. Spenser informed me that she had expressed some such intention. Mrs. Gregson wishes you to call upon her immediately, sir."

"She does, eh? What do you advise, Jeeves?"

"I think a trip abroad might prove enjoyable, sir."

I shook my head. "She'd come after me."

"Not if you went far enough afield, sir. There are excellent boats leaving every Wednesday and Saturday for New York."

"Jeeves," I said, "you are right, as always. Book the tickets.

# Archie Moffam

BETWEEN THE TALES collected in *My Man Jeeves* (1919) and *The Inimitable Jeeves* (1923), Wodehouse wrote eleven short stories starring Archibald Moffam. Archie shares a similar background with Reggie Pepper and Bertie Wooster, but he lacks their inherited wealth—which also means that he cannot afford a valet like Jeeves.

Encouraged by his relatives to seek his fortune in the new world, Archie travels to New York. There, he soon locks horns with Daniel Brewster, owner of the Cosmopolis hotel, and hilarious hijinks ensue.

The Archie Moffam stories were published in revised form as *The Indiscretions of Archie* (1921).

# The Man Who Married a Hotel

"I SAY, LADDIE!" said Archie.

"Sir?" replied the desk-clerk alertly. All the employees of the Hotel Cosmopolis were alert. It was one of the things on which Mr. Daniel Brewster, the proprietor, insisted. And as he was always wandering about the lobby of the hotel keeping a personal eye on affairs, it was never safe to relax.

"I want to see the manager."

"Is there anything I could do, sir?"

Archie looked at him doubtfully.

"Well, as a matter of fact, my dear old desk-clerk," he said, "I want to kick up a fearful row, and it hardly seems fair to lug you into it. Why you, I mean to say? The blighter whose head I want on a charger is the bally manager."

At this point a massive, grey-haired man, who had been standing close by, gazing on the lobby with an air of restrained severity, as if daring it to start anything, joined in the conversation.

"I am the manager," he said.

His eye was cold and hostile. Others, it seemed to say, might like Archie Moffam, but not he. Daniel Brewster was bristling for combat. What he had overheard had shocked him to the core of his being. The Hotel Cosmopolis was his own private, personal property, and the thing dearest to him in the world, after his daughter Lucille. He prided himself on the fact that his hotel was not like other New York hotels, which were run by impersonal companies and shareholders and boards of directors, and consequently lacked the paternal touch which made the Cosmopolis what it was. At other hotels things went wrong, and clients complained. At the Cosmopolis things never went wrong, because he was on the spot to see that they didn't, and as a result clients never complained. Yet here was this long, thin, string-bean of an Englishman actually registering annoyance and dissatisfaction before his very eyes.

"What is your complaint?" he enquired frigidly.

Archie attached himself to the top button of Mr. Brewster's coat, and was immediately dislodged by an irritable jerk of the other's substantial body.

"Listen, old thing! I came over to this country to nose about in search of a job, because there doesn't seem what you might call a general demand for my services in England. Directly I was demobbed, the family started talking about the Land of Opportunity and shot me on to a liner. The idea was that I might get hold of something in America—"

He got hold of Mr. Brewster's coat-button, and was again shaken off.

"Between ourselves, I've never done anything much in England, and I fancy the family were getting a bit fed. At any rate, they sent me over here—"

Mr. Brewster disentangled himself for the third time.

"I would prefer to postpone the story of your life," he said coldly, "and be informed what is your specific complaint against the Hotel Cosmopolis."

"Of course, yes. The jolly old hotel. I'm coming to that. Well, it was like this. A chappie on the boat told me that this was the best place to stop at in New York—"

"He was quite right," said Mr. Brewster.

"Was he, by Jove! Well, all I can say, then, is that the other New York hotels must be pretty moldy, if this is the best of the lot! I took a room here last night," said Archie quivering with self-pity, "and there was a beastly tap outside somewhere which went drip-drip-drip all night and kept me awake."

Mr. Brewster's annoyance deepened. He felt that a chink had been found in his armor. Not even the most paternal hotel-proprietor can keep an eye on every tap in his establishment.

"Drip-drip-drip!" repeated Archie firmly. "And I put my boots outside the door when I went to bed, and this morning they hadn't been touched. I give you my solemn word! Not touched."

"Naturally," said Mr. Brewster. "My employees are honest"

"But I wanted them cleaned, dash it!"

"There is a shoe-shining parlor in the basement. At the Cosmopolis shoes left outside bedroom doors are not cleaned."

"Then I think the Cosmopolis is a bally rotten hotel!"

Mr. Brewster's compact frame quivered. The unforgivable insult had been offered. Question the legitimacy of Mr. Brewster's parentage, knock Mr. Brewster down and

walk on his face with spiked shoes, and you did not irre-
mediably close all avenues to a peaceful settlement. But
make a remark like that about his hotel, and war was definitely declared.

"In that case," he said, stiffening, "I must ask you to
give up your room."

"I'm going to give it up! I wouldn't stay in the bally
place another minute."

Mr. Brewster walked away, and Archie charged round
to the cashier's desk to get his bill. It had been his intention in any case, though for dramatic purposes he concealed it from his adversary, to leave the hotel that morning. One of the letters of introduction which he had
brought over from England had resulted in an invitation
from a Mrs. van Tuyl to her house-party at Miami, and he
had decided to go there at once.

"Well," mused Archie, on his way to the station, "one
thing's certain. I'll never set foot in *that* bally place again!"

But nothing in this world is certain.

Mr. Daniel Brewster sat in his luxurious suite at the
Cosmopolis, smoking one of his admirable cigars and
chatting with his old friend, Professor Binstead. A
stranger who had only encountered Mr. Brewster in the
lobby of the hotel would have been surprised at the appearance of his sitting-room, for it had none of the rugged
simplicity which was the keynote of its owner's personal
appearance. Daniel Brewster was a man with a hobby. He
was what Parker, his valet, termed a connoozer. His edu-
cated taste in Art was one of the things which went to
make the Cosmopolis different from and superior to other

New York hotels. He had personally selected the tapestries in the dining-room and the various paintings throughout the building. And in his private capacity he was an enthusiastic collector of things which Professor Binstead, whose tastes lay in the same direction, would have stolen without a twinge of conscience if he could have got the chance.

The professor, a small man of middle age who wore tortoiseshell-rimmed spectacles, flitted covetously about the room, inspecting its treasures with a glistening eye. In a corner, Parker, a grave, lean individual, bent over the chafing-dish, in which he was preparing for his employer and his guest their simple lunch.

"Brewster," said Professor Binstead, pausing at the mantelpiece.

Mr. Brewster looked up amiably. He was in placid mood today. Two weeks and more had passed since the meeting with Archie recorded previously, and he had been able to dismiss that disturbing affair from his mind. Since then, everything had gone splendidly with Daniel Brewster, for he had just accomplished his ambition of the moment by completing the negotiations for the purchase of a site further down-town, on which he proposed to erect a new hotel. He liked building hotels. He had the Cosmopolis, his first-born, a summer hotel in the mountains, purchased in the previous year, and he was toying with the idea of running over to England and putting up another in London. That, however, would have to wait. Meanwhile, he would concentrate on this new one down-town. It had kept him busy and worried, arranging for securing the site; but his troubles were over now.

"Yes?" he said.

Professor Binstead had picked up a small china figure of delicate workmanship. It represented a warrior of pre-khaki days advancing with a spear upon some adversary who, judging from the contented expression on the warrior's face, was smaller than himself.

"Where did you get this?"

"That? Mawson, my agent, found it in a little shop on the east side."

"Where's the other? There ought to be another. These things go in pairs. They're valueless alone."

Mr. Brewster's brow clouded.

"I know that," he said shortly. "Mawson's looking for the other one everywhere. If you happen across it, I give you carte blanche to buy it for me."

"It must be somewhere."

"Yes. If you find it, don't worry about the expense. I'll settle up, no matter what it is."

"I'll bear it in mind," said Professor Binstead. "It may cost you a lot of money. I suppose you know that."

"I told you I don't care what it costs."

"It's nice to be a millionaire," sighed Professor Binstead.

"Luncheon is served, sir," said Parker.

He had stationed himself in a statutesque pose behind Mr. Brewster's chair, when there was a knock at the door. He went to the door, and returned with a telegram.

"Telegram for you, sir."

Mr. Brewster nodded carelessly. The contents of the chafing-dish had justified the advance advertising of their odor, and he was too busy to be interrupted.

"Put it down. And you needn't wait, Parker."

"Very good, sir."

The valet withdrew, and Mr. Brewster resumed his lunch.

"Aren't you going to open it?" asked Professor Binstead, to whom a telegram was a telegram.

"It can wait. I get them all day long. I expect it's from Lucille, saying what train she's making."

"She returns today?"

"Yes. Been at Miami." Mr. Brewster, having dwelt at adequate length on the contents of the chafing-dish, adjusted his glasses and took up the envelope. "I shall be glad—Great Godfrey!"

He sat staring at the telegram, his mouth open. His friend eyed him solicitously.

"No bad news, I hope?"

Mr. Brewster gurgled in a strangled way.

"Bad news? Bad—? Here, read it for yourself."

Professor Binstead, one of the three most inquisitive men in New York, took the slip of paper with gratitude.

"Returning New York today with darling Archie," he read. "Lots of love from us both. Lucille." He gaped at his host. "Who is Archie?" he enquired.

"Who is Archie?" echoed Mr. Brewster helplessly. "Who is—? That's just what I would like to know."

"'Darling Archie,'" murmured the professor, musing over the telegram. "'Returning today with darling Archie.' Strange!"

Mr. Brewster continued to stare before him. When you send your only daughter on a visit to Miami minus any entanglements and she mentions in a telegram that she has acquired a darling Archie, you are naturally startled. He rose from the table with a bound. It had occurred to him that by neglecting a careful study of his mail during the past week, as was his bad habit when busy, he had lost an opportunity of keeping abreast with current happenings. He recollected now that a letter had arrived from Lucille some time ago, and that he had put it away unopened till he should have leisure to read it. Lucille was a dear girl, he had felt, but her letters when on a vacation seldom contained anything that couldn't wait a few days for a reading. He sprang for his desk, rummaged among his papers, and found what he was seeking.

It was a long letter, and there was silence in the room for some moments while he mastered its contents. Then he turned to the professor, breathing heavily.

"Good heavens!"

"Yes?" said Professor Binstead eagerly. "Yes?"

"Good Lord!"

"Well?"

"Good gracious!"

"What is it?" demanded the professor in an agony.

Mr. Brewster sat down again with a thud.

"She's married!"

"Married!"

"Married! To an Englishman!"

"Bless my soul!"

"She says," proceeded Mr. Brewster, referring to the letter again, "that they were both so much in love that they simply had to slip off and get married, and she hopes I won't be cross. Cross!" gasped Mr. Brewster, gazing wildly at his friend.

"Very disturbing!"

"Disturbing! You bet it's disturbing! I don't know anything about the fellow. Never heard of him in my life. She says he wanted a quiet wedding because he thought a fellow looked such a chump getting married! And I must love him, because he's all set to love me very much!"

"Extraordinary!"

Mr. Brewster put the letter down.

"An Englishman!"

"I have met some very agreeable Englishmen," said Professor Binstead.

"I don't like Englishmen," growled Mr. Brewster. "Parker's an Englishman."

"Your valet?"

"Yes. I believe he wears my shirts on the sly,'" said Mr. Brewster broodingly, "If I catch him —! What would you do about this, Binstead?"

"Do?" The professor considered the point judiciary. "Well, really, Brewster, I do not see that there is anything you can do. You must simply wait and meet the man. Perhaps he will turn out an admirable son-in-law."

"H'm!" Mr. Brewster declined to take an optimistic view. "But an Englishman, Binstead!" he said with pathos. "Why," he went on, memory suddenly stirring, "there was an Englishman at this hotel only a week or two ago who went about knocking it in a way that would have amazed you! Said it was a rotten place! *My* hotel!"

Professor Binstead clicked his tongue sympathetically. He understood his friend's warmth.

AT ABOUT THE SAME moment that Professor Binstead was clicking his tongue in Mr. Brewster's sitting-room, Archie Moffam sat contemplating his bride in a drawing-room on the express from Miami. He was thinking that this was too good to be true. His brain had been in something of a whirl these last few days, but this was one thought that never failed to emerge clearly from the welter.

Mrs. Archie Moffam, *née* Lucille Brewster, was small and slender. She had a little animated face, set in a cloud of dark hair. She was so altogether perfect that Archie had frequently found himself compelled to take the marriage-certificate out of his inside pocket and study it furtively, to make himself realize that this miracle of good fortune had actually happened to him.

"Honestly, old bean—I mean, dear old thing—I mean, darling," said Archie, "I can't believe it!"

"What?"

"What I mean is, I can't understand why you should have married a blighter like me."

Lucille's eyes opened. She squeezed his hand.

"Why, you're the most wonderful thing in the world, precious!—Surely you know that?"

"Absolutely escaped my notice. Are you sure?"

"Of course I'm sure! You wonder-child! Nobody could see you without loving you!"

Archie heaved an ecstatic sigh. Then a thought crossed his mind. It was a thought which frequently came to mar his bliss.

"I say, I wonder if your father will think that!"

"Of course he will!"

"We rather sprung this, as it were, on the old lad," said Archie dubiously. "What sort of a man *is* your father?"

"Father's a darling, too."

"Rummy thing he should own that hotel," said Archie. "I had a frightful row with a blighter of a manager there just before I left for Miami. Your father ought to sack that chap. He was a blot on the landscape!"

It had been settled by Lucille during the journey that Archie should be broken gently to his father-in-law. That is to say, instead of bounding blithely into Mr. Brewster's presence hand in hand, the happy pair should separate for half an hour or so, Archie hanging around in the offing while Lucille saw her father and told him the whole story, or those chapters of it which she had omitted from her letter for want of space. Then, having impressed Mr. Brewster sufficiently with his luck in having acquired Archie for a son-in-law, she would lead him to where his bit of good fortune awaited him.

The program worked out admirably in its earlier stages. When the two emerged from Mr. Brewster's room to meet Archie, Brewster's general idea was that fortune had smiled upon him in an almost unbelievable fashion and had presented him with a son-in-law who combined in almost equal parts the more admirable characteristics of Apollo, Sir Galahad, and Marcus Aurelius. True, he had gathered in the course of the conversation that dear Archie had no occupation and no private means; but Mr. Brewster felt that a great-souled man like Archie didn't need them. You can't have everything, and Archie, according to Lucille's account, was practically a hundred per cent man in soul, looks, manners, amiability, and breeding. These are the things that count. Mr. Brewster proceeded to the lobby in a glow of optimism and geniality.

Consequently, when he perceived Archie, he got a bit of a shock.

"Hullo—ullo—ullo!" said Archie, advancing happily.

"Archie, darling, this is father," said Lucille.

"Good Lord!" said Archie.

There was one of those silences. Mr. Brewster looked at Archie. Archie gazed at Mr. Brewster. Lucille, perceiving without understanding why that the big introduction scene had stubbed its toe on some unlooked-for obstacle, waited anxiously for enlightenment. Meanwhile, Archie continued to inspect Mr. Brewster, and Mr. Brewster continued to drink in Archie.

After an awkward pause of about three and a quarter minutes, Mr. Brewster swallowed once or twice, and finally spoke.

"Lu!"

"Yes, father?"

"Is this true?"

Lucille's grey eyes clouded over with perplexity and apprehension.

"True?"

"Have you really inflicted this — *this* on me for a son-in-law?" Mr. Brewster swallowed a few more times, Archie the while watching with a frozen fascination the rapid shimmying of his new relative's Adam's-apple. "Go away! I want to have a few words alone with this — This — *Wassyourdamnname*?" he demanded, in an overwrought manner, addressing Archie for the first time.

"I told you, father. It's Moom."

"Moom?"

"It's spelt M-o-f-f-a-m, but pronounced Moom.

"To rhyme," said Archie, helpfully, "with Bluffing-hame."

"Lu," said Mr. Brewster, "run away! I want to speak to-to-to — "

"You called me *this* before," said Archie.

"You aren't angry, father, dear?" said Lucilla.

"Oh no! Oh no! I'm tickled to death!"

When his daughter had withdrawn, Mr. Brewster drew a long breath.

"Now then!" he said.

"Bit embarrassing, all this, what!" said Archie, chattily. "I mean to say, having met before in less happy circs and what not. Rum coincidence and so forth! How would it be to bury the jolly old hatchet—start a new life—forgive and forget—learn to love each other—and all that sort of rot? I'm game if you are. How do we go? Is it a bet?"

Mr. Brewster remained entirely unsoftened by this manly appeal to his better feelings.

"What the devil do you mean by marrying my daughter?"

Archie reflected.

"Well, it sort of happened, don't you know! You know how these things *are*! Young yourself once, and all that. I was most frightfully in love, and Lu seemed to think it wouldn't be a bad scheme, and one thing led to another, and—well, there you are, don't you know!"

"And I suppose you think you've done pretty well for yourself?"

"Oh, absolutely! As far as I'm concerned, everything's topping! I've never felt so braced in my life!"

"Yes!" said Mr. Brewster, with bitterness, "I suppose, from your view-point, everything *is* 'topping.' You haven't a cent to your name, and you've managed to fool a rich man's daughter into marrying you. I suppose you looked me up in Bradstreet before committing yourself?"

This aspect of the matter had not struck Archie until this moment.

"I say!" he observed, with dismay. "I never looked at it like that before! I can see that, from your point of view, this must look like a bit of a wash-out!"

"How do you propose to support Lucille, anyway?"

Archie ran a finger round the inside of his collar. He felt embarrassed, His father-in-law was opening up all kinds of new lines of thought.

"Well, there, old bean," he admitted, frankly, "you ra-ther have me!" He turned the matter over for a moment. "I had a sort of idea of, as it were, working, if you know what I mean."

"Working at what?"

"Now, there again you stump me somewhat! The general scheme was that I should kind of look round, you know, and nose about and buzz to and fro till something turned up. That was, broadly speaking, the notion!"

"And how did you suppose my daughter was to live while you were doing all this?"

"Well, I think," said Archie, "I *think* we rather expected *you* to rally round a bit for the nonce!"

"I see! You expected to live on me?"

"Well, you put it a bit crudely, but—as far as I had mapped anything out—that *was* what you might call the general scheme of procedure. You don't think much of it, what? Yes? No?"

Mr. Brewster exploded.

"No! I do not think much of it! Good God! You go out of my hotel—*my* hotel—calling it all the names you could think of—roasting it to beat the band—"

"Trifle hasty!" murmured Archie, apologetically. "Spoke without thinking. Dashed tap had gone *drip-drip-drip* all night—kept me awake—hadn't had breakfast—bygones be bygones—!"

"Don't interrupt! I say, you go out of my hotel, knocking it as no one has ever knocked it since it was built, and you sneak straight off and marry my daughter without my knowledge."

"Did think of wiring for blessing. Slipped the old bean, somehow. You know how one forgets things!"

"And now you come back and calmly expect me to fling my arms round you and kiss you, and support you for the rest of your life!"

"Only while I'm nosing about and buzzing to and fro."

"Well, I suppose I've got to support you. There seems no way out of it. I'll tell you exactly what I propose to do. You think my hotel is a pretty poor hotel, eh? Well, you'll have plenty of opportunity of judging, because you're coming to live here. I'll let you have a suite and I'll let you have your meals, but outside of that—nothing doing! Nothing doing! Do you understand what I mean?"

"Absolutely! You mean, 'Napoo!'"

"You can sign bills for a reasonable amount in my restaurant, and the hotel will look after your laundry. But not a cent do you get out me. And, if you want your shoes shined, you can pay for it yourself in the basement. If you leave them outside your door, I'll instruct the floor-waiter to throw them down the air-shaft. Do you understand? Good! Now, is there anything more you want to ask?"

Archie smiled a propitiatory smile.

"Well, as a matter of fact, I was going to ask if you would stagger along and have a bite with us in the grill-room?"

"I will not!"

"I'll sign the bill," said Archie, ingratiatingly. "You don't think much of it? Oh, right-o!"

# Dear Old Squiffy

ARCHIE INSERTED A FRESH cigarette in his long holder and began to smoke a little moodily. It was about a week after his disturbing adventures in J. B. Wheeler's studio, and life had ceased for the moment to be a thing of careless enjoyment. Mr. Wheeler, mourning over his lost home-brew and refusing, like Niobe, to be comforted, has suspended the sittings for the magazine cover, thus robbing Archie of his life-work. Mr. Brewster had not been in genial mood of late. And, in addition to all this, Lucille was away on a visit to a school-friend. And when Lucille went away, she took with her the sunshine. Archie was not surprised at her being popular and in demand among her friends, but that did not help him to become reconciled to her absence.

He gazed rather wistfully across the table at his friend, Roscoe Sherriff, the Press-agent, another of his Pen-and-Ink Club acquaintances. They had just finished lunch, and during the meal Sherriff, who, like most men of action, was fond of hearing the sound of his own voice and liked exercising it on the subject of himself, had been telling Archie a few anecdotes about his professional past. From these the latter had conceived a picture of Roscoe Sherriff's life as a prismatic thing of energy and adventure and well-paid withal—just the sort of life, in fact, which he would have enjoyed leading himself. He wished that he, too, like the Press-agent, could go about the place "slipping things over" and "putting things across." Daniel Brewster, he felt, would have beamed upon a son-in-law like Roscoe Sherriff.

"The more I see of America," sighed Archie, "the more it amazes me. All you birds seem to have been doing things from the cradle upwards. I wish I could do things!"

"Well, why don't you?"

Archie flicked the ash from his cigarette into the finger-bowl.

"Oh, I don't know, you know," he said, "Somehow, none of our family ever have. I don't know why it is, but whenever a Moffam starts out to do things he infallibly makes a bloomer. There was a Moffam in the Middle Ages who had a sudden spasm of energy and set out to make a pilgrimage to Jerusalem, dressed as a wandering friar. Rum ideas they had in those days."

"Did he get there?"

"Absolutely not! Just as he was leaving the front door his favorite hound mistook him for a tramp—or a varlet, or a scurvy knave, or whatever they used to call them at that time—and bit him in the fleshy part of the leg."

"Well, at least he started."

"Enough to make a chappie start, what?"

Roscoe Sherriff sipped his coffee thoughtfully. He was an apostle of Energy, and it seemed to him that he could make a convert of Archie and incidentally do himself a bit of good. For several days he had been, looking for someone like Archie to help him in a small matter which he had in mind.

"If you're really keen on doing things," he said, "there's something you can do for me right away."

Archie beamed. Action was what his soul demanded.

"Anything, dear boy, anything! State your case!"

"Would you have any objection to putting up a snake for me?"

"Putting up a snake?"

"Just for a day or two."

"But how do you mean, old soul? Put him up where?"

"Wherever you live. Where do you live? The Cosmopolis, isn't it? Of course! You married old Brewster's daughter. I remember reading about it."

"But, I say, laddie, I don't want to spoil your day and disappoint you and so forth, but my jolly old father-in-law would never let me keep a snake. Why, it's as much as I can do to make him let me stop on in the place."

"He wouldn't know."

"There's not much that goes on in the hotel that he doesn't know," said Archie, doubtfully.

"He mustn't know. The whole point of the thing is that it must be a dead secret."

Archie flicked some more ash into the finger-bowl.

"I don't seem absolutely to have grasped the affair in all its aspects, if you know what I mean," he said. "I mean to say—in the first place—why would it brighten your young existence if I entertained this snake of yours?"

"It's not mine. It belongs to Mme. Brudowska. You've heard of her, of course?"

"Oh yes. She's some sort of performing snake female in vaudeville or something, isn't she, or something of that species or order?"

"You're near it, but not quite right. She is the leading exponent of high-brow tragedy on any stage in the civilized world."

"Absolutely! I remember now. My wife lugged me to see her perform one night. It all comes back to me. She had me wedged in an orchestra-stall before I knew what I was up against, and then it was too late. I remember reading in some journal or other that she had a pet snake, given her by some Russian prince or other, what?"

"That," said Sherriff, "was the impression I intended to convey when I sent the story to the papers. I'm her press-agent. As a matter of fact, I bought Peter—its name's Peter—myself down on the East Side. I always believe in animals for press-agent stunts. I've nearly always had good results. But with Her Nibs I'm handicapped. Shackled, so to speak. You might almost say my genius is stifled. Or strangled, if you prefer it."

"Anything you say," agreed Archie, courteously, "But how? Why is your what-d'you-call-it what's-its-named?"

"She keeps me on a leash. She won't let me do anything with a kick in it. If I've suggested one rip-snorting stunt, I've suggested twenty, and every time she turns them down on the ground that that sort of thing is beneath the dignity of an artist in her position. It doesn't give a fellow a chance. So now I've made up my mind to do her good by stealth. I'm going to steal her snake."

"Steal it? Pinch it, as it were?"

"Yes. Big story for the papers, you see. She's grown very much attached to Peter. He's her mascot. I believe she's practically kidded herself into believing that Russian prince story. If I can sneak it away and keep it away for a day or two, she'll do the rest. She'll make such a fuss that the papers will be full of it."

"I see."

"Wow, any ordinary woman would work in with me. But not Her Nibs. She would call it cheap and degrading and a lot of other things. It's got to be a genuine steal, and, if I'm caught at it, I lose my job. So that's where you come in."

"But where am I to keep the jolly old reptile?"

"Oh, anywhere. Punch a few holes in a hat-box, and make it up a shakedown inside. It'll be company for you."

"Something in that. My wife's away just now and it's a bit lonely in the evenings."

"You'll never be lonely with Peter around. He's a great scout. Always merry and bright."

"He doesn't bite, I suppose, or sting or what-not?"

"He may what-not occasionally. It depends on the weather. But, outside of that, he's as harmless as a canary."

"Dashed dangerous things, canaries," said Archie, thoughtfully. "They peck at you."

"Don't weaken!" pleaded the press-agent.

"Oh, all right. I'll take him. By the way, touching the matter of browsing and sluicing. What do I feed him on?"

"Oh, anything. Bread-and-milk or fruit or soft-boiled egg or dog-biscuit or ants'-eggs. You know—anything you have yourself. Well, I'm much obliged for your hospitality. I'll do the same for you another time. Now I must be getting along to see to the practical end of the thing. By the way, Her Nibs lives at the Cosmopolis, too. Very convenient. Well, so long. See you later."

Archie, left alone, began for the first time to have serious doubts. He had allowed himself to be swayed by Mr. Sherriff's magnetic personality, but now that the other had removed himself he began to wonder if he had been entirely wise to lend his sympathy and co-operation to the scheme. He had never had intimate dealings with a snake before, but he had kept silkworms as a child, and there had been the deuce of a lot of fuss and unpleasantness over them. Getting into the salad and what-not. Something seemed to tell him that he was asking for trouble with a loud voice, but he had given his word and he supposed he would have to go through with it.

He lit another cigarette and wandered out into Fifth Avenue. His usually smooth brow was ruffled with care. Despite the eulogies which Sherriff had uttered concerning Peter, he found his doubts increasing. Peter might, as the Press-agent had stated, be a great scout, but was his little Garden of Eden on the fifth floor of the Cosmopolis Hotel likely to be improved by the advent of even the most amiable and winsome of serpents? However—

"Moffam! My dear fellow!"

The voice, speaking suddenly in his ear from behind, roused Archie from his reflections. Indeed, it roused him so effectually that he jumped a clear inch off the ground and bit his tongue. Revolving on his axis, he found himself confronting a middle-aged man with a face like a horse. The man was dressed in something of an old-world style. His clothes had an English cut. He had a drooping grey moustache. He also wore a grey bowler hat flattened at the crown—but who are we to judge him?

"Archie Moffam! I have been trying to find you all the morning."

Archie had placed him now. He had not seen General Mannister for several years—not, indeed, since the days when he used to meet him at the home of young Lord Seacliff, his nephew. Archie had been at Eton and Oxford with Seacliff, and had often visited him in the Long Vacation.

"Halloa, General! What ho, what ho! What on earth are you doing over here?"

"Let's get out of this crush, my boy." General Mannister steered Archie into a side-street, "That's better." He cleared his throat once or twice, as if embarrassed. "I've brought Seacliff over," he said, finally.

"Dear old Squiffy here? Oh, I say! Great work!"

General Mannister did not seem to share his enthusiasm. He looked like a horse with a secret sorrow. He coughed three times, like a horse who, in addition to a secret sorrow, had contracted asthma.

"You will find Seacliff changed," he said. "Let me see, how long is it since you and he met?"

Archie reflected.

"I was demobbed just about a year ago. I saw him in Paris about a year before that. The old egg got a bit of shrapnel in his foot or something, didn't he? Anyhow, I remember he was sent home."

"His foot is perfectly well again now. But, unfortunately, the enforced inaction led to disastrous results. You recollect, no doubt, that Seacliff always had a—a tendency;—a—a weakness—it was a family failing—"

"Mopping it up, do you mean? Shifting it? Looking on the jolly old stuff when it was red and what not, what?"

"Exactly."

Archie nodded.

"Dear old Squiffy was always rather a lad for the wassail-bowl. When I met him in Paris, I remember, he was quite tolerably blotto."

"Precisely. And the failing has, I regret to say, grown on him since he returned from the war. My poor sister was extremely worried. In fact, to cut a long story short, I induced him to accompany me to America. I am attached to the British Legation in Washington now, you know."

"Oh, really?"

"I wished Seacliff to come with me to Washington, but he insists on remaining in New York. He stated specifically that the thought of living in Washington gave him the—what was the expression he used?"

"The pip?"

"The pip. Precisely."

"But what was the idea of bringing him to America?"

"This admirable Prohibition enactment has rendered America—to my mind—the ideal place for a young man of his views." The General looked at his watch. "It is most fortunate that I happened to run into you, my dear fellow. My train for Washington leaves in another hour, and I have packing to do. I want to leave poor Seacliff in your charge while I am gone."

"Oh, I say! What!"

"You can look after him. I am credibly informed that even now there are places in New York where a determined young man may obtain the—er—stuff, and I should be infinitely obliged—and my poor sister would be infinitely grateful—if you would keep an eye on him." He hailed a taxi-cab. "I am sending Seacliff round to the Cosmopolis tonight. I am sure you, will do everything you can. Good-bye, my boy, good-bye."

Archie continued his walk. This, he felt, was beginning to be a bit thick. He smiled a bitter, mirthless smile as he recalled the fact that less than half an hour had elapsed since he had expressed a regret that he did not belong to the ranks of those who do things. Fate since then had certainly supplied him with jobs with a lavish hand. By bedtime he would be an active accomplice to a theft, valet and companion to a snake he had never met, and—as far as could gather the scope of his duties—a combination of nursemaid and private detective to dear old Squiffy.

It was past four o'clock when he returned to the Cosmopolis. Roscoe Sherriff was pacing the lobby of the hotel nervously, carrying a small hand-bag.

"Here you are at last! Good heavens, man, I've been waiting two hours."

"Sorry, old bean. I was musing a bit and lost track of the time."

The Press-agent looked cautiously round. There was nobody within earshot.

"Here he is!" he said.

"Who?"

"Peter."

"Where?" said Archie, staring blankly.

"In this bag. Did you expect to find him strolling arm-in-arm with me round the lobby? Here you are! Take him!"

He was gone. And Archie, holding the bag, made his way to the lift. The bag squirmed gently in his grip.

The only other occupant of the lift was a striking-looking woman of foreign appearance, dressed in a way that made Archie feel that she must be somebody or she couldn't look like that. Her face, too, seemed vaguely familiar. She entered the lift at the second floor where the tea-room is, and she had the contented expression of one who had tea'd to her satisfaction. She got off at the same floor as Archie, and walked swiftly, in a lithe, pantherist way, round the bend in the corridor. Archie followed more slowly. When he reached the door of his room, the passage was empty. He inserted the key in his door, turned it, pushed the door open, and pocketed the key. He was about to enter when the bag again squirmed gently in his grip.

From the days of Pandora, through the epoch of Bluebeard's wife, down to the present time, one of the chief failings of humanity has been the disposition to open things that were better closed. It would have been simple for Archie to have taken another step and put a door between himself and the world, but there came to him the irresistible desire to peep into the bag now — not three seconds later, but now. All the way up in the lift he had been battling with the temptation, and now he succumbed.

The bag was one of those simple bags with a thingummy which you press. Archie pressed it. And, as it opened, out popped the head of Peter. His eyes met Archie's. Over his head there seemed to be an invisible mark of interrogation. His gaze was curious, but kindly. He appeared to be saying to himself, "Have I found a friend?"

Serpents, or Snakes, says the Encyclopaedia, are reptiles of the saurian class Ophidia, characterised by an elongated, cylindrical, limbless, scaly form, and distinguished from lizards by the fact that the halves (*rami*) of the lower jaw are not solidly united at the chin, but movably connected by an elastic ligament. The vertebra are very numerous, gastrocentrous, and procoelous. And, of course, when they put it like that, you can see at once that a man might spend hours with combined entertainment and profit just looking at a snake.

Archie would no doubt have done this; but long before he had time really to inspect the halves (*rami*) of his new friend's lower jaw and to admire its elastic fittings, and long before the gastrocentrous and procoelous character of the other's vertebrae had made any real impression on him, a piercing scream almost at his elbow — startled him out of his scientific reverie. A door opposite had opened, and the woman of the elevator was standing staring at him with an expression of horror and fury that went through, him like a knife. It was the expression which, more than anything else, had made Mme. Brudowska what she was professionally. Combined with a deep voice and a sinuous walk, it enabled her to draw down a matter of a thousand dollars per week.

Indeed, though the fact gave him little pleasure, Archie, as a matter of fact, was at this moment getting about — including war-tax — two dollars and seventy-five cents worth of the great emotional star for nothing. For, having treated him gratis to the look of horror and fury, she now moved towards him with the sinuous walk and spoke in the tone which she seldom permitted herself to use before the curtain of act two, unless there was a whale of a situation that called for it in act one.

"Thief!"

It was the way she said it.

Archie staggered backwards as though he had been hit between the eyes, fell through the open door of his room, kicked it to with a flying foot, and collapsed on the bed. Peter, the snake, who had fallen on the floor with a squashy sound, looked surprised and pained for a moment; then, being a philosopher at heart, cheered up and began hunting for flies under the bureau.

Peril sharpens the intellect. Archie's mind as a rule worked in rather a languid and restful sort of way, but now it got going with a rush and a whir. He glared round the room. He had never seen a room so devoid of satisfactory cover. And then there came to him a scheme, a ruse. It offered a chance of escape. It was, indeed, a bit of all right.

Peter, the snake, loafing contentedly about the carpet, found himself seized by what the Encyclopaedia calls the "distensible gullet" and looked up reproachfully. The next moment he was in his bag again; and Archie, bounding silently into the bathroom, was tearing the cord off his dressing-gown.

There came a banging at the door. A voice spoke sternly. A masculine voice this time.

"Say! Open this door!"

Archie rapidly attached the dressing-gown cord to the handle of the bag, leaped to the window, opened it, tied the cord to a projecting piece of iron on the sill, lowered Peter and the bag into the depths, and closed the window again. The whole affair took but a few seconds. Generals have received the thanks of their nations for displaying less resource on the field of battle.

He opened the door. Outside stood the bereaved woman, and beside her a bullet-headed gentleman with a bowler hat on the back of his head, in whom Archie recognized the hotel detective.

The hotel detective also recognized Archie, and the stern cast of his features relaxed. He even smiled a rusty but propitiatory smile. He imagined—erroneously—that Archie, being the son-in-law of the owner of the hotel, had a pull with that gentleman; and he resolved to proceed warily lest he jeopardize his job.

"Why, Mr. Moffam!" he said, apologetically. "I didn't know it was you I was disturbing."

"Always glad to have a chat," said Archie, cordially. "What seems to be the trouble?"

"My snake!" cried the queen of tragedy. "Where is my snake?"

Archie, looked at the detective. The detective looked at Archie.

"This lady," said the detective, with a dry little cough, "thinks her snake is in your room, Mr. Moffam."

"Snake?"

"Snake's what the lady said."

"My snake! My Peter!" Mme. Brudowska's voice shook with emotion. "He is here—here in this room."

Archie shook his head.

"No snakes here! Absolutely not! I remember noticing when I came in."

"The snake is here—here in this room. This man had it in a bag! I saw him! He is a thief!"

"Easy, ma'am!" protested the detective. "Go easy! This gentleman is the boss's son-in-law."

"I care not who he is! He has my snake! Here—here in this room!"

"Mr. Moffam wouldn't go round stealing snakes."

"Rather not," said Archie. "Never stole a snake in my life. None of the Moffams have ever gone about stealing snakes. Regular family tradition! Though I once had an uncle who kept gold-fish."

"Here he is! Here! My Peter!"

Archie looked at the detective. The detective looked at Archie. "We must humor her!" their glances said.

"Of course," said Archie, "if you'd like to search the room, what? What I mean to say is, this is Liberty Hall. Everybody welcome! Bring the kiddies!"

"I will search the room!" said Mme. Brudowska.

The detective glanced apologetically at Archie.

"Don't blame me for this, Mr. Moffam," he urged.

"Rather not! Only too glad you've dropped in!"

He took up an easy attitude against the window, and watched the empress of the emotional drama explore. Presently she desisted, baffled. For an instant she paused, as though about to speak, then swept from the room. A moment later a door banged across the passage.

"How do they get that way?" queried the detective, "Well, g'bye, Mr. Moffam. Sorry to have butted in."

The door closed. Archie waited a few moments, then went to the window and hauled in the slack. Presently the bag appeared over the edge of the window-sill.

"Good God!" said Archie.

In the rush and swirl of recent events he must have omitted to see that the clasp that fastened the bag was properly closed; for the bag, as it jumped on to the window-sill, gaped at him like a yawning face. And inside it there was nothing.

Archie leaned as far out of the window as he could manage without committing suicide. Far below him, the traffic took its usual course and the pedestrians moved to and fro upon the pavements. There was no crowding, no excitement. Yet only a few moments before a long green snake with three hundred ribs, a distensible gullet, and gastrocentrous vertebras must have descended on that street like the gentle rain from Heaven upon the place beneath. And nobody seemed even interested. Not for the first time since he had arrived in America, Archie marvelled at the cynical detachment of the New Yorker, who permits himself to be surprised at nothing.

He shut the window and moved away with a heavy heart. He had not had the pleasure of an extended acquaintanceship with Peter, but he had seen enough of him to realize his sterling qualities. Somewhere beneath Peter's three hundred ribs there had lain a heart of gold, and Archie mourned for his loss.

Archie had a dinner and theatre engagement that night, and it was late when he returned to the hotel. He found his father-in-law prowling restlessly about the lobby. There seemed to be something on Mr. Brewster's mind. He came up to Archie with a brooding frown on his square face.

"Who's this man Seacliff?" he demanded, without preamble. "I hear he's a friend of yours."

"Oh, you've met him, what?" said Archie. "Had a nice little chat together, yes? Talked of this and that, no!"

"We have not said a word to each other."

"Really? Oh, well, dear old Squiffy is one of those strong, silent fellers you know. You mustn't mind if he's a bit dumb. He never says much, but it's whispered round the clubs that he thinks a lot. It was rumored in the spring of nineteen-thirteen that Squiffy was on the point of making a bright remark, but it never came to anything."

Mr. Brewster struggled with his feelings.

"Who is he? You seem to know him."

"Oh yes. Great pal of mine, Squiffy. We went through Eton, Oxford, and the Bankruptcy Court together. And here's a rummy coincidence. When they examined *me*, I had no assets. And, when they examined Squiffy, *he* had no assets! Rather extraordinary, what?"

Mr. Brewster seemed to be in no mood for discussing coincidences.

"I might have known he was a friend of yours!" he said, bitterly. "Well, if you want to see him, you'll have to do it outside my hotel."

"Why, I thought he was stopping here."

"He is—tonight. Tomorrow he can look for some other hotel to break up."

"Great Scot! Has dear old Squiffy been breaking the place up?"

Mr. Brewster snorted.

"I am informed that this precious friend of yours entered my grill-room at eight o'clock. He must have been completely intoxicated, though the head waiter tells me he noticed nothing at the time."

Archie nodded approvingly.

"Dear old Squiffy was always like that. It's a gift. However woozled he might be, it was impossible to detect it with the naked eye. I've seen the dear old chap many a time whiffled to the eyebrows, and looking as sober as a bishop. Soberer! When did it begin to dawn on the lads in the grill-room that the old egg had been pushing the boat out?"

"The head waiter," said Mr. Brewster, with cold fury, "tells me that he got a hint of the man's condition when he suddenly got up from his table and went the round of the room, pulling off all the table-cloths, and breaking everything that was on them. He then threw a number of rolls at the diners, and left. He seems to have gone straight to bed."

"Dashed sensible of him, what? Sound, practical chap, Squiffy. But where on earth did he get the—er—materials?"

"From his room. I made enquiries. He has six large cases in his room."

"Squiffy always was a chap of infinite resource! Well, I'm dashed sorry this should have happened, don't you know."

"If it hadn't been for you, the man would never have come here." Mr. Brewster brooded coldly. "I don't know why it is, but ever since you came to this hotel I've had nothing but trouble."

"Dashed sorry!" said Archie, sympathetically.

"Grrh!" said Mr. Brewster.

Archie made his way meditatively to the lift. The injustice of his father-in-law's attitude pained him. It was absolutely rotten and all that to be blamed for everything that went wrong in the Hotel Cosmopolis.

While this conversation was in progress, Lord Seacliff was enjoying a refreshing sleep in his room on the fourth floor. Two hours passed. The noise of the traffic in the street below faded away. Only the rattle of an occasional belated cab broke the silence. In the hotel all was still. Mr. Brewster had gone to bed. Archie, in his room, smoked meditatively. Peace may have been said to reign.

At half-past two Lord Seacliff awoke. His hours of slumber were always irregular. He sat up in bed and switched the light on. He was a shock-headed young man with a red face and a hot brown eye. He yawned and stretched himself. His head was aching a little. The room seemed to him a trifle close. He got out of bed and threw open the window. Then, returning to bed, he picked up a book and began to read. He was conscious of feeling a little jumpy, and reading generally sent him to sleep.

Much has been written on the subject of bed-books. The general consensus of opinion is that a gentle, slow-moving story makes the best opiate. If this be so, dear old Squiffy's choice of literature had been rather injudicious. His book was *The Adventures of Sherlock Holmes*, and the particular story which he selected for perusal was the one entitled, "The Speckled Band." He was not a great reader, but, when he read, he liked something with a bit of zip to it.

Squiffy became absorbed. He had read the story before, but a long time back, and its complications were fresh to him. The tale, it may be remembered, deals with the activities of an ingenious gentleman who kept a snake, and used to loose it into people's bedrooms as a preliminary to collecting on their insurance. It gave Squiffy pleasant thrills, for he had always had a particular horror of snakes. As a child, he had shrunk from visiting the serpent house at the zoo; and, later, when he had come to man's estate and had put off childish things, and settled down in real earnest to his self-appointed mission of drinking up all the alcoholic fluid in England, the distaste for Ophidia had lingered. To a dislike for real snakes had been added a maturer shrinking from those which existed only in his imagination. He could still recall his emotions on the occasion, scarcely three months before, when he had seen a long, green serpent which a majority of his contemporaries had assured him wasn't there.

Squiffy read on:—

*Suddenly another sound became audible—a very gentle, soothing sound, like that of a small jet of steam escaping continuously from a kettle.*

Lord Seacliff looked up from his book with a start Imagination was beginning to play him tricks. He could have sworn that he had actually heard that identical sound. It had seemed to come from the window. He listened again. No! All was still. He returned to his book and went on reading.

*It was a singular sight that met our eyes. Beside the table, on a wooden chair, sat Doctor Grimesby Rylott, clad in a long dressing-gown. His chin was cocked upward and his eyes were fixed in a dreadful, rigid stare at the corner of the ceiling. Round his brow he had a peculiar yellow band, with brownish speckles, which seemed to be bound tightly round his head.*

*I took a step forward. In an instant his strange head-gear began to move, and there reared itself from among his hair the squat, diamond-shaped head and puffed neck of a loathsome serpent...*

"Ugh!" said Squiffy.

He closed the book and put it down. His head was aching worse than ever. He wished now that he had read something else. No fellow could read himself to sleep with this sort of thing. People ought not to write this sort of thing.

His heart gave a bound. There it was again, that hissing sound. And this time he was sure it came from the window.

He looked at the window, and remained staring, frozen. Over the sill, with a graceful, leisurely movement, a green snake was crawling. As it crawled, it raised its head and peered from side to side, like a shortsighted man looking for his spectacles. It hesitated a moment on the edge of the sill, then wriggled to the floor and began to cross the room. Squiffy stared on.

It would have pained Peter deeply, for he was a snake of great sensibility, if he had known how much his entrance had disturbed the occupant of the room. He himself had no feeling but gratitude for the man who had opened the window and so enabled him to get in out of the rather nippy night air. Ever since the bag had swung open and shot him out onto the sill of the window below Archie's, he had been waiting patiently for something of the kind to happen. He was a snake who took things as they came, and was prepared to rough it a bit if necessary; but for the last hour or two he had been hoping that somebody would do something practical in the way of getting him in out of the cold. When at home, he had an eiderdown quilt to sleep on, and the stone of the window-sill was a little trying to a snake of regular habits. He crawled thankfully across the floor under Squiffy's bed. There was a pair of trousers there, for his host had undressed when not in a frame of mind to fold his clothes neatly and place them upon a chair. Peter looked the trousers over. They were not an eiderdown quilt, but they would serve. He curled up in them and went to sleep. He had had an exciting day, and was glad to turn in.

After about ten minutes, the tension of Squiffy's attitude relaxed. His heart, which had seemed to suspend its operations, began beating again. Reason reasserted itself. He peeped cautiously under the bed. He could see nothing.

Squiffy was convinced. He told himself that he had never really believed in Peter as a living thing. It stood to reason that there couldn't really be a snake in his room. The window looked out on emptiness. His room was several stories above the ground. There was a stern, set expression on Squiffy's face as he climbed out of bed. It was the expression of a man who is turning over a new leaf, starting a new life. He looked about the room for some implement which would carry out the deed he had to do, and finally pulled out one of the curtain-rods. Using this as a lever, he broke open the topmost of the six cases which stood in the corner. The soft wood cracked and split. Squiffy drew out a straw-covered bottle. For a moment he stood looking at it, as a man might gaze at a friend on the point of death. Then, with a sudden determination, he went into the bathroom. There was a crash of glass and a gurgling sound.

Half an hour later the telephone in Archie's room rang. "I say, Archie, old top," said the voice of Squiffy.

"Halloa, old bean! Is that you?"

"I say, could you pop down here for a second? I'm rather upset."

"Absolutely! Which room?"

"Four-forty-one."

"I'll be with you eftsoons or right speedily."

"Thanks, old man."

"What appears to be the difficulty?"

"Well, as a matter of fact, I thought I saw a snake!"

"A snake!"

"I'll tell you all about it when you come down."

Archie found Lord Seacliff seated on his bed. An arresting aroma of mixed drinks pervaded the atmosphere.

"I say! What?" said Archie, inhaling.

"That's all right. I've been pouring my stock away. Just finished the last bottle."

"But why?"

"I told you. I thought I saw a snake!"

"Green?"

Squiffy shivered slightly.

"Frightfully green!"

Archie hesitated. He perceived that there are moments when silence is the best policy. He had been worrying himself over the unfortunate case of his friend, and now that Fate seemed to have provided a solution, it would be rash to interfere merely to ease the old bean's mind. If Squiffy was going to reform because he thought he had seen an imaginary snake, better not to let him know that the snake was a real one.

"Dashed serious!" he said.

"Bally dashed serious!" agreed Squiffy. "I'm going to cut it out!"

"Great scheme!"

"You don't think," asked Squiffy, with a touch of hopefulness, "that it could have been a real snake?"

"Never heard of the management supplying them."

"I thought it went under the bed."

"Well, take a look."

Squiffy shuddered.

"Not me! I say, old top, you know, I simply can't sleep in this room now. I was wondering if you could give me a doss somewhere in yours."

"Rather! I'm in five-forty-one. Just above. Trot along up. Here's the key. I'll tidy up a bit here, and join you in a minute."

Squiffy put on a dressing-gown and disappeared. Archie looked under the bed. From the trousers the head of Peter popped up with its usual expression of amiable enquiry. Archie nodded pleasantly, and sat down on the bed. The problem of his little friend's immediate future wanted thinking over.

He lit a cigarette and remained for a while in thought. Then he rose. An admirable solution had presented itself. He picked Peter up and placed him in the pocket of his dressing-gown. Then, leaving the room, he mounted the stairs till he reached the seventh floor. Outside a room half-way down the corridor he paused.

From within, through the open transom, came the rhythmical snoring of a good man taking his rest after the labors of the day. Mr. Brewster was always a heavy sleeper.

"There's always a way," thought Archie, philosophically, "if a chappie only thinks of it."

His father-in-law's snoring took on a deeper note. Archie extracted Peter from his pocket and dropped him gently through the transom.

# Washy Makes His Presence Felt

THE LOBBY OF THE Cosmopolis Hotel was a favorite stamping-ground of Mr. Daniel Brewster, its proprietor. He liked to wander about there, keeping a paternal eye on things, rather in the manner of the Jolly Innkeeper (hereinafter to be referred to as Mine Host) of the old-fashioned novel. Customers who, hurrying in to dinner, tripped over Mr. Brewster, were apt to mistake him for the hotel detective — for his eye was keen and his aspect a trifle austere — but, nevertheless, he was being as jolly an innkeeper as he knew how. His presence in the lobby supplied a personal touch to the Cosmopolis which other New York hotels lacked, and it undeniably made the girl at the book-stall extraordinarily civil to her clients, which was all to the good.

Most of the time Mr. Brewster stood in one spot and just looked thoughtful; but now and again he would wander to the marble slab behind which he kept the desk-clerk and run his eye over the register, to see who had booked rooms — like a child examining the stocking on Christmas morning to ascertain what Santa Claus had brought him.

As a rule, Mr. Brewster concluded this performance by shoving the book back across the marble slab and resuming his meditations. But one night a week or two after the Sausage Chappie's sudden restoration to the normal, he varied this procedure by starting rather violently, turning purple, and uttering an exclamation which was manifestly an exclamation of chagrin. He turned abruptly and cannoned into Archie, who, in company with Lucille, happened to be crossing the lobby at the moment on his way to dine in their suite.

Mr. Brewster apologized gruffly; then, recognizing his victim, seemed to regret having done so.

"Oh, it's you! Why can't you look where you're going?" he demanded. He had suffered much from his son-in-law.

"Frightfully sorry," said Archie, amiably. "Never thought you were going to fox-trot backwards all over the fairway."

"You mustn't bully Archie," said Lucille, severely, attaching herself to her father's back hair and giving it a punitive tug, "because he's an angel, and I love him, and you must learn to love him, too."

"Give you lessons at a reasonable rate," murmured Archie.

Mr. Brewster regarded his young relative with a lowering eye.

"What's the matter, father darling?" asked Lucille. "You seem upset"

"I am upset!" Mr. Brewster snorted. "Some people have got a nerve!" He glowered forbiddingly at an inoffensive young man in a light overcoat who had just entered, and the young man, though his conscience was quite clear and Mr. Brewster an entire stranger to him, stopped dead, blushed, and went out again—to dine elsewhere. "Some people have got the nerve of an army mule!"

"Why, what's happened?"

"Those darned McCalls have registered here!"

"No!"

"Bit beyond me, this," said Archie, insinuating himself into the conversation. "Deep waters and what not! Who are the McCalls?"

"Some people father dislikes," said Lucille. "And they've chosen his hotel to stop at. But, father dear, you mustn't mind. It's really a compliment. They've come because they know it's the best hotel in New York."

"Absolutely!" said Archie. "Good accommodation for man and beast! All the comforts of home! Look on the bright side, old bean. No good getting the wind up. Cheerio, old companion!"

"Don't call me old companion!"

"Eh, what? Oh, right-o!"

Lucille steered her husband out of the danger zone, and they entered the lift.

"Poor father!" she said, as they went to their suite, "it's a shame. They must have done it to annoy him. This man McCall has a place next to some property father bought in Westchester, and he's bringing a law-suit against father about a bit of land which he claims belongs to him. He might have had the tact to go to another hotel. But, after all, I don't suppose it was the poor little fellow's fault. He does whatever his wife tells him to."

"We all do that," said Archie the married man.

Lucille eyed him fondly.

"Isn't it a shame, precious, that all husbands haven't nice wives like me?"

"When I think of you, by Jove," said Archie, fervently, "I want to babble, absolutely babble!"

"Oh, I was telling you about the McCalls. Mr. McCall is one of those little, meek men, and his wife's one of those big, bullying women. It was she who started all the trouble with father. Father and Mr. McCall were very fond of each other till she made him begin the suit. I feel sure she made him come to this hotel just to annoy father. Still, they've probably taken the most expensive suite in the place, which is something."

Archie was at the telephone. His mood was now one of quiet peace. Of all the happenings which went to make up existence in New York, he liked best the cozy *tete-a-tete* dinners with Lucille in their suite, which, owing to their engagements—for Lucille was a popular girl, with many friends—occurred all too seldom.

"Touching now the question of browsing and sluicing," he said. "I'll be getting them to send along a waiter."

"Oh, good gracious!"

"What's the matter?"

"I've just remembered. I promised faithfully I would go and see Jane Murchison today. And I clean forgot. I must rush."

"But light of my soul, we are about to eat. Pop around and see her after dinner."

"I can't. She's going to a theatre tonight."

"Give her the jolly old miss-in-baulk, then, for the nonce, and spring round tomorrow."

"She's sailing for England tomorrow morning, early. No, I must go and see her now. What a shame! She's sure to make me stop to dinner, I tell you what. Order something for me, and, if I'm not back in half an hour, start."

"Jane Murchison," said Archie, "is a bally nuisance."

"Yes. But I've known her since she was eight."

"If her parents had had any proper feeling," said Archie, "they would have drowned her long before that."

He unhooked the receiver, and asked despondently to be connected with Room Service. He thought bitterly of the exigent Jane, whom he recollected dimly as a tall female with teeth. He half thought of going down to the grill-room on the chance of finding a friend there, but the waiter was on his way to the room. He decided that he might as well stay where he was.

The waiter arrived, booked the order, and departed. Archie had just completed his toilet after a shower-bath when a musical clinking without announced the advent of the meal. He opened the door. The waiter was there with a table congested with things under covers, from which escaped a savory and appetizing odor. In spite of his depression, Archie's soul perked up a trifle.

Suddenly he became aware that he was not the only person present who was deriving enjoyment from the scent of the meal. Standing beside the waiter and gazing wistfully at the foodstuffs was a long, thin boy of about sixteen. He was one of those boys who seem all legs and knuckles. He had pale red hair, sandy eyelashes, and a long neck; and his eyes, as he removed them from the table and raised them to Archie's, had a hungry look. He reminded Archie of a half-grown, half-starved hound.

"That smells good!" said the long boy. He inhaled deeply. "Yes, sir," he continued, as one whose mind is definitely made up, "that smells good!"

Before Archie could reply, the telephone bell rang. It was Lucille, confirming her prophecy that the pest Jane would insist on her staying to dine.

"Jane," said Archie, into the telephone, "is a pot of poison. The waiter is here now, setting out a rich banquet, and I shall have to eat two of everything by myself."

He hung up the receiver, and, turning, met the pale eye of the long boy, who had propped himself up in the doorway.

"Were you expecting somebody to dinner?" asked the boy.

"Why, yes, old friend, I was."

"I wish—"

"Yes?"

"Oh, nothing."

The waiter left. The long boy hitched his back more firmly against the doorpost, and returned to his original theme.

"That surely does smell good!" He basked a moment in the aroma. "Yes, sir! I'll tell the world it does!"

Archie was not an abnormally rapid thinker, but he began at this point to get a clearly defined impression that this lad, if invited, would waive the formalities and consent to join his meal. Indeed, the idea Archie got was that, if he were not invited pretty soon, he would invite himself.

"Yes," he agreed. "It doesn't smell bad, what!"

"It smells *good*!" said the boy. "Oh, doesn't it! Wake me up in the night and ask me if it doesn't!"

"*Poulet en casserole*," said Archie.

"Golly!" said the boy, reverently.

There was a pause. The situation began to seem to Archie a trifle difficult. He wanted to start his meal, but it began to appear that he must either do so under the penetrating gaze of his new friend or else eject the latter forcibly. The boy showed no signs of ever wanting to leave the doorway.

"You've dined, I suppose, what?" said Archie.

"I never dine."

"What!"

"Not really dine, I mean. I only get vegetables and nuts and things."

"Dieting?"

"Mother is."

"I don't absolutely catch the drift, old bean," said Archie. The boy sniffed with half-closed eyes as a wave of perfume from the *poulet en casserole* floated past him. He seemed to be anxious to intercept as much of it as possible before it got through the door.

"Mother's a food-reformer," he vouchsafed. "She lectures on it. She makes Pop and me live on vegetables and nuts and things."

Archie was shocked. It was like listening to a tale from the abyss.

"My dear old chap, you must suffer agonies—absolute shooting pains!" He had no hesitation now. Common humanity pointed out his course. "Would you care to join me in a bite now?"

"Would I!" The boy smiled a wan smile. "Would I! Just stop me on the street and ask me!"

"Come on in, then," said Archie, rightly taking this peculiar phrase for a formal acceptance. "And close the door. The fatted calf is getting cold."

Archie was not a man with a wide visiting-list among people with families, and it was so long since he had seen a growing boy in action at the table that he had forgotten what sixteen is capable of doing with a knife and fork, when it really squares its elbows, takes a deep breath, and gets going. The spectacle which he witnessed was consequently at first a little unnerving. The long boy's idea of trifling with a meal appeared to be to swallow it whole and reach out for more. He ate like a starving Eskimo. Archie, in the time he had spent in the trenches making the world safe for the working-man to strike in, had occasionally been quite peckish, but he sat dazed before this majestic hunger. This was real eating.

There was little conversation. The growing boy evidently did not believe in table-talk when he could use his mouth for more practical purposes. It was not until the final roll had been devoured to its last crumb that the guest found leisure to address his host. Then he leaned back with a contented sigh.

"Mother," said the human python, "says you ought to chew every mouthful thirty-three times...."

"Yes, sir! Thirty-three times!" He sighed again, "I haven't ever had meal like that."

"All right, was it, what?"

"Was it! Was it! Call me up on the 'phone and ask me! — Yes, sir! — Mother's tipped off these darned waiters not to serve-me anything but vegetables and nuts and things, darn it!"

"The mater seems to have drastic ideas about the good old feed-bag, what!"

"I'll say she has! Pop hates it as much as me, but he's scared to kick. Mother says vegetables contain all the proteins you want. Mother says, if you eat meat, your blood-pressure goes all blooey. Do you think it does?"

"Mine seems pretty well in the pink."

"She's great on talking," conceded the boy. "She's out tonight somewhere, giving a lecture on Rational Eating to some ginks. I'll have to be slipping up to our suite before she gets back." He rose, sluggishly. "That isn't a bit of roll under that napkin, is it?" he asked, anxiously.

Archie raised the napkin.

"No. Nothing of that species."

"Oh, well!" said the boy, resignedly. "Then I believe I'll be going. Thanks very much for the dinner."

"Not a bit, old top. Come again if you're ever trickling round in this direction."

The long boy removed himself slowly, loath to leave. At the door he cast an affectionate glance back at the table.

"Some meal!" he said, devoutly. "Considerable meal!"

Archie lit a cigarette. He felt like a Boy Scout who has done his day's Act of Kindness.

On the following morning it chanced that Archie needed a fresh supply of tobacco. It was his custom, when this happened, to repair to a small shop on Sixth Avenue which he had discovered accidentally in the course of his rambles about the great city. His relations with Jno. Blake, the proprietor, were friendly and intimate. The discovery that Mr. Blake was English and had, indeed, until a few years back maintained an establishment only a dozen doors or so from Archie's London club, had served as a bond.

Today he found Mr. Blake in a depressed mood. The tobacconist was a hearty, red-faced man, who looked like an English sporting publican—the kind of man who wears a fawn-colored top-coat and drives to the Derby in a dog-cart; and usually there seemed to be nothing on his mind except the vagaries of the weather, concerning which he was a great conversationalist. But now moodiness had claimed him for its own. After a short and melancholy "Good morning," he turned to the task of measuring out the tobacco in silence.

Archie's sympathetic nature was perturbed. "What's the matter, laddie?" he enquired. "You would seem to be feeling a bit of an onion this bright morning, what, yes, no? I can see it with the naked eye."

Mr. Blake grunted sorrowfully.

"I've had a knock, Mr. Moffam."

"Tell me all, friend of my youth."

Mr. Blake, with a jerk of his thumb, indicated a poster which hung on the wall behind the counter. Archie had noticed it as he came in, for it was designed to attract the eye. It was printed in black letters on a yellow ground, and ran as follows:

CLOVER-LEAF SOCIAL AND OUTING CLUB

GRAND CONTEST

PIE-EATING CHAMPIONSHIP OF THE WEST SIDE

SPIKE O'DOWD
(Champion)

vs.

BLAKE'S UNKNOWN

FOR A PURSE OF $50 AND SIDE-BET

Archie examined this document gravely. It conveyed nothing to him except—what he had long suspected—that his sporting-looking friend had sporting blood as well as that kind of exterior. He expressed a kindly hope that the other's Unknown would bring home the bacon.

Mr. Blake laughed one of those hollow, mirthless laughs.

"There ain't any blooming Unknown," he said, bitterly. This man had plainly suffered. "Yesterday, yes, but not now."

Archie sighed.

"In the midst of life—Dead?" he enquired, delicately.

"As good as," replied the stricken tobacconist. He cast aside his artificial restraint and became voluble. Archie was one of those sympathetic souls in whom even strangers readily confided their most intimate troubles. He was to those in travail of spirit very much what catnip is to a cat. "It's 'ard, sir, it's blooming 'ard! I'd got the event all sewed up in a parcel, and now this young feller-me-lad 'as to give me the knock. This lad of mine—sort of cousin 'e is; comes from London, like you and me—'as always 'ad, ever since he landed in this country, a most amazing knack of stowing away grub. 'E'd been a bit underfed these last two or three years over in the old country, what with food restrictions and all, and 'e took to the food over 'ere amazing. I'd 'ave backed 'im against a ruddy orstridge! Orstridge! I'd 'ave backed 'im against 'arff a dozen orstridges—take 'em on one after the other in the same ring on the same evening—and given 'em a handicap, too! 'E was a jewel, that boy. I've seen him polish off four pounds of steak and mealy potatoes and then look round kind of wolfish, as much as to ask when dinner was going to begin! That's the kind of a lad 'e was till this very morning. 'E would have out-swallowed this 'ere O'Dowd without turning a hair, as a relish before 'is tea! I'd got a couple of 'undred dollars on 'im, and thought myself lucky to get the odds. And now—"

Mr. Blake relapsed into a tortured silence.

"But what's the matter with the blighter? Why can't he go over the top? Has he got indigestion?"

"Indigestion?" Mr. Blaife laughed another of his hollow laughs. "You couldn't give that boy indigestion if you fed 'im in on safety-razor blades. Religion's more like what 'e's got."

"Religion?"

"Well, you can call it that. Seems last night, instead of goin' and resting 'is mind at a picture-palace like I told him to, 'e sneaked off to some sort of a lecture down on Eighth Avenue. 'E said 'e'd seen a piece about it in the papers, and it was about Rational Eating, and that kind of attracted 'im. 'E sort of thought 'e might pick up a few hints, like. 'E didn't know what rational eating was, but it sounded to 'im as if it must be something to do with food, and 'e didn't want to miss it. 'E came in here just now," said Mr. Blake, dully, "and 'e was a changed lad! Scared to death 'e was! Said the way 'e'd been goin' on in the past, it was a wonder 'e'd got any stummick left! It was a lady that give the lecture, and this boy said it was amazing what she told 'em about blood-pressure and things 'e didn't even know 'e 'ad. She showed 'em pictures, coloured pictures, of what 'appens inside the injudicious eater's stummick who doesn't chew his food, and it was like a battlefield! 'E said 'e would no more think of eatin' a lot of pie than 'e would of shootin' 'imself, and anyhow eating pie would be a quicker death. I reasoned with 'im, Mr. Moffam, with tears in my eyes. I asked 'im was he goin' to chuck away fame and wealth just because a woman who didn't know what she was talking about had shown him a lot of faked pictures. But there wasn't any doin' anything with him. 'E give me the knock and 'opped it down the street to buy nuts." Mr. Blake moaned. "Two 'undred dollars and more gone pop, not to talk of the fifty dollars 'e would have won and me to get twenty-five of!"

Archie took his tobacco and walked pensively back to the hotel. He was fond of Jno. Blake, and grieved for the trouble that had come upon him. It was odd, he felt, how things seemed to link themselves up together. The woman who had delivered the fateful lecture to injudicious eaters could not be other than the mother of his young guest of last night. An uncomfortable woman! Not content with starving her own family — Archie stopped in his tracks. A pedestrian, walking behind him, charged into his back, but Archie paid no attention. He had had one of those sudden, luminous ideas, which help a man who does not do much thinking as a rule to restore his average. He stood there for a moment, almost dizzy at the brilliance of his thoughts; then hurried on. Napoleon, he mused as he walked, must have felt rather like this after thinking up a hot one to spring on the enemy.

As if Destiny were suiting her plans to his, one of the first persons he saw as he entered the lobby of the Cosmopolis was the long boy. He was standing at the bookstall, reading as much of a morning paper as could be read free under the vigilant eyes of the presiding girl. Both he and she were observing the unwritten rules which govern these affairs—to wit, that you may read without interference as much as can be read without touching the paper. If you touch the paper, you lose, and have to buy.

"Well, well, well!" said Archie. "Here we are again, what!" He prodded the boy amiably in the lower ribs. "You're just the chap I was looking for. Got anything on for the time being?"

The boy said he had no engagements.

"Then I want you to stagger round with me to a chappie I know on Sixth Avenue. It's only a couple of blocks away. I think I can do you a bit of good. Put you on to something tolerably ripe, if you know what I mean. Trickle along, laddie. You don't need a hat."

They found Mr. Blake brooding over his troubles in an empty shop.

"Cheer up, old thing!" said Archie. "The relief expedition has arrived." He directed his companion's gaze to the poster. "Cast your eye over that. How does that strike you?"

The long boy scanned the poster. A gleam appeared in his rather dull eye.

"Well?"

"Some people have all the luck!" said the long boy, feelingly.

"Would you like to compete, what?"

The boy smiled a sad smile.

"Would I! Would I! Say! ..."

"I know," interrupted Archie. "Wake you up in the night and ask you! I knew I could rely on you, old thing." He turned to Mr. Blake. "Here's the fellow you've been wanting to meet. The finest left-and-right-hand eater east of the Rockies! He'll fight the good fight for you."

Mr. Blake's English training had not been wholly over-come by residence in New York. He still retained a nice eye for the distinctions of class.

"But this is young gentleman's a young gentleman," he urged, doubtfully, yet with hope shining in his eye. "He wouldn't do it."

"Of course, he would. Don't be ridic, old thing."

"Wouldn't do what?" asked the boy.

"Why save the old homestead by taking on the champion. Dashed sad case, between ourselves! This poor egg's nominee has given him the raspberry at the eleventh hour, and only you can save him. And you owe it to him to do something you know, because it was your jolly old mater's lecture last night that made the nominee quit. You must charge in and take his place. Sort of poetic justice, don't you know, and what not!" He turned to Mr. Blake. "When is the conflict supposed to start? Two-thirty? You haven't any important engagement for two-thirty, have you?"

"No. Mother's lunching at some ladies' club, and giving a lecture afterwards. I can slip away."

Archie patted his head.

"Then leg it where glory waits you, old bean!"

The long boy was gazing earnestly at the poster. It seemed to fascinate him.

"Pie!" he said in a hushed voice.

The word was like a battle-cry.

AT ABOUT NINE O'CLOCK next morning, in a suite at the Hotel Cosmopolis, Mrs. Cora Bates McCall, the eminent lecturer on Rational Eating, was seated at breakfast with

her family. Before her sat Mr. McCall, a little hunted-look-
ing man, the natural peculiarities of whose face were ac-
centuated by a pair of glasses of semicircular shape, like
half-moons with the horns turned up. Behind these, Mr.
McCall's eyes played a perpetual game of peekaboo, now
peering over them, anon ducking down and hiding behind them. He was sipping a cup of anti-caffeine. On his
right, toying listlessly with a plateful of cereal, sat his son,
Washington. Mrs. McCall herself was eating a slice of
Health Bread and nut butter. For she practiced as well as
preached the doctrines which she had striven for so many
years to inculcate in an unthinking populace. Her day always began with a light but nutritious breakfast, at which
a peculiarly uninviting cereal, which looked and tasted
like an old straw hat that had been run through a meat
chopper, competed for first place in the dislike of her husband and son with a more than usually offensive brand of
imitation coffee. Mr. McCall was inclined to think that he
loathed the imitation coffee rather more than the cereal,
but Washington held strong views on the latter's superior
ghastliness. Both Washington and his father, however,
would have been fair-minded enough to admit that it was
a close thing.

Mrs. McCall regarded her offspring with grave approval.

"I am glad to see, Lindsay," she said to her husband,
whose eyes sprang dutifully over the glass fence as he
heard his name, "that Washy has recovered his appetite.
When he refused his dinner last night, I was afraid that he
might be sickening for something. Especially as he had
quite a flushed look. You noticed his flushed look?"

"He did look flushed."

"Very flushed. And his breathing was almost stertorous. And, when he said that he had no appetite, I am bound to say that I was anxious. But he is evidently perfectly well this morning. You do feel perfectly well this morning, Washy?"

The heir of the McCall's looked up from his cereal. He was a long, thin boy of about sixteen, with pale red hair, sandy eyelashes, and a long neck.

"Uh-huh," he said.

Mrs. McCall nodded.

"Surely now you will agree, Lindsay, that a careful and rational diet is what a boy needs? Washy's constitution is superb. He has a remarkable stamina, and I attribute it entirely to my careful supervision of his food. I shudder when I think of the growing boys who are permitted by irresponsible people to devour meat, candy, pie—" She broke off. "What is the matter, Washy?"

It seemed that the habit of shuddering at the thought of pie ran in the McCall family, for at the mention of the word a kind of internal shimmy had convulsed Washington's lean frame, and over his face there had come an expression that was almost one of pain. He had been reaching out his hand for a slice of Health Bread, but now he withdrew it rather hurriedly and sat back breathing hard.

"I'm all right," he said, huskily.

"Pie," proceeded Mrs. McCall, in her platform voice. She stopped again abruptly. "Whatever is the matter, Washington? You are making me feel nervous."

"I'm all right."

Mrs. McCall had lost the thread of her remarks. Moreover, having now finished her breakfast, she was inclined for a little light reading. One of the subjects allied to the matter of dietary on which she felt deeply was the question of reading at meals. She was of the opinion that the strain on the eye, coinciding with the strain on the digestion, could not fail to give the latter the short end of the contest; and it was a rule at her table that the morning paper should not even be glanced at till the conclusion of the meal. She said that it was upsetting to begin the day by reading the paper, and events were to prove that she was occasionally right.

All through breakfast the New York Chronicle had been lying neatly folded beside her plate. She now opened it, and, with a remark about looking for the report of her yesterday's lecture at the Butterfly Club, directed her gaze at the front page, on which she hoped that an editor with the best interests of the public at heart had decided to place her.

Mr. McCall, jumping up and down behind his glasses, scrutinized her face closely as she began to read. He always did this on these occasions, for none knew better than he that his comfort for the day depended largely on some unknown reporter whom he had never met. If this unseen individual had done his work properly and as befitted the importance of his subject, Mrs. McCall's mood for the next twelve hours would be as uniformly sunny as it was possible for it to be. But sometimes the fellows scamped their job disgracefully; and once, on a day which lived in Mr. McCall's memory, they had failed to make a report at all.

Today, he noted with relief, all seemed to be well. The report actually was on the front page, an honor rarely accorded to his wife's utterances. Moreover, judging from the time it took her to read the thing, she had evidently been reported at length.

"Good, my dear?" he ventured. "Satisfactory?"

"Eh?" Mrs. McCall smiled meditatively. "Oh, yes, excellent. They have used my photograph, too. Not at all badly reproduced."

"Splendid!" said Mr. McCall.

Mrs. McCall gave a sharp shriek, and the paper fluttered from her hand.

"My dear!" said Mr. McCall, with concern.

His wife had recovered the paper, and was reading with burning eyes. A bright wave of color had flowed over her masterful features. She was breathing as stertorously as ever her son Washington had done on the previous night.

"Washington!"

A basilisk glare shot across the table and turned the long boy to stone—all except his mouth, which opened feebly.

"Washington! Is this true?"

Washy closed his mouth, then let it slowly open again.

"My dear!" Mr. McCall's voice was alarmed. "What is it?" His eyes had climbed up over his glasses and remained there. "What is the matter? Is anything wrong?"

"Wrong! Read for yourself!"

Mr. McCall was completely mystified. He could not even formulate a guess at the cause of the trouble. That it appeared to concern his son Washington seemed to be the one solid fact at his disposal, and that only made the matter still more puzzling. Where, Mr. McCall asked himself, did Washington come in?

He looked at the paper, and received immediate enlightenment. Headlines met his eyes:

GOOD STUFF IN THIS BOY.
ABOUT A TON OF IT.

SON OF CORA BATES McCALL
FAMOUS FOOD-REFORM LECTURER
WINS PIE-EATING CHAMPIONSHIP OF
WEST SIDE.

There followed a lyrical outburst. So uplifted had the reporter evidently felt by the importance of his news that he had been unable to confine himself to prose:

*My children, if you fail to shine or triumph in your special line; if, let us say, your hopes are bent on some day being President, and folks ignore your proper worth, and say you've not a chance on earth—Cheer up! for in these stirring days Fame may be won in many ways. Consider, when your spirits fall, the case of Washington McCall.*

*Yes, cast your eye on Washy, please! He looks just like a piece of cheese: he's not a brilliant sort of chap: he has a dull and vacant map: his eyes are blank, his face is red, his ears stick out beside his head. In fact, to end these compliments, he would be dear at thirty cents. Yet Fame has welcomed to her Hall this self-same Washington McCall.*

*His mother (née Miss Cora Bates) is one who frequently orates upon the proper kind of food which every menu should include. With eloquence the world she weans from chops and steaks and pork and beans. Such horrid things she'd like to crush, and make us live on milk and mush. But oh! the thing that makes her sigh is when she sees us eating pie. (We heard her lecture last July upon "The Nation's Menace—Pie.") Alas, the hit it made was small with Master Washington McCall.*

*For yesterday we took a trip to see the great Pie Championship, where men with bulging cheeks and eyes consume vast quantities of pies. A fashionable West Side crowd beheld the champion, Spike O'Dowd, endeavour to defend his throne against an upstart, Blake's Unknown. He wasn't an Unknown at all. He was young Washington McCall.*

*We freely own we'd give a leg if we could borrow, steal, or beg the skill old Homer used to show. (He wrote the Iliad, you know.) Old Homer swung a wicked pen, but we are ordinary men, and cannot even start to dream of doing justice to our theme. The subject of that great repast is too magnificent and vast. We can't describe (or even try) the way those rivals wolfed their pie. Enough to say that, when for hours each had extended all his pow'rs, toward the quiet evenfall O'Dowd succumbed to young McCall.*

*The champion was a willing lad. He gave the public all he had. His was a genuine fighting soul. He'd lots of speed and much control. No yellow streak did he evince. He tackled applepie and mince. This was the motto on his shield—"O'Dowds may burst. They never yield." His eyes began to start and roll. He eased his belt another hole. Poor fellow! With a single glance one saw that he had not a chance. A python would have had to crawl and own defeat from young McCall.*

*At last, long last, the finish came. His features overcast with shame, O'Dowd, who'd faltered once or twice, declined to eat another slice. He tottered off, and kindly men rallied around with oxygen. But Washy, Cora Bates's son, seemed disappointed it was done. He somehow made those present feel he'd barely started on his meal. We ask him, "Aren't you feeling bad?" "Me!" said the lion-hearted lad. "Lead me"—he started for the street — "where I can get a bite to eat!" Oh, what a lesson does it teach to all of us, that splendid speech! How better can the curtain fall on Master Washington McCall!*

Mr. McCall read this epic through, then he looked at his son. He first looked at him over his glasses, then through his glasses, then over his glasses again, then through his glasses once more. A curious expression was in his eyes. If such a thing had not been so impossible, one would have said that his gaze had in it something of respect, of admiration, even of reverence.

"But how did they find out your name?" he asked, at length.

Mrs. McCall exclaimed impatiently.

"Is *that* all you have to say?"

"No, no, my dear, of course not, quite so. But the point struck me as curious."

"Wretched boy," cried Mrs. McCall, "were you insane enough to reveal your name?"

Washington wriggled uneasily. Unable to endure the piercing stare of his mother, he had withdrawn to the window, and was looking out with his back turned. But even there he could feel her eyes on the back of his neck.

"I didn't think it 'ud matter," he mumbled. "A fellow with tortoiseshell-rimmed specs asked me, so I told him. How was I to know —"

His stumbling defense was cut short by the opening of the door.

"Hallo-allo-allo! What ho! What ho!"

Archie was standing in the doorway, beaming ingratiatingly on the family.

The apparition of an entire stranger served to divert the lightning of Mrs. McCall's gaze from the unfortunate

Washy. Archie, catching it between the eyes, blinked and held on to the wall. He had begun to regret that he had yielded so weakly to Lucille's entreaty that he should look in on the McCalls and use the magnetism of his personality upon them in the hope of inducing them to settle the lawsuit. He wished, too, if the visit had to be paid that he had postponed it till after lunch, for he was never at his strongest in the morning. But Lucille had urged him to go now and get it over, and here he was.

"I think," said Mrs. McCall, icily, "that you must have mistaken your room."

Archie rallied his shaken forces.

"Oh, no. Rather not. Better introduce myself, what? My name's Moffam, you know. I'm old Brewster's son-in-law, and all that sort of rot, if you know what I mean." He gulped and continued. "I've come about this jolly old lawsuit, don't you know."

Mr. McCall seemed about to speak, but his wife anticipated him.

"Mr. Brewster's attorneys are in communication with ours. We do not wish to discuss the matter."

Archie took an uninvited seat, eyed the Health Bread on the breakfast table for a moment with frank curiosity, and resumed his discourse.

"No, but I say, you know! I'll tell you what happened. I hate to totter in where I'm not wanted and all that, but my wife made such a point of it. Rightly or wrongly she regards me as a bit of a hound in the diplomacy line, and she begged me to look you up and see whether we couldn't do something about settling the jolly old thing. I mean to say, you know, the old bird—old Brewster, you know—is considerably perturbed about the affair—hates the thought of being in a posish where he has either got to bite his old pal McCall in the neck or be bitten by him — and — well, and so forth, don't you know! How about it?" He broke off. "Great Scot! I say, what!"

So engrossed had he been in his appeal that he had not observed the presence of the pie-eating champion, between whom and himself a large potted plant intervened. But now Washington, hearing the familiar voice, had moved from the window and was confronting him with an accusing stare.

"*He* made me do it!" said Washy, with the stern joy a sixteen-year-old boy feels when he sees somebody on to whose shoulders he can shift trouble from his own. "That's the fellow who took me to the place!"

"What are you talking about, Washington?"

"I'm telling you! He got me into the thing."

"Do you mean this — this —" Mrs. McCall shuddered. "Are you referring to this pie-eating contest?"

"You bet I am!"

"Is this true?" Mrs. McCall glared stonily at Archie, "Was it you who lured my poor boy into that — that —"

"Oh, absolutely. The fact is, don't you know, a dear old pal of mine who runs a tobacco shop on Sixth Avenue was rather in the soup. He had backed a chappie against the champion, and the chappie was converted by one of your lectures and swore off pie at the eleventh hour. Dashed hard luck on the poor chap, don't you know! And then I got the idea that our little friend here was the one to step in and save the situash, so I broached the matter to him. And I'll tell you one thing," said Archie, handsomely, "I don't know what sort of a capacity the original chappie had, but I'll bet he wasn't in your son's class. Your son has to be seen to be believed! Absolutely! You ought to be proud of him!" He turned in friendly fashion to Washy. "Rummy we should meet again like this! Never dreamed I should find you here. And, by Jove, it's absolutely marvellous how fit you look after yesterday. I had a sort of idea you would be groaning on a bed of sickness and all that."

There was a strange gurgling sound in the background. It resembled something getting up steam. And this, curiously enough, is precisely what it was. The thing that was getting up steam was Mr. Lindsay McCall.

The first effect of the Washy revelations on Mr. McCall had been merely to stun him. It was not until the arrival of Archie that he had had leisure to think; but since Archie's entrance he had been thinking rapidly and deeply.

For many years Mr. McCall had been in a state of suppressed revolution. He had smoldered, but had not dared to blaze. But this startling upheaval of his fellow-sufferer, Washy, had acted upon him like a high explosive. There was a strange gleam in his eye, a gleam of determination. He was breathing hard.

"Washy!"

His voice had lost its deprecating mildness. It rang strong and clear.

"Yes, pop?"

"How many pies did you eat yesterday?"

Washy considered.

"A good few."

"How many? Twenty?"

"More than that. I lost count. A good few."

"And you feel as well as ever?"

"I feel fine."

Mr. McCall dropped his glasses. He glowered for a moment at the breakfast table. His eye took in the Health Bread, the imitation coffee-pot, the cereal, the nut-butter. Then with a swift movement he seized the cloth, jerked it forcibly, and brought the entire contents rattling and crashing to the floor.

"Lindsay!"

Mr. McCall met his wife's eye with quiet determination. It was plain that something had happened in the hinterland of Mr. McCall's soul.

"Cora," he said, resolutely, "I have come to a decision. I've been letting you run things your own way a little too long in this family. I'm going to assert myself. For one thing, I've had all I want of this food-reform foolery. Look at Washy! Yesterday that boy seems to have consumed anything from a couple of hundredweight to a ton of pie, and he has thriven on it! Thriven! I don't want to hurt your feelings, Cora, but Washington and I have drunk our last cup of anti-caffeine! If you care to go on with the stuff, that's your look-out. But Washy and I are through."

He silenced his wife with a masterful gesture and turned to Archie. "And there's another thing. I never liked the idea of that lawsuit, but I let you talk me into it. Now I'm going to do things my way. Mr. Moffam, I'm glad you looked in this morning. I'll do just what you want. Take me to Dan Brewster now, and let's call the thing off, and shake hands on it."

"Are you mad, Lindsay?"

It was Cora Bates McCall's last shot. Mr. McCall paid no attention to it. He was shaking hands with Archie.

"I consider you, Mr. Moffam," he said, "the most sensible young man I have ever met!"

Archie blushed modestly.

"Awfully good of you, old bean," he said. "I wonder if you'd mind telling my jolly old father-in-law that? It'll be a bit of news for him!

# The Oldest Member

AFTER THE ARCHIE MOFFAM stories, Wodehouse wrote several tales centering on golf. These are narrated by the "Oldest Member" of a fictional club, mostly to pass on his wisdom to younger golfers.

If Archie resembles Reggie Pepper and Bertie Wooster, the Oldest Member recalls Jeeves. Though the golf stories are not as well known as many of Wodehouse's other series, they are among his funniest works.

Wodehouse wrote twenty-five Oldest Member stories. All but two are collected in *The Clicking of Cuthbert* (1922), *The Heart of a Goof* (1926), and *Nothing Serious* (1950).

# The Clicking of Cuthbert

THE YOUNG MAN CAME into the smoking-room of the club-house and flung his bag with a clatter on the floor. He sank moodily into an arm-chair and pressed the bell.

"Waiter!"

"Sir?"

The young man pointed at the bag with every evidence of distaste.

"You may have these clubs," he said. "Take them away. If you don't want them yourself, give them to one of the caddies."

Across the room the Oldest Member gazed at him with a grave sadness through the smoke of his pipe. His eye was deep and dreamy—the eye of a man who, as the poet says, has seen Golf steadily and seen it whole.

"You are giving up golf?" he said.

He was not altogether unprepared for such an attitude on the young man's part: for from his eyrie on the terrace above the ninth green he had observed him start out on the afternoon's round and had seen him lose a couple of balls in the lake at the second hole after taking seven strokes at the first.

"Yes!" cried the young man fiercely. "Forever, dam-mit! Footling game! Blanked infernal fat-headed silly ass of a game! Nothing but a waste of time."

The Sage winced.

"Don't say that, my boy."

"But I do say it. What earthly good is golf? Life is stern and life is earnest. We live in a practical age. All round us we see foreign competition making itself unpleasant. And we spend our time playing golf! What do we get out of it? Is golf any use? That's what I'm asking you. Can you name me a single case where devotion to this pestilential pastime has done a man any practical good?"

The Sage smiled gently.

"I could name a thousand."

"One will do."

"I will select," said the Sage, "from the innumerable memories that rush to my mind, the story of Cuthbert Banks."

"Never heard of him."

"Be of good cheer," said the Oldest Member. "You are going to hear of him now."

IT WAS IN THE PICTURESQUE little settlement of Wood Hills (said the Oldest Member) that the incidents occurred which I am about to relate. Even if you have never been in Wood Hills, that suburban paradise is probably familiar to you by name. Situated at a convenient distance from the city, it combines in a notable manner the advantages of town life with the pleasant surroundings and healthful air of the country. Its inhabitants live in commodious houses, standing in their own grounds, and enjoy so many luxuries—such as gravel soil, main drainage, electric light, telephone, baths (h. and c.), and company's own water, that you might be pardoned for imagining life to be so ideal for them that no possible improvement could be added to their lot. Mrs. Willoughby Smethurst was under no such delusion. What Wood Hills needed to make it perfect, she realized, was Culture. Material comforts are all very well, but, if the *summum bonum* is to be achieved, the Soul also demands a look in, and it was Mrs. Smethurst's unfaltering resolve that never while she had her strength should the Soul be handed the loser's end. It was her intention to make Wood Hills a center of all that was most cultivated and refined, and, golly! how she had succeeded. Under her presidency the Wood Hills Literary and Debating Society had tripled its membership.

But there is always a fly in the ointment, a caterpillar in the salad. The local golf club, an institution to which Mrs. Smethurst strongly objected, had also tripled its membership; and the division of the community into two rival camps, the Golfers and the Cultured, had become more marked than ever. This division, always acute, had attained now to the dimensions of a Schism. The rival sects treated one another with a cold hostility.

Unfortunate episodes came to widen the breach. Mrs. Smethurst's house adjoined the links, standing to the right of the fourth tee: and, as the Literary Society was in the habit of entertaining visiting lecturers, many a golfer had foozled his drive owing to sudden loud outbursts of applause coinciding with his down-swing. And not long before this story opens a sliced ball, whizzing in at the open window, had come within an ace of incapacitating Raymond Parsloe Devine, the rising young novelist (who rose at that moment a clear foot and a half) from any further exercise of his art. Two inches, indeed, to the right and Raymond must inevitably have handed in his dinner-pail.

To make matters worse, a ring at the front-door bell followed almost immediately, and the maid ushered in a young man of pleasing appearance in a sweater and baggy knickerbockers who apologetically but firmly insisted on playing his ball where it lay, and, what with the shock of the lecturer's narrow escape and the spectacle of the intruder standing on the table and working away with a niblick, the afternoon's session had to be classed as a complete frost. Mr. Devine's determination, from which no argument could swerve him, to deliver the rest of his lecture in the coal-cellar gave the meeting a jolt from which it never recovered.

I have dwelt upon this incident, because it was the means of introducing Cuthbert Banks to Mrs. Smethurst's niece, Adeline. As Cuthbert, for it was he who had so nearly reduced the muster-roll of rising novelists by one, hopped down from the table after his stroke, he was suddenly aware that a beautiful girl was looking at him intently. As a matter of fact, everyone in the room was looking at him intently, none more so than Raymond Parsloe Devine, but none of the others were beautiful girls. Long as the members of Wood Hills Literary Society were on brain, they were short on looks, and, to Cuthbert's excited eye, Adeline Smethurst stood out like a jewel in a pile of coke.

He had never seen her before, for she had only arrived at her aunt's house on the previous day, but he was perfectly certain that life, even when lived in the midst of gravel soil, main drainage, and company's own water, was going to be a pretty poor affair if he did not see her again. Yes, Cuthbert was in love: and it is interesting to record, as showing the effect of the tender emotion on a man's game, that twenty minutes after he had met Adeline he did the short eleventh in one, and as near as a toucher got a three on the four-hundred-yard twelfth.

I will skip lightly over the intermediate stages of Cuthbert's courtship and come to the moment when—at the annual ball in aid of the local Cottage Hospital, the only occasion during the year on which the lion, so to speak, lay down with the lamb, and the Golfers and the Cultured met on terms of easy comradeship, their differences temporarily laid aside—he proposed to Adeline and was badly stymied.

That fair, soulful girl could not see him with a spyglass.

"Mr. Banks," she said, "I will speak frankly."

"Charge right ahead," assented Cuthbert.

"Deeply sensible as I am of—"

"I know. Of the honor and the compliment and all that. But, passing lightly over all that guff, what seems to be the trouble? I love you to distraction—"

"Love is not everything."

"You're wrong," said Cuthbert, earnestly. "You're right off it. Love—" And he was about to dilate on the theme when she interrupted him.

"I am a girl of ambition."

"And very nice, too," said Cuthbert.

"I am a girl of ambition," repeated Adeline, "and I realize that the fulfilment of my ambitions must come through my husband. I am very ordinary myself—"

"What!" cried Cuthbert. "You ordinary? Why, you are a pearl among women, the queen of your sex. You can't have been looking in a glass lately. You stand alone.

Simply alone. You make the rest look like battered re-paints."

"Well," said Adeline, softening a trifle, "I believe I am fairly good-looking—"

"Anybody who was content to call you fairly good-looking would describe the Taj Mahal as a pretty nifty tomb."

"But that is not the point. What I mean is, if I marry a nonentity I shall be a nonentity myself for ever. And I would sooner die than be a nonentity."

"And, if I follow your reasoning, you think that that lets me out?"

"Well, really, Mr. Banks, have you done anything, or are you likely ever to do anything worth while?"

Cuthbert hesitated.

"It's true," he said, "I didn't finish in the first ten in the Open, and I was knocked out in the semi-final of the Amateur, but I won the French Open last year."

"The—what?"

"The French Open Championship. Golf, you know."

"Golf! You waste all your time playing golf. I admire a man who is more spiritual, more intellectual."

A pang of jealousy rent Cuthbert's bosom.

"Like What's-his-name Devine?" he said, sullenly.

"Mr. Devine," replied Adeline, blushing faintly, "is going to be a great man. Already he has achieved much. The critics say that he is more Russian than any other young English writer."

"And is that good?"

"Of course it's good."

"I should have thought the wheeze would be to be more English than any other young English writer."

"Nonsense! Who wants an English writer to be English? You've got to be Russian or Spanish or something to be a real success. The mantle of the great Russians has descended on Mr. Devine."

"From what I've heard of Russians, I should hate to have that happen to me."

"There is no danger of that," said Adeline scornfully.

"Oh! Well, let me tell you that there is a lot more in me than you think."

"That might easily be so."

"You think I'm not spiritual and intellectual," said Cuthbert, deeply moved. "Very well. Tomorrow I join the Literary Society."

Even as he spoke the words his leg was itching to kick himself for being such a chump, but the sudden expression of pleasure on Adeline's face soothed him; and he went home that night with the feeling that he had taken on something rather attractive. It was only in the cold, grey light of the morning that he realized what he had let himself in for.

I do not know if you have had any experience of suburban literary societies, but the one that flourished under the eye of Mrs. Willoughby Smethurst at Wood Hills was rather more so than the average. With my feeble powers of narrative, I cannot hope to make clear to you all that Cuthbert Banks endured in the next few weeks. And, even if I could, I doubt if I should do so. It is all very well to excite pity and terror, as Aristotle recommends, but there are limits. In the ancient Greek tragedies it was an iron-clad rule that all the real rough stuff should take place off-stage, and I shall follow this admirable principle. It will suffice if I say merely that J. Cuthbert Banks had a thin time. After attending eleven debates and fourteen lectures on *vers libre* Poetry, the Seventeenth-Century Essayists, the Neo-Scandinavian Movement in Portuguese Literature, and other subjects of a similar nature, he grew so enfeebled that, on the rare occasions when he had time for a visit to the links, he had to take a full iron for his mashie shots.

It was not simply the oppressive nature of the debates and lectures that sapped his vitality. What really got right in amongst him was the torture of seeing Adeline's adoration of Raymond Parsloe Devine. The man seemed to have made the deepest possible impression upon her plastic emotions. When he spoke, she leaned forward with parted lips and looked at him. When he was not speaking—which was seldom—she leaned back and looked at him. And when he happened to take the next seat to her, she leaned sideways and looked at him. One glance at Mr. Devine would have been more than enough for Cuthbert; but Adeline found him a spectacle that never palled. She could not have gazed at him with a more rapturous intensity if she had been a small child and he a saucer of ice-cream. All this Cuthbert had to witness while still endeavoring to retain the possession of his faculties sufficiently to enable him to duck and back away if somebody suddenly asked him what he thought of the somber realism of Vladimir Brusiloff. It is little wonder that he tossed in bed, picking at the coverlet, through sleepless nights, and had to have all his waistcoats taken in three inches to keep them from sagging.

This Vladimir Brusiloff to whom I have referred was the famous Russian novelist, and, owing to the fact of his being in the country on a lecturing tour at the moment, there had been something of a boom in his works. The Wood Hills Literary Society had been studying them for weeks, and never since his first entrance into intellectual circles had Cuthbert Banks come nearer to throwing in the towel. Vladimir specialized in grey studies of hopeless misery, where nothing happened till page three hundred and eighty, when the moujik decided to commit suicide. It was tough going for a man whose deepest reading hitherto had been Vardon on the Push-Shot, and there can be no greater proof of the magic of love than the fact that Cuthbert stuck it without a cry. But the strain was terrible and I am inclined to think that he must have cracked, had it not been for the daily reports in the papers of the internecine strife which was proceeding so briskly in Russia. Cuthbert was an optimist at heart, and it seemed to him that, at the rate at which the inhabitants of that interesting country were murdering one another, the supply of Russian novelists must eventually give out.

One morning, as he tottered down the road for the short walk which was now almost the only exercise to which he was equal, Cuthbert met Adeline. A spasm of anguish flitted through all his nerve-centers as he saw that she was accompanied by Raymond Parsloe Devine.

"Good morning, Mr. Banks," said Adeline.

"Good morning," said Cuthbert hollowly.

"Such good news about Vladimir Brusiloff."

"Dead?" said Cuthbert, with a touch of hope.

"Dead? Of course not. Why should he be? No, Aunt Emily met his manager after his lecture at Queen's Hall yesterday, and he has promised that Mr. Brusiloff shall come to her next Wednesday reception."

"Oh, ah!" said Cuthbert, dully.

"I don't know how she managed it. I think she must have told him that Mr. Devine would be there to meet him."

"But you said he was coming," argued Cuthbert.

"I shall be very glad," said Raymond Devine, "of the opportunity of meeting Brusiloff."

"I'm sure," said Adeline, "he will be very glad of the opportunity of meeting you."

"Possibly," said Mr. Devine. "Possibly. Competent critics have said that my work closely resembles that of the great Russian Masters."

"Your psychology is so deep."

"Yes, yes."

"And your atmosphere."

"Quite."

Cuthbert in a perfect agony of spirit prepared to withdraw from this love-feast. The sun was shining brightly, but the world was black to him. Birds sang in the tree-tops, but he did not hear them. He might have been a moujik for all the pleasure he found in life.

"You will be there, Mr. Banks?" said Adeline, as he turned away.

"Oh, all right," said Cuthbert.

When Cuthbert had entered the drawing-room on the following Wednesday and had taken his usual place in a distant corner where, while able to feast his gaze on Adeline, he had a sporting chance of being overlooked or mistaken for a piece of furniture, he perceived the great Russian thinker seated in the midst of a circle of admiring females. Raymond Parsloe Devine had not yet arrived.

His first glance at the novelist surprised Cuthbert. Doubtless with the best motives, Vladimir Brusiloff had permitted his face to become almost entirely concealed behind a dense zareba of hair, but his eyes were visible through the undergrowth, and it seemed to Cuthbert that there was an expression in them not unlike that of a cat in a strange backyard surrounded by small boys. The man looked forlorn and hopeless, and Cuthbert wondered whether he had had bad news from home.

This was not the case. The latest news which Vladimir Brusiloff had had from Russia had been particularly cheering. Three of his principal creditors had perished in the last massacre of the bourgeoisie, and a man whom he owed for five years for a samovar and a pair of overshoes had fled the country, and had not been heard of since. It was not bad news from home that was depressing Vladimir. What was wrong with him was the fact that this was the eighty-second suburban literary reception he had been compelled to attend since he had landed in the country on his lecturing tour, and he was sick to death of it. When his agent had first suggested the trip, he had signed on the dotted line without an instant's hesitation. Worked out in rubles, the fees offered had seemed just about right. But now, as he peered through the brushwood at the faces round him, and realized that eight out of ten of those present had manuscripts of some sort concealed on their persons, and were only waiting for an opportunity to whip them out and start reading, he wished that he had stayed at his quiet home in Nijni-Novgorod, where the worst thing that could happen to a fellow was a brace of bombs coming in through the window and mixing themselves up with his breakfast egg.

At this point in his meditations he was aware that his hostess was looming up before him with a pale young

man in horn-rimmed spectacles at her side. There was in
Mrs. Smethurst's demeanor something of the unction of
the master-of-ceremonies at the big fight who introduces
the earnest gentleman who wishes to challenge the winner.

"Oh, Mr. Brusiloff," said Mrs. Smethurst, "I do so want
you to meet Mr. Raymond Parsloe Devine, whose work I
expect you know. He is one of our younger novelists."

The distinguished visitor peered in a wary and defensive manner through the shrubbery, but did not speak. In-
wardly he was thinking how exactly like Mr. Devine was
to the eighty-one other younger novelists to whom he had
been introduced at various hamlets throughout the country. Raymond Parsloe Devine bowed courteously, while
Cuthbert, wedged into his corner, glowered at him.

"The critics," said Mr. Devine, "have been kind enough
to say that my poor efforts contain a good deal of the Russian spirit. I owe much to the great Russians. I have been
greatly influenced by Sovietski."

Down in the forest something stirred. It was Vladimir
Brusiloff's mouth opening, as he prepared to speak. He
was not a man who prattled readily, especially in a foreign
tongue. He gave the impression that each word was exca-
vated from his interior by some up-to-date process of min-
ing. He glared bleakly at Mr. Devine, and allowed three
words to drop out of him.

"Sovietski no good!"

He paused for a moment, set the machinery working
again, and delivered five more at the pithead.

"I spit me of Sovietski!"

There was a painful sensation. The lot of a popular idol
is in many ways an enviable one, but it has the drawback

of uncertainty. Here today and gone tomorrow. Until this moment Raymond Parsloe Devine's stock had stood at something considerably over par in Wood Hills intellectual circles, but now there was a rapid slump. Hitherto he had been greatly admired for being influenced by Sovietski, but it appeared now that this was not a good thing to be. It was evidently a rotten thing to be. The law could not touch you for being influenced by Sovietski, but there is an ethical as well as a legal code, and this it was obvious that Raymond Parsloe Devine had transgressed. Women drew away from him slightly, holding their skirts. Men looked at him censoriously. Adeline Smethurst started violently, and dropped a tea-cup. And Cuthbert Banks, doing his popular imitation of a sardine in his corner, felt for the first time that life held something of sunshine.

Raymond Parsloe Devine was plainly shaken, but he made an adroit attempt to recover his lost prestige.

"When I say I have been influenced by Sovietski, I mean, of course, that I was once under his spell. A young writer commits many follies. I have long since passed through that phase. The false glamour of Sovietski has ceased to dazzle me. I now belong whole-heartedly to the school of Nastikoff."

There was a reaction. People nodded at one another sympathetically. After all, we cannot expect old heads on young shoulders, and a lapse at the outset of one's career should not be held against one who has eventually seen the light.

"Nastikoff no good," said Vladimir Brusiloff, coldly. He paused, listening to the machinery.

"Nastikoff worse than Sovietski."

He paused again.

"I spit me of Nastikoff!" he said.

This time there was no doubt about it. The bottom had dropped out of the market, and Raymond Parsloe Devine Preferred were down in the cellar with no takers. It was clear to the entire assembled company that they had been all wrong about Raymond Parsloe Devine. They had allowed him to play on their innocence and sell them a pup. They had taken him at his own valuation, and had been cheated into admiring him as a man who amounted to something, and all the while he had belonged to the school of Nastikoff. You never can tell. Mrs. Smethurst's guests were well-bred, and there was consequently no violent demonstration, but you could see by their faces what they felt. Those nearest Raymond Parsloe jostled to get further away. Mrs. Smethurst eyed him stonily through a raised lorgnette. One or two low hisses were heard, and over at the other end of the room somebody opened the window in a marked manner.

Raymond Parsloe Devine hesitated for a moment, then, realizing his situation, turned and slunk to the door. There was an audible sigh of relief as it closed behind him.

Vladimir Brusiloff proceeded to sum up.

"No novelists any good except me. Sovietski—yah! Nastikoff—bah! I spit me of zem all. No novelists anywhere any good except me. P. G. Wodehouse and Tolstoi not bad. Not good, but not bad. No novelists any good except me."

And, having uttered this dictum, he removed a slab of cake from a near-by plate, steered it through the jungle, and began to champ.

It is too much to say that there was a dead silence. There could never be that in any room in which Vladimir

Brusiloff was eating cake. But certainly what you might call the general chit-chat was pretty well down and out. Nobody liked to be the first to speak. The members of the Wood Hills Literary Society looked at one another timidly. Cuthbert, for his part, gazed at Adeline; and Adeline gazed into space. It was plain that the girl was deeply stirred. Her eyes were opened wide, a faint flush crimsoned her cheeks, and her breath was coming quickly.

Adeline's mind was in a whirl. She felt as if she had been walking gaily along a pleasant path and had stopped suddenly on the very brink of a precipice. It would be idle to deny that Raymond Parsloe Devine had attracted her extraordinarily. She had taken him at his own valuation as an extremely hot potato, and her hero-worship had gradually been turning into love. And now her hero had been shown to have feet of clay. It was hard, I consider, on Raymond Parsloe Devine, but that is how it goes in this world. You get a following as a celebrity, and then you run up against another bigger celebrity and your admirers desert you. One could moralize on this at considerable length, but better not, perhaps. Enough to say that the glamour of Raymond Devine ceased abruptly in that moment for Adeline, and her most coherent thought at this juncture was the resolve, as soon as she got up to her room, to burn the three signed photographs he had sent her and to give the autographed presentation set of his books to the grocer's boy.

Mrs. Smethurst, meanwhile, having rallied somewhat, was endeavoring to set the feast of reason and flow of soul going again.

"And how do you like England, Mr. Brusiloff?" she asked.

The celebrity paused in the act of lowering another segment of cake.

"Dam good," he replied, cordially.

"I suppose you have travelled all over the country by this time?"

"You said it," agreed the Thinker.

"Have you met many of our great public men?"

"Yais—Yais—Quite a few of the nibs—Lloyid Gorge, I meet him. But—" beneath the matting a discontented expression came into his face, and his voice took on a peevish note. "But I not meet your real great men—your Arbmishel, your Arreevadon—I not meet them. That's what gives me the pipovitch. Have you ever met Arbmishel and Arreevadon?"

A strained, anguished look came into Mrs. Smethurst's face and was reflected in the faces of the other members of the circle. The eminent Russian had sprung two entirely new ones on them, and they felt that their ignorance was about to be exposed. What would Vladimir Brusiloff think of the Wood Hills Literary Society? The reputation of the Wood Hills Literary Society was at stake, trembling in the balance, and coming up for the third time. In dumb agony Mrs. Smethurst rolled her eyes about the room searching for someone capable of coming to the rescue. She drew blank.

And then, from a distant corner, there sounded a deprecating cough, and those nearest Cuthbert Banks saw that he had stopped twisting his right foot round his left ankle and his left foot round his right ankle and was sitting up with a light of almost human intelligence in his eyes.

"Er—" said Cuthbert, blushing as every eye in the room seemed to fix itself on him, "I think he means Abe Mitchell and Harry Vardon."

"Abe Mitchell and Harry Vardon?" repeated Mrs. Smethurst, blankly. "I never heard of—"

"Yais! Yais! Most! Very!" shouted Vladimir Brusiloff, enthusiastically. "Arbmishel and Arreevadon. You know them, yes, what, no, perhaps?"

"I've played with Abe Mitchell often, and I was partnered with Harry Vardon in last year's Open."

The great Russian uttered a cry that shook the chandelier.

"You play in ze Open? Why," he demanded reproachfully of Mrs. Smethurst, "was I not been introduced to this young man who play in opens?"

"Well, really," faltered Mrs. Smethurst. "Well, the fact is, Mr. Brusiloff—"

She broke off. She was unequal to the task of explaining, without hurting anyone's feelings, that she had always regarded Cuthbert as a piece of cheese and a blot on the landscape.

"Introduce me!" thundered the Celebrity.

"Why, certainly, certainly, of course. This is Mr.—"

She looked appealingly at Cuthbert.

"Banks," prompted Cuthbert.

"Banks!" cried Vladimir Brusiloff. "Not Cootaboot Banks?"

"Is your name Cootaboot?" asked Mrs. Smethurst, faintly.

"Well, it's Cuthbert."

"Yais! Yais! Cootaboot!" There was a rush and swirl, as the effervescent Muscovite burst his way through the throng and rushed to where Cuthbert sat. He stood for a moment eyeing him excitedly, then, stooping swiftly, kissed him on both cheeks before Cuthbert could get his guard up. "My dear young man, I saw you win ze French Open. Great! Great! Grand! Superb! Hot stuff, and you can say I said so! Will you permit one who is but eighteen at Nijni-Novgorod to salute you once more?"

And he kissed Cuthbert again. Then, brushing aside one or two intellectuals who were in the way, he dragged up a chair and sat down.

"You are a great man!" he said.

"Oh, no," said Cuthbert modestly.

"Yais! Great. Most! Very! The way you lay your approach-putts dead from anywhere!"

"Oh, I don't know."

Mr. Brusiloff drew his chair closer.

"Let me tell you one vairy funny story about putting. It was one day I play at Nijni-Novgorod with the pro against Lenin and Trotsky, and Trotsky had a two-inch putt for the hole. But, just as he addresses the ball, someone in the crowd he tries to assassinate Lenin with a rewolver—you know that is our great national sport, trying to assassinate Lenin with rewolwers—and the bang puts Trotsky off his stroke and he goes five yards past the hole, and then Lenin, who is rather shaken, you understand, he misses again himself, and we win the hole and match and I clean up three hundred and ninety-six thousand rubles, or fifteen shillings in your money. Some gameovitch! And now let me tell you one other vairy funny story—"

Desultory conversation had begun in murmurs over the rest of the room, as the Wood Hills intellectuals politely endeavored to conceal the fact that they realized that they were about as much out of it at this re-union of twin souls as cats at a dog-show. From time to time they started as Vladimir Brusiloff's laugh boomed out. Perhaps it was a consolation to them to know that he was enjoying himself.

As for Adeline, how shall I describe her emotions? She was stunned. Before her very eyes the stone which the builders had rejected had become the main thing, the hundred-to-one shot had walked away with the race. A rush of tender admiration for Cuthbert Banks flooded her heart. She saw that she had been all wrong. Cuthbert, whom she had always treated with a patronizing superiority, was really a man to be looked up to and worshipped. A deep, dreamy sigh shook Adeline's fragile form.

Half an hour later Vladimir and Cuthbert Banks rose.

"Goot-a-bye, Mrs. Smet-thirst," said the Celebrity. "Zank you for a most charming visit. My friend Cootaboot and me we go now to shoot a few holes. You will lend me clobs, friend Cootaboot?"

"Any you want."

"The niblicksky is what I use most. Goot-a-bye, Mrs. Smet-thirst."

They were moving to the door, when Cuthbert felt a light touch on his arm. Adeline was looking up at him tenderly.

"May I come, too, and walk round with you?"

Cuthbert's bosom heaved.

"Oh," he said, with a tremor in his voice, "that you would walk round with me for life!"

Her eyes met his.

"Perhaps," she whispered, softly, "it could be arranged."

"AND SO," (CONCLUDED the Oldest Member), "you see that golf can be of the greatest practical assistance to a man in Life's struggle. Raymond Parsloe Devine, who was no player, had to move out of the neighborhood immediately, and is now, I believe, writing scenarios out in California for the Flicker Film Company. Adeline is married to Cuthbert, and it was only his earnest pleading which prevented her from having their eldest son christened Abe Mitchell Ribbed-Faced Mashie Banks, for she is now as keen a devotee of the great game as her husband. Those who know them say that theirs is a union so devoted, so—"

The Sage broke off abruptly, for the young man had rushed to the door and out into the passage. Through the open door he could hear him crying passionately to the waiter to bring back his clubs.

# Ordeal by Golf

A PLEASANT BREEZE PLAYED among the trees on the terrace outside the Marvis Bay Golf and Country Club. It ruffled the leaves and cooled the forehead of the Oldest Member, who, as was his custom of a Saturday afternoon, sat in the shade on a rocking-chair, observing the younger generation as it hooked and sliced in the valley below. The eye of the Oldest Member was thoughtful and reflective. When it looked into yours you saw in it that perfect peace, that peace beyond understanding, which comes at its maximum only to the man who has given up golf.

The Oldest Member has not played golf since the rubber-cored ball superseded the old dignified gutty. But as a spectator and philosopher he still finds pleasure in the pastime. He is watching it now with keen interest. His gaze, passing from the lemonade which he is sucking through a straw, rests upon the Saturday foursome which is struggling raggedly up the hill to the ninth green. Like all Saturday foursomes, it is in difficulties. One of the patients is zigzagging about the fairway like a liner pursued by submarines. Two others seem to be digging for buried treasure, unless—it is too far off to be certain—they are killing snakes. The remaining cripple, who has just foozled a mashie-shot, is blaming his caddie. His voice, as he upbraids the innocent child for breathing during his up-swing, comes clearly up the hill.

The Oldest Member sighs. His lemonade gives a sympathetic gurgle. He puts it down on the table.

HOW FEW MEN (says the Oldest Member) possess the proper golfing temperament! How few indeed, judging by the sights I see here on Saturday afternoons, possess any qualification at all for golf except a pair of baggy knicker-bockers and enough money to enable them to pay for the drinks at the end of the round. The ideal golfer never loses his temper. When I played, I never lost my temper. Some-times, it is true, I may, after missing a shot, have broken my club across my knees; but I did it in a calm and judicial spirit, because the club was obviously no good and I was going to get another one anyway. To lose one's temper at golf is foolish. It gets you nothing, not even relief. Imitate the spirit of Marcus Aurelius. "Whatever may befall thee," says that great man in his Meditations, "it was preor-dained for thee from everlasting. Nothing happens to an-ybody which he is not fitted by nature to bear." I like to think that this noble thought came to him after he had sliced a couple of new balls into the woods, and that he jotted it down on the back of his score-card. For there can be no doubt that the man was a golfer, and a bad golfer at that. Nobody who had not had a short putt stop on the edge of the hole could possibly have written the words: "That which makes the man no worse than he was makes life no worse. It has no power to harm, without or within." Yes, Marcus Aurelius undoubtedly played golf, and all the evidence seems to indicate that he rarely went round in under a hundred and twenty. The niblick was his club.

Speaking of Marcus Aurelius and the golfing temperament recalls to my mind the case of young Mitchell
Holmes. Mitchell, when I knew him first, was a promising
young man with a future before him in the Paterson Dyeing and Refining Company, of which my old friend, Alexander Paterson, was the president. He had many engag-
ing qualities—among them an unquestioned ability to imitate a bulldog quarrelling with a Pekingese in a way
which had to be heard to be believed. It was a gift which
made him much in demand at social gatherings in the
neighborhood, marking him off from other young men
who could only almost play the mandolin or recite bits of
Gunga Din; and no doubt it was this talent of his which
first sowed the seeds of love in the heart of Millicent Boyd.
Women are essentially hero-worshippers, and when a
warm-hearted girl like Millicent has heard a personable
young man imitating a bulldog and a Pekingese to the applause of a crowded drawing-room, and has been able to
detect the exact point at which the Pekingese leaves off
and the bulldog begins, she can never feel quite the same
to other men. In short, Mitchell and Millicent were engaged, and were only waiting to be married till the former
could bite the Dyeing and Refining Company's ear for a
bit of extra salary.

Mitchell Holmes had only one fault. He lost his temper
when playing golf. He seldom played a round without becoming piqued, peeved, or—in many cases—chagrined.
The caddies on our links, it was said, could always worst
other small boys in verbal argument by calling them some
of the things they had heard Mitchell call his ball on dis-
covering it in a cuppy lie. He had a great gift of language,
and he used it unsparingly. I will admit that there was

some excuse for the man. He had the makings of a brilliant golfer, but a combination of bad luck and inconsistent play invariably robbed him of the fruits of his skill. He was the sort of player who does the first two holes in one under bogey and then takes an eleven at the third. The least thing upset him on the links. He missed short putts because of the uproar of the butterflies in the adjoining meadows.

It seemed hardly likely that this one kink in an otherwise admirable character would ever seriously affect his working or professional life, but it did. One evening, as I was sitting in my garden, Alexander Paterson was announced. A glance at his face told me that he had come to ask my advice. Rightly or wrongly, he regarded me as one capable of giving advice. It was I who had changed the whole current of his life by counselling him to leave the wood in his bag and take a driving-iron off the tee; and in one or two other matters, like the choice of a putter (so much more important than the choice of a wife), I had been of assistance to him.

Alexander sat down and fanned himself with his hat, for the evening was warm. Perplexity was written upon his fine face.

"I don't know what to do," he said.

"Keep the head still—slow back—don't press," I said, gravely. There is no better rule for a happy and successful life.

"It's nothing to do with golf this time," he said. "It's about the treasurership of my company. Old Smithers retires next week, and I've got to find a man to fill his place."

"That should be easy. You have simply to select the most deserving from among your other employees."

"But which is the most deserving? That's the point. There are two men who are capable of holding the job quite adequately. But then I realize how little I know of their real characters. It is the treasurership, you understand, which has to be filled. Now, a man who was quite good at another job might easily get wrong ideas into his head when he became a treasurer. He would have the handling of large sums of money. In other words, a man who in ordinary circumstances had never been conscious of any desire to visit the more distant portions of South America might feel the urge, so to speak, shortly after he became a treasurer. That is my difficulty. Of course, one always takes a sporting chance with any treasurer; but how am I to find out which of these two men would give me the more reasonable opportunity of keeping some of my money?"

I did not hesitate a moment. I held strong views on the subject of character-testing.

"The only way," I said to Alexander, "of really finding out a man's true character is to play golf with him. In no other walk of life does the cloven hoof so quickly display itself. I employed a lawyer for years, until one day I saw him kick his ball out of a heel-mark. I removed my business from his charge next morning. He has not yet run off with any trust-funds, but there is a nasty gleam in his eye, and I am convinced that it is only a question of time. Golf, my dear fellow, is the infallible test. The man who can go into a patch of rough alone, with the knowledge that only God is watching him, and play his ball where it lies, is the man who will serve you faithfully and well. The man who can smile bravely when his putt is diverted by one of those beastly wormcasts is pure gold right through. But the man who is hasty, unbalanced, and violent on the links will display the same qualities in the wider field of everyday life. You don't want an unbalanced treasurer, do you?"

"Not if his books are likely to catch the complaint."

"They are sure to. Statisticians estimate that the average of crime among good golfers is lower than in any class of the community except possibly bishops. Since Willie Park won the first championship at Prestwick in the year 1860 there has, I believe, been no instance of an Open Champion spending a day in prison. Whereas the bad golfers—and by bad I do not mean incompetent, but black-souled—the men who fail to count a stroke when they miss the globe; the men who never replace a divot; the men who talk while their opponent is driving; and the men who let their angry passions rise—these are in and out of Wormwood Scrubbs all the time. They find it hardly worth while to get their hair cut in their brief intervals of liberty."

Alexander was visibly impressed.

"That sounds sensible, by George!" he said.

"It is sensible."

"I'll do it! Honestly, I can't see any other way of deciding between Holmes and Dixon."

I started.

"Holmes? Not Mitchell Holmes?"

"Yes. Of course you must know him? He lives here, I believe."

"And by Dixon do you mean Rupert Dixon?"

"That's the man. Another neighbor of yours."

I confess that my heart sank. It was as if my ball had fallen into the pit which my niblick had dug. I wished heartily that I had thought of waiting to ascertain the names of the two rivals before offering my scheme. I was extremely fond of Mitchell Holmes and of the girl to whom he was engaged to be married. Indeed, it was I who had sketched out a few rough notes for the lad to use when proposing; and results had shown that he had put my stuff across well. And I had listened many a time with a sympathetic ear to his hopes in the matter of securing a rise of salary which would enable him to get married. Somehow, when Alexander was talking, it had not occurred to me that young Holmes might be in the running for so important an office as the treasurership. I had ruined the boy's chances. Ordeal by golf was the one test which he could not possibly undergo with success. Only a miracle could keep him from losing his temper, and I had expressly warned Alexander against such a man.

When I thought of his rival my heart sank still more. Rupert Dixon was rather an unpleasant young man, but the worst of his enemies could not accuse him of not possessing the golfing temperament. From the drive off the tee to the holing of the final putt he was uniformly suave.

WHEN ALEXANDER HAD gone, I sat in thought for some time. I was faced with a problem. Strictly speaking, no doubt, I had no right to take sides; and, though secrecy had not been enjoined upon me in so many words, I was very well aware that Alexander was under the impression that I would keep the thing under my hat and not reveal to either party the test that awaited him. Each candidate was, of course, to remain ignorant that he was taking part in anything but a friendly game.

But when I thought of the young couple whose future depended on this ordeal, I hesitated no longer. I put on my hat and went round to Miss Boyd's house, where I knew that Mitchell was to be found at this hour.

The young couple were out in the porch, looking at the moon. They greeted me heartily, but their heartiness had rather a tinny sound, and I could see that on the whole they regarded me as one of those things which should not happen. But when I told my story their attitude changed. They began to look on me in the pleasanter light of a guardian, philosopher, and friend.

"Wherever did Mr. Paterson get such a silly idea?" said Miss Boyd, indignantly. I had—from the best motives— concealed the source of the scheme. "It's ridiculous!"

"Oh, I don't know," said Mitchell. "The old boy's crazy about golf. It's just the sort of scheme he would cook up. Well, it dishes me!"

"Oh, come!" I said.

"It's no good saying 'Oh, come!' You know perfectly well that I'm a frank, outspoken golfer. When my ball goes off nor'-nor'-east when I want it to go due west I can't help expressing an opinion about it. It is a curious phenomenon which calls for comment, and I give it. Similarly, when I top my drive, I have to go on record as saying that I did not do it intentionally. And it's just these trifles, as far as I can make out, that are going to decide the thing."

"Couldn't you learn to control yourself on the links, Mitchell, darling?" asked Millicent. "After all, golf is only a game!"

Mitchell's eyes met mine, and I have no doubt that mine showed just the same look of horror which I saw in his. Women say these things without thinking. It does not mean that there is any kink in their character. They simply don't realize what they are saying.

"Hush!" said Mitchell, huskily, patting her hand and overcoming his emotion with a strong effort. "Hush, dearest!"

TWO OR THREE DAYS LATER I met Millicent coming from the post-office. There was a new light of happiness in her eyes, and her face was glowing.

"Such a splendid thing has happened," she said. "After Mitchell left that night I happened to be glancing through a magazine, and I came across a wonderful advertisement. It began by saying that all the great men in history owed their success to being able to control themselves, and that Napoleon wouldn't have amounted to anything if he had not curbed his fiery nature, and then it said that we can all be like Napoleon if we fill in the accompanying blank order-form for Professor Orlando Rollitt's wonderful book, *Are You Your Own Master?* absolutely free for five days and then seven shillings, but you must write at once because the demand is enormous and pretty soon it may be too late. I wrote at once, and luckily I was in time, because Professor Rollitt did have a copy left, and it's just arrived. I've been looking through it, and it seems splendid."

She held out a small volume. I glanced at it. There was a frontispiece showing a signed photograph of Professor Orlando Rollitt controlling himself in spite of having long white whiskers, and then some reading matter, printed between wide margins. One look at the book told me the professor's methods. To be brief, he had simply swiped

Marcus Aurelius's best stuff, the copyright having expired some two thousand years ago, and was retailing it as his own. I did not mention this to Millicent. It was no affair of mine. Presumably, however obscure the necessity, Professor Rollitt had to live.

"I'm going to start Mitchell on it today. Don't you think this is good? 'Thou seest how few be the things which if a man has at his command his life flows gently on and is divine.' I think it will be wonderful if Mitchell's life flows gently on and is divine for seven shillings, don't you?"

AT THE CLUB-HOUSE THAT evening I encountered Rupert Dixon. He was emerging from a shower-bath, and looked as pleased with himself as usual.

"Just been going round with old Paterson," he said. "He was asking after you. He's gone back to town in his car."

I was thrilled. So the test had begun!

"How did you come out?" I asked.

Rupert Dixon smirked. A smirking man, wrapped in a bath towel, with a wisp of wet hair over one eye, is a repellent sight.

"Oh, pretty well. I won by six and five. In spite of having poisonous luck."

I felt a gleam of hope at these last words.

"Oh, you had bad luck?"

"The worst. I over-shot the green at the third with the best brassey-shot I've ever made in my life—and that's saying a lot—and lost my ball in the rough beyond it."

"And I suppose you let yourself go, eh?"

"Let myself go?"

"I take it that you made some sort of demonstration?"

"Oh, no. Losing your temper doesn't get you anywhere at golf. It only spoils your next shot."

I went away heavy-hearted. Dixon had plainly come through the ordeal as well as any man could have done. I expected to hear every day that the vacant treasurership had been filled, and that Mitchell had not even been called upon to play his test round. I suppose, however, that Alexander Paterson felt that it would be unfair to the other competitor not to give him his chance, for the next I heard of the matter was when Mitchell Holmes rang me up on the Friday and asked me if I would accompany him round the links next day in the match he was playing with Alexander, and give him my moral support.

"I shall need it," he said. "I don't mind telling you I'm pretty nervous. I wish I had had longer to get the stranglehold on that *Are You Your Own Master?* stuff. I can see, of course, that it is the real tabasco from start to finish, and absolutely as mother makes it, but the trouble is I've only had a few days to soak it into my system. It's like trying to patch up a motor car with string. You never know when the thing will break down. Heaven knows what will happen if I sink a ball at the water-hole. And something seems to tell me I am going to do it."

There was a silence for a moment.

"Do you believe in dreams?" asked Mitchell.

"Believe in what?"

"Dreams."

"What about them?"

"I said, 'Do you believe in dreams?' Because last night I dreamed that I was playing in the final of the Open Championship, and I got into the rough, and there was a cow there, and the cow looked at me in a sad sort of way and said, 'Why don't you use the two-V grip instead of the interlocking?' At the time it seemed an odd sort of thing to happen, but I've been thinking it over and I wonder if there isn't something in it. These things must be sent to us for a purpose."

"You can't change your grip on the day of an important match."

"I suppose not. The fact is, I'm a bit jumpy, or I wouldn't have mentioned it. Oh, well! See you tomorrow at two."

THE DAY WAS BRIGHT AND sunny, but a tricky cross-wind was blowing when I reached the club-house. Alexander Paterson was there, practicing swings on the first tee; and almost immediately Mitchell Holmes arrived, accompanied by Millicent.

"Perhaps," said Alexander, "we had better be getting under way. Shall I take the honor?"

"Certainly," said Mitchell.

Alexander teed up his ball.

Alexander Paterson has always been a careful rather than a dashing player. It is his custom, a sort of ritual, to take two measured practice-swings before addressing the ball, even on the putting-green. When he does address the ball he shuffles his feet for a moment or two, then pauses, and scans the horizon in a suspicious sort of way, as if he had been expecting it to play some sort of a trick on him when he was not looking. A careful inspection seems to convince him of the horizon's bona fides, and he turns his attention to the ball again. He shuffles his feet once more, then raises his club. He waggles the club smartly over the ball three times, then lays it behind the globule. At this point he suddenly peers at the horizon again, in the apparent hope of catching it off its guard. This done, he raises his club very slowly, brings it back very slowly till it almost touches the ball, raises it again, brings it down again, raises it once more, and brings it down for the third time. He then stands motionless, wrapped in thought, like some Indian fakir contemplating the infinite. Then he raises his club again and replaces it behind the ball. Finally he quivers all over, swings very slowly back, and drives the ball for about a hundred and fifty yards in a dead straight line.

It is a method of procedure which proves sometimes a little exasperating to the highly strung, and I watched Mitchell's face anxiously to see how he was taking his first introduction to it. The unhappy lad had blenched visibly. He turned to me with the air of one in pain.

"Does he always do that?" he whispered.

"Always," I replied.

"Then I'm done for! No human being could play golf against a one-ring circus like that without blowing up!"

I said nothing. It was, I feared, only too true. Well-poised as I am, I had long since been compelled to give up playing with Alexander Paterson, much as I esteemed him. It was a choice between that and resigning from the Baptist Church.

At this moment Millicent spoke. There was an open book in her hand. I recognized it as the life-work of Professor Rollitt.

"Think on this doctrine," she said, in her soft, modulated voice, "that to be patient is a branch of justice, and that men sin without intending it."

Mitchell nodded briefly, and walked to the tee with a firm step.

"Before you drive, darling," said Millicent, "remember this. Let no act be done at haphazard, nor otherwise than according to the finished rules that govern its kind."

The next moment Mitchell's ball was shooting through the air, to come to rest two hundred yards down the course. It was a magnificent drive. He had followed the counsel of Marcus Aurelius to the letter.

An admirable iron-shot put him in reasonable proximity to the pin, and he holed out in one under bogey with one of the nicest putts I have ever beheld. And when at the next hole, the dangerous water-hole, his ball soared over the pond and lay safe, giving him bogey for the hole, I began for the first time to breathe freely. Every golfer has his day, and this was plainly Mitchell's. He was playing faultless golf. If he could continue in this vein, his unfortunate failing would have no chance to show itself.

The third hole is long and tricky. You drive over a ravine—or possibly into it. In the latter event you breathe a prayer and call for your niblick. But, once over the ravine, there is nothing to disturb the equanimity. Bogey is five, and a good drive, followed by a brassey-shot, will put you within easy mashie-distance of the green.

Mitchell cleared the ravine by a hundred and twenty yards. He strolled back to me, and watched Alexander go through his ritual with an indulgent smile. I knew just how he was feeling. Never does the world seem so sweet and fair and the foibles of our fellow human beings so little irritating as when we have just swatted the pill right on the spot.

"I can't see why he does it," said Mitchell, eyeing Alexander with a toleration that almost amounted to affection. "If I did all those Swedish exercises before I drove, I should forget what I had come out for and go home." Alexander concluded the movements, and landed a bare three yards on the other side of the ravine. "He's what you would call a steady performer, isn't he? Never varies!"

Mitchell won the hole comfortably. There was a jauntiness about his stance on the fourth tee which made me a little uneasy. Over-confidence at golf is almost as bad as timidity.

My apprehensions were justified. Mitchell topped his ball. It rolled twenty yards into the rough, and nestled under a dock-leaf. His mouth opened, then closed with a snap. He came over to where Millicent and I were standing.

"I didn't say it!" he said. "What on earth happened then?"

"Search men's governing principles," said Millicent, "and consider the wise, what they shun and what they cleave to."

"Exactly," I said. "You swayed your body."

"And now I've got to go and look for that infernal ball."

"Never mind, darling," said Millicent. "Nothing has such power to broaden the mind as the ability to investigate systematically and truly all that comes under thy observation in life."

"Besides," I said, "you're three up."

"I shan't be after this hole."

He was right. Alexander won it in five, one above bogey, and regained the honor.

Mitchell was a trifle shaken. His play no longer had its first careless vigor. He lost the next hole, halved the sixth, lost the short seventh, and then, rallying, halved the eighth.

The ninth hole, like so many on our links, can be a perfectly simple four, although the rolling nature of the green makes bogey always a somewhat doubtful feat; but, on the other hand, if you foozle your drive, you can easily achieve double figures. The tee is on the farther side of the pond, beyond the bridge, where the water narrows almost to the dimensions of a brook. You drive across this water and over a tangle of trees and under-growth on the other bank. The distance to the fairway cannot be more than sixty yards, for the hazard is purely a mental one, and yet how many fair hopes have been wrecked there!

Alexander cleared the obstacles comfortably with his customary short, straight drive, and Mitchell advanced to the tee.

I think the loss of the honor had been preying on his mind. He seemed nervous. His up-swing was shaky, and he swayed back perceptibly. He made a lunge at the ball, sliced it, and it struck a tree on the other side of the water and fell in the long grass. We crossed the bridge to look for it; and it was here that the effect of Professor Rollitt began definitely to wane.

"Why on earth don't they mow this darned stuff?" demanded Mitchell, querulously, as he beat about the grass with his niblick.

"You have to have rough on a course," I ventured.

"Whatever happens at all," said Millicent, "happens as it should. Thou wilt find this true if thou shouldst watch narrowly."

"That's all very well," said Mitchell, watching narrowly in a clump of weeds but seeming unconvinced. "I believe the Greens Committee run this bally club purely in the interests of the caddies. I believe they encourage lost balls, and go halves with the little beasts when they find them and sell them!"

Millicent and I exchanged glances. There were tears in her eyes.

"Oh, Mitchell! Remember Napoleon!"

"Napoleon! What's Napoleon got to do with it? Napoleon never was expected to drive through a primeval forest. Besides, what did Napoleon ever do? Where did Napoleon get off, swanking round as if he amounted to something? Poor fish! All he ever did was to get hammered at Waterloo!"

Alexander rejoined us. He had walked on to where his ball lay.

"Can't find it, eh? Nasty bit of rough, this!"

"No, I can't find it. But tomorrow some miserable, chinless, half-witted reptile of a caddie with pop eyes and eight hundred and thirty-seven pimples will find it, and will sell it to someone for sixpence! No, it was a brand-new ball. He'll probably get a shilling for it. That'll be sixpence for himself and sixpence for the Greens Committee. No wonder they're buying cars quicker than the makers can supply them. No wonder you see their wives going about in mink coats and pearl necklaces. Oh, dash it! I'll drop another!"

"In that case," Alexander pointed out, "you will, of course, under the rules governing match-play, lose the hole."

"All right, then. I'll give up the hole."

"Then that, I think, makes me one up on the first nine," said Alexander. "Excellent! A very pleasant, even game."

"Pleasant! On second thought I don't believe the Greens Committee let the wretched caddies get any of the loot. They hang round behind trees till the deal's concluded, and then sneak out and choke it out of them!"

I saw Alexander raise his eyebrows. He walked up the hill to the next tee with me.

"Rather a quick-tempered young fellow, Holmes!" he said, thoughtfully. "I should never have suspected it. It just shows how little one can know of a man, only meeting him in business hours."

I tried to defend the poor lad.

"He has an excellent heart, Alexander. But the fact is — we are such old friends that I know you will forgive my mentioning it — your style of play gets, I fancy, a little on his nerves."

"My style of play? What's wrong with my style of play?"

"Nothing is actually wrong with it, but to a young and ardent spirit there is apt to be something a trifle upsetting in being, compelled to watch a man play quite so slowly as you do. Come now, Alexander, as one friend to another, is it necessary to take two practice-swings before you putt?"

"Dear, dear!" said Alexander. "You really mean to say that that upsets him? Well, I'm afraid I am too old to change my methods now."

I had nothing more to say.

As we reached the tenth tee, I saw that we were in for a few minutes' wait. Suddenly I felt a hand on my arm. Millicent was standing beside me, dejection written on her face. Alexander and young Mitchell were some distance away from us.

"Mitchell doesn't want me to come round the rest of the way with him," she said, despondently. "He says I make him nervous."

I shook my head.

"That's bad! I was looking on you as a steadying influence."

"I thought I was, too. But Mitchell says no. He says my being there keeps him from concentrating."

"Then perhaps it would be better for you to remain in the club-house till we return. There is, I fear, dirty work ahead."

A choking sob escaped the unhappy girl.

"I'm afraid so. There is an apple tree near the thirteenth hole, and Mitchell's caddie is sure to start eating apples. I am thinking of what Mitchell will do when he hears the crunching when he is addressing his ball."

"That is true."

"Our only hope," she said, holding out Professor Rollitt's book, "is this. Will you please read him extracts when you see him getting nervous? We went through the book last night and marked all the passages in blue pencil which might prove helpful. You will see notes against them in the margin, showing when each is supposed to be used."

It was a small favor to ask. I took the book and gripped her hand silently. Then I joined Alexander and Mitchell on the tenth tee. Mitchell was still continuing his speculations regarding the Greens Committee.

"The hole after this one," he said, "used to be a short hole. There was no chance of losing a ball. Then, one day, the wife of one of the Greens Committee happened to mention that the baby needed new shoes, so now they've tacked on another hundred and fifty yards to it. You have to drive over the brow of a hill, and if you slice an eighth of an inch you get into a sort of No Man's Land, full of rocks and bushes and crevices and old pots and pans. The Greens Committee practically live there in the summer. You see them prowling round in groups, encouraging each other with merry cries as they fill their sacks. Well, I'm going to fool them today. I'm going to drive an old ball which is just hanging together by a thread. It'll come to pieces when they pick it up!"

Golf, however, is a curious game—a game of fluctuations. One might have supposed that Mitchell, in such a frame of mind, would have continued to come to grief. But at the beginning of the second nine he once more found his form. A perfect drive put him in position to reach the tenth green with an iron-shot, and, though the ball was several yards from the hole, he laid it dead with his approach-putt and holed his second for a bogey four. Alexander could only achieve a five, so that they were all square again.

The eleventh, the subject of Mitchell's recent criticism, is certainly a tricky hole, and it is true that a slice does land the player in grave difficulties. Today, however, both men kept their drives straight, and found no difficulty in securing fours.

"A little more of this," said Mitchell, beaming, "and the Greens Committee will have to give up piracy and go back to work."

The twelfth is a long, dog-leg hole, bogey five. Alexander plugged steadily round the bend, holing out in six, and Mitchell, whose second shot had landed him in some long grass, was obliged to use his niblick. He contrived, however, to halve the hole with a nicely-judged mashie-shot to the edge of the green.

Alexander won the thirteenth. It is a three hundred and sixty yard hole, free from bunkers. It took Alexander three strokes to reach the green, but his third laid the ball dead; while Mitchell, who was on in two, required three putts.

"That reminds me," said Alexander, chattily, "of a story I heard. Friend calls out to a beginner, 'How are you getting on, old man?' and the beginner says, 'Splendidly. I just made three perfect putts on the last green!'"

Mitchell did not appear amused. I watched his face anxiously. He had made no remark, but the missed putt which would have saved the hole had been very short, and I feared the worst. There was a brooding look in his eye as we walked to the fourteenth tee.

There are few more picturesque spots in the whole of the countryside than the neighborhood of the fourteenth tee. It is a sight to charm the nature-lover's heart.

But, if golf has a defect, it is that it prevents a man being a whole-hearted lover of nature. Where the layman sees waving grass and romantic tangles of undergrowth, your golfer beholds nothing but a nasty patch of rough from which he must divert his ball. The cry of the birds, wheeling against the sky, is to the golfer merely something that may put him off his putt. As a spectator, I am fond of the ravine at the bottom of the slope. It pleases the eye. But, as a golfer, I have frequently found it the very devil.

The last hole had given Alexander the honor again. He drove even more deliberately than before. For quite half a minute he stood over his ball, pawing at it with his driving-iron like a cat investigating a tortoise. Finally he dispatched it to one of the few safe spots on the hillside. The drive from this tee has to be carefully calculated, for, if it be too straight, it will catch the slope and roll down into the ravine.

Mitchell addressed his ball. He swung up, and then, from immediately behind him came a sudden sharp crunching sound. I looked quickly in the direction whence it came. Mitchell's caddie, with a glassy look in his eyes, was gnawing a large apple. And even as I breathed a silent prayer, down came the driver, and the ball, with a terrible slice on it, hit the side of the hill and bounded into the ravine.

There was a pause—a pause in which the world stood still. Mitchell dropped his club and turned. His face was working horribly.

"Mitchell!" I cried. "My boy! Reflect! Be calm!"

"Calm! What's the use of being calm when people are chewing apples in thousands all round you? What is this, anyway—a golf match or a pleasant day's outing for the children of the poor? Apples! Go on, my boy, take another bite. Take several. Enjoy yourself! Never mind if it seems to cause me a fleeting annoyance. Go on with your lunch! You probably had a light breakfast, eh, and are feeling a little peckish, yes? If you will wait here, I will run to the clubhouse and get you a sandwich and a bottle of ginger-ale. Make yourself quite at home, you lovable little fellow! Sit down and have a good time!"

I turned the pages of Professor Rollitt's book feverishly. I could not find a passage that had been marked in blue pencil to meet this emergency. I selected one at random.

"Mitchell," I said, "one moment. How much time he gains who does not look to see what his neighbor says or does, but only at what he does himself, to make it just and holy."

"Well, look what I've done myself! I'm somewhere down at the bottom of that dashed ravine, and it'll take me a dozen strokes to get out. Do you call that just and holy? Here, give me that book for a moment!"

He snatched the little volume out of my hands. For an instant he looked at it with a curious expression of loathing, then he placed it gently on the ground and jumped on it a few times. Then he hit it with his driver. Finally, as if feeling that the time for half measures had passed, he took a little run and kicked it strongly into the long grass.

He turned to Alexander, who had been an impassive spectator of the scene.

"I'm through!" he said. "I concede the match. Goodbye. You'll find me in the bay!"

"Going swimming?"

"No. Drowning myself."

A gentle smile broke out over my old friend's usually grave face. He patted Mitchell's shoulder affectionately.

"Don't do that, my boy," he said. "I was hoping you would stick around the office awhile as treasurer of the company."

Mitchell tottered. He grasped my arm for support. Everything was very still. Nothing broke the stillness but the humming of the bees, the murmur of the distant wavelets, and the sound of Mitchell's caddie going on with his apple.

"What!" cried Mitchell.

"The position," said Alexander, "will be falling vacant very shortly, as no doubt you know. It is yours, if you care to accept it."

"You mean—you mean—you're going to give me the job?"

"You have interpreted me exactly."

Mitchell gulped. So did his caddie. One from a spiritual, the other from a physical cause.

"If you don't mind excusing me," said Mitchell, huskily, "I think I'll be popping back to the club-house. Someone I want to see."

He disappeared through the trees, running strongly. I turned to Alexander.

"What does this mean?" I asked. "I am delighted, but what becomes of the test?"

My old friend smiled gently.

"The test," he replied, "has been eminently satisfactory. Circumstances, perhaps, have compelled me to modify the original idea of it, but nevertheless it has been a completely successful test. Since we started out, I have been doing a good deal of thinking, and I have come to the conclusion that what the Paterson Dyeing and Refining Company really needs is a treasurer whom I can beat at golf. And I have discovered the ideal man. Why," he went on, a look of holy enthusiasm on his fine old face, "do you realize that I can always lick the stuffing out of that boy, good player as he is, simply by taking a little trouble? I can make him get the wind up every time, simply by taking one or two extra practice-swings! That is the sort of man I need for a responsible post in my office."

"But what about Rupert Dixon?" I asked.

He gave a gesture of distaste.

"I wouldn't trust that man. Why, when I played with him, everything went wrong, and he just smiled and didn't say a word. A man who can do that is not the man to trust with the control of large sums of money. It wouldn't be safe. Why, the fellow isn't honest! He can't be." He paused for a moment. "Besides," he added, thoughtfully, "he beat me by six and five. What's the good of a treasurer who beats the boss by six and five?"

# The Long Hole

THE YOUNG MAN, AS HE sat filling his pipe in the club-house smoking-room, was inclined to be bitter.

"If there's one thing that gives me a pain squarely in the center of the gizzard," he burst out, breaking a silence that had lasted for some minutes, "it's a golf-lawyer. They oughtn't to be allowed on the links."

The Oldest Member, who had been meditatively putting himself outside a cup of tea and a slice of seed-cake, raised his white eyebrows.

"The Law," he said, "is an honorable profession. Why should its practitioners be restrained from indulgence in the game of games?"

"I don't mean actual lawyers," said the young man, his acerbity mellowing a trifle under the influence of tobacco. "I mean the blighters whose best club is the book of rules. You know the sort of excrescences. Every time you think you've won a hole, they dig out Rule eight hundred and fifty-three, section two, sub-section four, to prove that you've disqualified yourself by having an ingrowing toe-nail. Well, take my case." The young man's voice was high and plaintive. "I go out with that man Hemmingway to play an ordinary friendly round—nothing depending on it except a measly ball—and on the seventh he pulls me up and claims the hole simply because I happened to drop my niblick in the bunker. Oh, well, a tick's a tick, and there's nothing more to say, I suppose."

The Sage shook his head.

"Rules are rules, my boy, and must be kept. It is odd that you should have brought up this subject, for only a moment before you came in I was thinking of a somewhat curious match which ultimately turned upon a question of the rule-book. It is true that, as far as the actual prize was concerned, it made little difference. But perhaps I had better tell you the whole story from the beginning."

The young man shifted uneasily in his chair.

"Well, you know, I've had a pretty rotten time this afternoon already—"

"I will call my story," said the Sage, tranquilly, "'The Long Hole,' for it involved the playing of what I am inclined to think must be the longest hole in the history of golf. In its beginnings the story may remind you of one I once told you about Peter Willard and James Todd, but you will find that it develops in quite a different manner. Ralph Bingham—"

"I half promised to go and see a man—"

"But I will begin at the beginning," said the Sage. "I see that you are all impatience to hear the full details."

RALPH BINGHAM AND Arthur Jukes (said the Oldest Member) had never been friends—their rivalry was too keen to admit of that—but it was not till Amanda Trivett came to stay here that a smoldering distaste for each other burst out into the flames of actual enmity. It is ever so. One of the poets, whose name I cannot recall, has a passage, which I am unable at the moment to remember, in one of his works, which for the time being has slipped my mind, which hits off admirably this age-old situation. The gist of his remarks is that lovely woman rarely fails to start something. In the weeks that followed her arrival, being in the same room with the two men was like dropping in on a reunion of Capulets and Montagues.

You see, Ralph and Arthur were so exactly equal in their skill on the links that life for them had for some time past resolved itself into a silent, bitter struggle in which first one, then the other, gained some slight advantage. If Ralph won the May medal by a stroke, Arthur would be one ahead in the June competition, only to be nosed out again in July. It was a state of affairs which, had they been men of a more generous stamp, would have bred a mutual respect, esteem, and even love. But I am sorry to say that, apart from their golf, which was in a class of its own as far as this neighborhood was concerned, Ralph Bingham and Arthur Jukes were a sorry pair—and yet, mark you, far from lacking in mere superficial good looks. They were handsome fellows, both of them, and well aware of the fact; and when Amanda Trivett came to stay they simply straightened their ties, twirled their moustaches, and expected her to do the rest.

But there they were disappointed. Perfectly friendly though she was to both of them, the love-light was conspicuously absent from her beautiful eyes. And it was not long before each had come independently to a solution of this mystery. It was plain to them that the whole trouble lay in the fact that each neutralized the other's attractions. Arthur felt that, if he could only have a clear field, all would be over except the sending out of the wedding invitations; and Ralph was of the opinion that, if he could just call on the girl one evening without finding the place all littered up with Arthur, his natural charms would swiftly bring home the bacon. And, indeed, it was true that they had no rivals except themselves. It happened at the moment that Woodhaven was very short of eligible bachelors. We marry young in this delightful spot, and all the likely men were already paired off. It seemed that, if Amanda Trivett intended to get married, she would have to select either Ralph Bingham or Arthur Jukes. A dreadful choice.

IT HAD NOT OCCURRED to me at the outset that my position in the affair would be anything closer than that of a detached and mildly interested spectator. Yet it was to me that Ralph came in his hour of need. When I returned home one evening, I found that my man had brought him in and laid him on the mat in my sitting-room.

I offered him a chair and a cigar, and he came to the point with commendable rapidity.

"Leigh," he said, directly he had lighted his cigar, "is too small for Arthur Jukes and myself."

"Ah, you have been talking it over and decided to move?" I said, delighted. "I think you are perfectly right. Leigh is over-built. Men like you and Jukes need a lot of space. Where do you think of going?"

"I'm not going."

"But I thought you said—"

"What I meant was that the time has come when one of us must leave."

"Oh, only one of you?" It was something, of course, but I confess I was disappointed, and I think my disappointment must have shown in my voice; for he looked at me, surprised.

"Surely you wouldn't mind Jukes going?" he said.

"Why, certainly not. He really is going, is he?"

A look of saturnine determination came into Ralph's face.

"He is. He thinks he isn't, but he is."

I failed to understand him, and said so. He looked cautiously about the room, as if to reassure himself that he could not be overheard.

"I suppose you've noticed," he said, "the disgusting way that man Jukes has been hanging round Miss Trivett, boring her to death?"

"I have seen them together sometimes."

"I love Amanda Trivett!" said Ralph.

"Poor girl!" I sighed.

"I beg your pardon?"

"Poor girl!" I said. "I mean, to have Arthur Jukes hanging round her."

"That's just what I think," said Ralph Bingham. "And that's why we're going to play this match."

"What match?"

"This match we've decided to play. I want you to act as one of the judges, to go along with Jukes and see that he doesn't play any of his tricks. You know what he is! And in a vital match like this—"

"How much are you playing for?"

"The whole world!"

"I beg your pardon?"

"The whole world. It amounts to that. The loser is to leave Leigh for good, and the winner stays on and marries Amanda Trivett. We have arranged all the details. Rupert Bailey will accompany me, acting as the other judge."

"And you want me to go round with Jukes?"

"Not round," said Ralph Bingham. "Along."

"What is the distinction?"

"We are not going to play a round. Only one hole."

"Sudden death, eh?"

"Not so very sudden. It's a longish hole. We start on the first tee here and hole out in the town in the doorway of the Majestic Hotel in Royal Square. A distance, I imagine, of about sixteen miles."

I was revolted. About that time a perfect epidemic of freak matches had broken out in the club, and I had strongly opposed them from the start. George Willis had begun it by playing a medal round with the pro, George's first nine against the pro's complete eighteen. After that came the contest between Herbert Widgeon and Montague Brown, the latter, a twenty-four handicap man, being entitled to shout "Boo!" three times during the round at moments selected by himself. There had been many more of these degrading travesties on the sacred game, and I had writhed to see them. Playing freak golf-matches is to my mind like ragging a great classical melody. But of the whole collection this one, considering the sentimental interest and the magnitude of the stakes, seemed to me the most terrible. My face, I imagine, betrayed my disgust, for Bingham attempted extenuation.

"It's the only way," he said. "You know how Jukes and I are on the links. We are as level as two men can be. This, of course, is due to his extraordinary luck. Everybody knows that he is the world's champion fluker. I, on the other hand, invariably have the worst luck. The consequence is that in an ordinary round it is always a toss-up which of us wins. The test we propose will eliminate luck. After sixteen miles of give-and-take play, I am certain—

that is to say, the better man is certain to be ahead. That is what I meant when I said that Arthur Jukes would shortly be leaving Leigh. Well, may I take it that you will consent to act as one of the judges?"

I considered. After all, the match was likely to be historic, and one always feels tempted to hand one's name down to posterity.

"Very well," I said.

"Excellent. You will have to keep a sharp eye on Jukes, I need scarcely remind you. You will, of course, carry a book of the rules in your pocket and refer to them when you wish to refresh your memory. We start at daybreak, for, if we put it off till later, the course at the other end might be somewhat congested when we reached it. We want to avoid publicity as far as possible. If I took a full iron and hit a policeman, it would excite a remark."

"It would. I can tell you the exact remark which it would excite."

"We will take bicycles with us, to minimize the fatigue of covering the distance. Well, I am glad that we have your co-operation. At daybreak tomorrow on the first tee, and don't forget to bring your rule-book."

THE ATMOSPHERE BROODING over the first tee when I reached it on the following morning, somewhat resembled that of a dueling-ground in the days when these affairs were sealed with rapiers or pistols. Rupert Bailey, an old friend of mine, was the only cheerful member of the party. I am never at my best in the early morning, and the two rivals glared at each other with silent sneers. I had never supposed till that moment that men ever really sneered at one another outside the movies, but these two were indisputably doing so. They were in the mood when men say "Pshaw!"

They tossed for the honor, and Arthur Jukes, having won, drove off with a fine ball that landed well down the course. Ralph Bingham, having teed up, turned to Rupert Bailey.

"Go down on to the fairway of the seventeenth," he said. "I want you to mark my ball."

Rupert stared.

"The seventeenth!"

"I am going to take that direction," said Ralph, pointing over the trees.

"But that will land your second or third shot in the lake."

"I have provided for that. I have a flat-bottomed boat moored close by the sixteenth green. I shall use a mashie-niblick and chip my ball aboard, row across to the other side, chip it ashore, and carry on. I propose to go across country as far as Woodfield. I think it will save me a stroke or two."

I gasped. I had never before realized the man's devilish cunning. His tactics gave him a flying start. Arthur, who had driven straight down the course, had as his objective the high road, which adjoins the waste ground beyond the first green. Once there, he would play the orthodox game by driving his ball along till he reached the bridge. While Arthur was winding along the high road, Ralph would have cut off practically two sides of a triangle. And it was hopeless for Arthur to imitate his enemy's tactics now. From where his ball lay he would have to cross a wide tract of marsh in order to reach the seventeenth fairway —

an impossible feat. And, even if it had been feasible, he had no boat to take him across the water.

He uttered a violent protest. He was an unpleasant young man, almost—it seems absurd to say so, but almost as unpleasant as Ralph Bingham; yet at the moment I am bound to say I sympathized with him.

"What are you doing?" he demanded. "You can't play fast and loose with the rules like that."

"To what rule do you refer?" said Ralph, coldly.

"Well, that bally boat of yours is a hazard, isn't it? And you can't row a hazard about all over the place."

"Why not?"

The simple question seemed to take Arthur Jukes aback.

"Why not?" he repeated. "Why not? Well, you can't. That's why."

"There is nothing in the rules," said Ralph Bingham, "against moving a hazard. If a hazard can be moved without disturbing the ball, you are at liberty, I gather, to move it wherever you please. Besides, what is all this about moving hazards? I have a perfect right to go for a morning row, haven't I? If I were to ask my doctor, he would probably actually recommend it. I am going to row my boat across the sound. If it happens to have my ball on board, that is not my affair. I shall not disturb my ball, and I shall play it from where it lies. Am I right in saying that the rules enact that the ball shall be played from where it lies?"

We admitted that it was.

"Very well, then," said Ralph Bingham. "Don't let us waste any more time. We will wait for you at Woodfield."

He addressed his ball, and drove a beauty over the trees. It flashed out of sight in the direction of the seventeenth tee. Arthur and I made our way down the hill to play our second.

IT IS A CURIOUS TRAIT OF the human mind that, however little personal interest one may have in the result, it is impossible to prevent oneself taking sides in any event of a competitive nature. I had embarked on this affair in a purely neutral spirit, not caring which of the two won and only sorry that both could not lose. Yet, as the morning wore on, I found myself almost unconsciously becoming distinctly pro-Jukes. I did not like the man. I objected to his face, his manners, and the color of his tie. Yet there was something in the dogged way in which he struggled against adversity which touched me and won my grudging support. Many men, I felt, having been so outmaneuvered at the start, would have given up the contest in despair; but Arthur Jukes, for all his defects, had the soul of a true golfer. He declined to give up. In grim silence he hacked his ball through the rough till he reached the high road; and then, having played twenty-seven, set himself resolutely to propel it on its long journey.

It was a lovely morning, and, as I bicycled along, keeping a fatherly eye on Arthur's activities, I realized for the first time in my life the full meaning of that exquisite phrase of Coleridge: "Clothing the palpable and familiar / With golden exhalations of the dawn," for in the pellucid air everything seemed weirdly beautiful, even Arthur Jukes' heather-mixture knickerbockers, of which hitherto I had never approved. The sun gleamed on their seat, as he bent to make his shots, in a cheerful and almost a poetic way. The birds were singing gaily in the hedgerows, and such was my uplifted state that I, too, burst into song, until Arthur petulantly desired me to refrain, on the plea that, though he yielded to no man in his enjoyment of farmyard imitations in their proper place, I put him off his stroke. And so we passed through Bayside in silence and started to cover that long stretch of road which ends in the railway bridge and the gentle descent into Woodfield.

Arthur was not doing badly. He was at least keeping them straight. And in the circumstances straightness was to be preferred to distance. Soon after leaving Little Hadley he had become ambitious and had used his brassey with disastrous results, slicing his fifty-third into the rough on the right of the road. It had taken him ten with the niblick to get back on to the car tracks, and this had taught him prudence.

He was now using his putter for every shot, and, except when he got trapped in the cross-lines at the top of the hill just before reaching Bayside, he had been in no serious difficulties. He was playing a nice easy game, getting the full face of the putter on to each shot.

At the top of the slope that drops down into Woodfield High Street he paused.

"I think I might try my brassey again here," he said. "I have a nice lie."

"Is it wise?" I said.

He looked down the hill.

"What I was thinking," he said, "was that with it I might wing that man Bingham. I see he is standing right out in the middle of the fairway."

I followed his gaze. It was perfectly true. Ralph Bingham was leaning on his bicycle in the roadway, smoking a cigarette. Even at this distance one could detect the man's disgustingly complacent expression. Rupert Bailey was sitting with his back against the door of the Wood-field Garage, looking rather used up. He was a man who liked to keep himself clean and tidy, and it was plain that the cross-country trip had done him no good. He seemed to be scraping mud off his face. I learned later that he had had the misfortune to fall into a ditch just beyond Bayside.

"No," said Arthur. "On second thoughts, the safe game is the one to play. I'll stick to the putter."

We dropped down the hill, and presently came up with the opposition. I had not been mistaken in thinking that Ralph Bingham looked complacent. The man was smirking.

"Playing three hundred and ninety-six," he said, as we drew near. "How are you?"

I consulted my score-card.

"We have played a snappy seven hundred and eleven." I said.

Ralph exulted openly. Rupert Bailey made no comment. He was too busy with the alluvial deposits on his person.

"Perhaps you would like to give up the match?" said Ralph to Arthur.

"Tchah!" said Arthur.

"Might just as well."

"Pah!" said Arthur.

"You can't win now."

"Pshaw!" said Arthur.

I am aware that Arthur's dialogue might have been brighter, but he had been through a trying time.

Rupert Bailey sidled up to me.

"I'm going home," he said.

"Nonsense!" I replied. "You are in an official capacity. You must stick to your post. Besides, what could be nicer than a pleasant morning ramble?"

"Pleasant morning ramble my number nine foot!" he replied, peevishly. "I want to get back to civilization and set an excavating party with pickaxes to work on me."

"You take too gloomy a view of the matter. You are a little dusty. Nothing more."

"And it's not only the being buried alive that I mind. I cannot stick Ralph Bingham much longer."

"You have found him trying?"

"Trying! Why, after I had fallen into that ditch and was coming up for the third time, all the man did was simply to call to me to admire an infernal iron shot he had just made. No sympathy, mind you! Wrapped up in himself. Why don't you make your man give up the match? He can't win."

"I refuse to admit it. Much may happen between here and Royal Square."

I have seldom known a prophecy more swiftly fulfilled. At this moment the doors of the Woodfield Garage opened and a small car rolled out with a grimy young man in a sweater at the wheel. He brought the machine out into the road, and alighted and went back into the garage, where we heard him shouting unintelligibly to someone in the rear premises. The car remained puffing and panting against the curb.

Engaged in conversation with Rupert Bailey, I was paying little attention to this evidence of an awakening world, when suddenly I heard a hoarse, triumphant cry from Arthur Jukes, and, turned, I perceived his ball dropping neatly into the car's interior. Arthur himself, brandishing a niblick, was dancing about in the fairway.

"Now what about your moving hazards?" he cried.

At this moment the man in the sweater returned, carrying a spanner. Arthur Jukes sprang towards him.

"I'll give you five pounds to drive me to Royal Square," he said.

I do not know what the sweater-clad young man's engagements for the morning had been originally, but nothing could have been more obliging than the ready way in which he consented to revise them at a moment's notice. I dare say you have noticed that the sturdy peasantry of our beloved land respond to an offer of five pounds as to a bugle-call.

"You're on," said the youth.

"Good!" said Arthur Jukes.

"You think you're darned clever," said Ralph Bingham.

"I know it," said Arthur.

"Well, then," said Ralph, "perhaps you will tell us how you propose to get the ball out of the car when you reach Royal Square?"

"Certainly," replied Arthur. "You will observe on the side of the vehicle a convenient handle which, when turned, opens the door. The door thus opened, I shall chip my ball out!"

"I see," said Ralph. "Yes, I never thought of that."

There was something in the way the man spoke that I did not like. His mildness seemed to me suspicious. He had the air of a man who has something up his sleeve. I was still musing on this when Arthur called to me impatiently to get in. I did so, and we drove off. Arthur was in great spirits. He had ascertained from the young man at the wheel that there was no chance of the opposition being able to hire another car at the garage. This machine was his own property, and the only other one at present in the shop was suffering from complicated trouble of the oiling-system and would not be able to be moved for at least another day.

I, however, shook my head when he pointed out the advantages of his position. I was still wondering about Ralph.

"I don't like it," I said.

"Don't like what?"

"Ralph Bingham's manner."

"Of course not," said Arthur. "Nobody does. There have been complaints on all sides."

"I mean, when you told him how you intended to get the ball out of the car."

"What was the matter with him?"

"He was too—ha!"

"How do you mean he was too—ha?"

"I have it!"

"What?"

"I see the trap he was laying for you. It has just dawned on me. No wonder he didn't object to your opening the door and chipping the ball out. By doing so you would forfeit the match."

"Nonsense! Why?"

"Because," I said, "it is against the rules to tamper with a hazard. If you had got into a sand-bunker, would you smooth away the sand? If you had put your shot under a tree, could your caddie hold up the branches to give you a clear shot? Obviously you would disqualify yourself if you touched that door."

Arthur's jaw dropped.

"What! Then how the deuce am I to get it out?"

"That," I said, gravely, "is a question between you and your Maker."

It was here that Arthur Jukes forfeited the sympathy which I had begun to feel for him. A crafty, sinister look came into his eyes.

"Listen!" he said. "It'll take them an hour to catch up with us. Suppose, during that time, that door happened to open accidentally, as it were, and close again? You wouldn't think it necessary to mention the fact, eh? You would be a good fellow and keep your mouth shut, yes? You might even see your way to go so far as to back me up in a statement to the effect that I hooked it out with my—?"

I was revolted.

"I am a golfer," I said, coldly, "and I obey the rules."

"Yes, but—"

"Those rules were drawn up by—"—I bared my head reverently—"by the Committee of the Royal and Ancient at St. Andrews. I have always respected them, and I shall not deviate on this occasion from the policy of a lifetime."

Arthur Jukes relapsed into a moody silence. He broke it once, crossing the West Street Bridge, to observe that he would like to know if I called myself a friend of his—a question which I was able to answer with a whole-hearted negative. After that he did not speak till the car drew up in front of the Majestic Hotel in Royal Square.

Early as the hour was, a certain bustle and animation already prevailed in that center of the city, and the spectacle of a man in a golf-coat and plus-four knickerbockers hacking with a niblick at the floor of a car was not long in collecting a crowd of some dimensions. Three messenger-boys, four typists, and a gentleman in full evening-dress, who obviously possessed or was friendly with someone who possessed a large cellar, formed the nucleus of it; and they were joined about the time when Arthur addressed the ball in order to play his nine hundred and fifteenth by six news-boys, eleven charladies, and perhaps a dozen assorted loafers, all speculating with the liveliest interest as to which particular asylum had had the honor of sheltering Arthur before he had contrived to elude the vigilance of his custodians.

Arthur had prepared for some such contingency. He suspended his activities with the niblick, and drew from his pocket a large poster, which he proceeded to hang over the side of the car. It read:

COME
TO
MCCLURG
and MACDONALD,
18 WEST 49th STREET,
for ALL GOLFING
SUPPLIES.

His knowledge of psychology had not misled him. Directly they gathered that he was advertising something, the crowd declined to look at it; they melted away, and Arthur returned to his work in solitude.

He was taking a well-earned rest after playing his eleven hundred and fifth, a nice niblick shot with lots of wrist behind it, when out of Bridle Street there trickled a weary-looking golf-ball, followed in the order named by Ralph Bingham, resolute but going a trifle at the knees, and Rupert Bailey on a bicycle. The latter, on whose face and limbs the mud had dried, made an arresting spectacle.

"What are you playing?" I inquired.

"Eleven hundred," said Rupert. "We got into a casual dog."

"A casual dog?"

"Yes, just before the bridge. We were coming along nicely, when a stray dog grabbed our nine hundred and ninety-eighth and took it nearly back to Woodfield, and we had to start all over again. How are you getting on?"

"We have just played our eleven hundred and fifth. A nice even game." I looked at Ralph's ball, which was lying close to the curb. "You are farther from the hole, I think. Your shot, Bingham."

Rupert Bailey suggested breakfast. He was a man who was altogether too fond of creature comforts. He had not the true golfing spirit.

"Breakfast!" I exclaimed.

"Breakfast," said Rupert, firmly. "If you don't know what it is, I can teach you in half a minute. You play it with a pot of coffee, a knife and fork, and about a hundred-weight of scrambled eggs. Try it. It's a pastime that grows on you."

I was surprised when Ralph Bingham supported the suggestion. He was so near holing out that I should have supposed that nothing would have kept him from finishing the match. But he agreed heartily.

"Breakfast," he said, "is an excellent idea. You go along in. I'll follow in a moment. I want to buy a paper."

We went into the hotel, and a few minutes later he joined us. Now that we were actually at the table, I confess that the idea of breakfast was by no means repugnant to me. The keen air and the exercise had given me an appetite, and it was some little time before I was able to assure the waiter definitely that he could cease bringing orders of scrambled eggs. The others having finished also, I suggested a move. I was anxious to get the match over and be free to go home.

We filed out of the hotel, Arthur Jukes leading. When I had passed through the swing-doors, I found him gazing perplexedly up and down the street.

"What is the matter?" I asked.

"It's gone!"

"What has gone?"

"The car!"

"Oh, the car?" said Ralph Bingham. "That's all right. Didn't I tell you about that? I bought it just now and engaged the driver as my chauffeur, I've been meaning to buy a car for a long time. A man ought to have a car."

"Where is it?" said Arthur, blankly. The man seemed dazed.

"I couldn't tell you to a mile or two," replied Ralph. "I told the man to drive to Glasgow. Why? Had you any message for him?"

"But my ball was inside it!"

"Now that," said Ralph, "is really unfortunate! Do you mean to tell me you hadn't managed to get it out yet? Yes, that is a little awkward for you. I'm afraid it means that you lose the match."

"Lose the match?"

"Certainly. The rules are perfectly definite on that point. A period of five minutes is allowed for each stroke. The player who fails to make his stroke within that time loses the hole. Unfortunate, but there it is!"

Arthur Jukes sank down on the path and buried his face in his hands. He had the appearance of a broken man. Once more, I am bound to say, I felt a certain pity for him. He had certainly struggled gamely, and it was hard to be beaten like this on the post.

"Playing eleven hundred and one," said Ralph Bingham, in his odiously self-satisfied voice, as he addressed his ball. He laughed jovially. A messenger-boy had paused close by and was watching the proceedings gravely. Ralph Bingham patted him on the head.

"Well, sonny," he said, "what club would you use here?"

"I claim the match!" cried Arthur Jukes, springing up. Ralph Bingham regarded him coldly.

"I beg your pardon?"

"I claim the match!" repeated Arthur Jukes. "The rules say that a player who asks advice from any person other than his caddie shall lose the hole."

"This is absurd!" said Ralph, but I noticed that he had turned pale.

"I appeal to the judges."

"We sustain the appeal," I said, after a brief consultation with Rupert Bailey. "The rule is perfectly clear."

"But you had lost the match already by not playing within five minutes," said Ralph, vehemently.

"It was not my turn to play. You were farther from the pin."

"Well, play now. Go on! Let's see you make your shot."

"There is no necessity," said Arthur, frigidly. "Why should I play when you have already disqualified yourself?"

"I claim a draw!"

"I deny the claim."

"I appeal to the judges."

"Very well. We will leave it to the judges."

I consulted with Rupert Bailey. It seemed to me that Arthur Jukes was entitled to the verdict. Rupert, who, though an amiable and delightful companion, had always been one of Nature's fat-heads, could not see it. We had to go back to our principals and announce that we had been unable to agree.

"This is ridiculous," said Ralph Bingham. "We ought to have had a third judge."

At this moment, who should come out of the hotel but Amanda Trivett! A veritable goddess from the machine.

"It seems to me," I said, "that you would both be well advised to leave the decision to Miss Trivett. You could have no better referee."

"I'm game," said Arthur Jukes.

"Suits me," said Ralph Bingham.

"Why, whatever are you all doing here with your golf-clubs?" asked the girl, wonderingly.

"These two gentlemen," I explained, "have been playing a match, and a point has arisen on which the judges do not find themselves in agreement. We need an unbiased outside opinion, and we should like to put it up to you. The facts are as follows: ..."

Amanda Trivett listened attentively, but, when I had finished, she shook her head.

"I'm afraid I don't know enough about the game to be able to decide a question like that," she said.

"Then we must consult St. Andrews," said Rupert Bailey.

"I'll tell you who might know," said Amanda Trivett, after a moment's thought.

"Who is that?" I asked.

"My fiancé. He has just come back from a golfing holiday. That's why I'm in town this morning. I've been to meet him. He is very good at golf. He won a medal at Little-Mudbury-in-the-Wold the day before he left."

There was a tense silence. I had the delicacy not to look at Ralph or Arthur. Then the silence was broken by a sharp crack. Ralph Bingham had broken his mashie-niblick across his knee. From the direction where Arthur Jukes was standing there came a muffled gulp.

"Shall I ask him?" said Amanda Trivett.

"Don't bother," said Ralph Bingham.

"It doesn't matter," said Arthur Jukes.

Made in the USA
Las Vegas, NV
02 February 2021